B
NEHRU
GRIFFIT
1989
C1

Griffith, Kenneth, 1921-
The discovery of Nehru : an experience of India / Kenneth Griffith. -- London : M. Joseph ; New York, N.Y. : Viking Penguin, 1989.
viii, 216 p. ; 25 cm.
Includes index.
ISBN 0-07-813175-4

A-P

1. Nehru, Jawaharlal, 1889-1964. 2. Griffith, Kenneth, 1921- 3. Prime ministers--India--Biography. I. Title.

Wa wln90-305018

The Discovery of Nehru

AN EXPERIENCE OF INDIA

The Discovery of Nehru

AN EXPERIENCE OF INDIA

Kenneth Griffith

Michael Joseph
LONDON

Dedicated to my European colleagues: Alan Birkinshaw, Jonathan Griffith and Chiara Peretti, who suffered with me in India.

And to the 799.999 million Indians, whom I was not expected to meet and who have to suffer, not for two years, but for their entire lives.

Kenneth Griffith.

MICHAEL JOSEPH LTD

Published by the Penguin Group
27 Wrights Lane, London W8 5TZ, England
Viking Penguin Inc., 40 West 23rd Street, New York, New York 10010, USA
Penguin Books Australia Ltd, Ringwood, Victoria, Australia
Penguin Books Canada Ltd, 2801 John Street, Markham, Ontario, Canada L3R 1B4
Penguin Books (NZ) Ltd, 182–190 Wairau Road, Auckland 10, New Zealand

Penguin Books Ltd, Registered Offices: Harmondsworth, Middlesex, England

First published 1989

Set in Meridien 11/13 pt

Printed and bound in Great Britain by
Richard Clay Ltd, Bungay, Suffolk

A CIP catalogue record for this book is available from the British Library

ISBN 0 7181 3175 4

CONTENTS

PREFACE

This book is a record of my curious meanderings through Indian events. It is simply a slice of my unpredictable life as far as India is concerned. My uneasy childhood dreams of joining the British Army and of being sent to the Northwest Frontier of what was then India; of Prime Minister Indira Gandhi inviting me to talk to her about world affairs and India in particular. Of going to India for the first time as a film actor, of going again to make one of my factual films about Robert Clive, Clive of India. And then Mrs Gandhi inviting me to her home in Delhi and, while sitting together on a chaise longue, saying to me: 'Perhaps, Mr Griffith, you would consider making a film for India about the life of my father [Jawaharlal Nehru, first Prime Minister of India].' And, finally, my going to India and doing that privileged but onerous job for the Indian Government.

This book culminates with the making of that Nehru film. But I have written about it *all*: at least to the extent of what is held in my head. Human experience, I have found, is a clambering ramble and I have recorded the Indian pieces here. The truth is often apparently inconsequential, but I believe that a diamond is best appreciated in a blue clay. Anyway, it is all here – as I remember it.

The making of the Nehru film, which I have called *But I Have Promises to Keep*, admits to unexpected problems in the structuring of this book. For reasons that are incomprehensible to Western minds, the first six months of my sojourn in India was a sort of vacuum, which only an Easterner could begin to understand. Nothing, so far as the Nehru film went, was allowed to happen. So I filled my days, weeks and months with other contemplations; particularly with an on the spot study of the Indian Mutiny of 1857 or, as it is understandably called by many Indians, The First War of Independence.

Then at the end of our filming of Nehru's life, there was again an unusual period of thin duties for me in India while the film was technically completed in Britain. And again I filled all spare time with a maximum of probing in other Indian directions, and that is in this book. As far as the Andaman and Nicobar Islands go, they were a happy ending to a hard Indian experience, but on top of that I have been informed that very few Europeans have been allowed to visit these islands since 1947. Indeed, the Roman Catholic Bishop of the Andaman and Nicobar Islands asked me how had I been allowed in – His Holiness the Pope's Emissary had been refused permission.

In this book my adventures are recounted because they happened to me on Indian territory. And they are as significant to this overall story as my nervous boyhood dreams of being dressed in khaki at the Khyber Pass. Perhaps it was *all meant* by an Indian Mysticism beyond my Welsh understanding to head me towards a greater 'Discovery of Nehru'.

CHAPTER ONE

The Sea Wolves to *Clive of India*

I had had no experience of dealing with professional politicians – apart from screaming at Lloyd George, 'Give Labour a chance', when I was four years old at the behest of my Uncle Reggie who was then known as a 'Bolshi' – until Huw Wheldon said to me, thirty years later: 'Kenneth, would you make a film for us (the British Broadcasting Corporation's television service) on your enthusiasm?' Also pushing me was young David Attenborough (then head of BBC2).

Huw Wheldon, the man who led British television to its creative zenith, had long thought well of me as an actor and through this interest had learnt of my passionate preoccupation with the implications of history. If one wishes to understand this world's contemporary problems begin by examining the historical cause of them.

Huw Wheldon and David Attenborough wanted me to combine my histrionic ability with my strong feelings for the value of historical truth. Those two were stylish leaders: 'You can do what you like; go where you like and there'll be no censorship,' so spoke Huw. Those fortunate television programme-makers who knew him will recognise the rare spirit. Well, after overcoming my astonishment at the unexpectedness of the offer, I had a go and in due course found myself in the world's biggest pulpit, preaching sermons on the grandest of scales. And thus I began to meet professional politicians once again – I mean since my encounter with Lloyd George. This I had not foreseen: they took an interest in what I was achieving and they (the friendly ones) approached me.

Indeed, I have foreseen very little in my life. Caring

people, like Huw Wheldon, have either pointed the way or realities have suddenly presented themselves, stark and unsettling, in my path. Yes, I did sense the difference between hissing my truth into a friend's ear and hissing it, equally truthfully, into a camera's lens. It must be interesting to contemplate that difference. I suspect that we all adjust our messages to the capacity of the specific listener, but the larger the group, the less possible this tempering becomes. Finally, when the words and physical appearance are being directed at millions of unknown people one can only fall back on the inner self and tell one's truth with as much professional skill as possible.

I digress; I had not properly contemplated the effect that my opinions could have on the anonymous millions. It came as a shock. I had been invited into that kitchen, I had entered of my own volition and I found the heat and the spitting oil very disturbing. But what a privilege! As long as you stick to your truth – what a privilege! There is a heavy responsibility; there is an obligation to work diligently and to examine non-stop one's poor human honesty and to hold on to that; there is nothing, except that, between oneself and the Black Pit.

I have had a whacking share of praise and a whacking share of abuse. But I know more acutely what I have done and not done than anyone else. When the praise comes I can only say, 'Thank you for telling me,' and these days I begin to add, 'And your encouraging words help to offset the attacks on me. Thank you!' Praise and blame are both very hot but I will stay in that kitchen for as long as I have access and for as long as I can stand up and think.

The heat became intense some years ago when I felt an overwhelming impulse to put forward on film, to British people, above all, the fundamental Irish Republican point of view. I had first felt uneasy about Britain's role in Irish national affairs when I was about nine years old in 1930. Years later I shared a home with Peter O'Toole and he talked to me about – among many other matters! – Michael

Collins and Ireland's non-stop war to remove the Union Jack. Now I know of no better way to communicate a universal truth to uninformed people than through the unbroken saga of a human life. So my colleagues and I made a film on the life of Michael Collins. I called it *Hang Out Your Brightest Colours*. And did the fat fly in the kitchen! The Independent Broadcasting Authority began secretly to suppress the film. I remember a great fear in my stomach that the Powers Whoever They Are would silently succeed, but Hallelujah! the Press – and the more responsible Press – took an interest and this led to members of the House of Commons looking at the film for themselves.

I was confined, in a very friendly manner, to a little office inside ATV House at Marble Arch in London by Sir (as he then was) Lew Grade. Lord Grade (as he is now) understandably wanted to appease the Discreet Eminence of the IBA. I was reading a book when there was a knock on my door. Into the room came Michael Foot and about eight or nine other distinguished British Socialists. I remember Neil Kinnock. I had met none of them before. Michael Foot said something to the effect that they didn't know exactly what to say to me; that they had all seen the Michael Collins film and for his part it was perhaps the most powerful political film he had ever seen. He said he didn't know what they could do about the suppression of the film but that he and his colleagues would have a meeting and that they would do their best. Of course, the film has never been seen on television – which has proved to be a damned pity for Britain and a damned pity for the majority of human beings on the island of Ireland; come to think of it, probably for all of them, in the long run. We British should understand the historical cause of the conflict in Ireland and until we do honestly investigate it the obscene Troubles will continue. The tragedy is that Britain is the root cause of those Troubles and we lack the character to face up to the fundamental responsibility and guilt.

Anyway I was now in the political field without any

doubt; I even found myself inside 10 Downing Street where Ireland was significantly discussed with me. But enough of the Irish Question; this book is about the Indian Question.

What is of relevant significance is that I was not aiming at political influence, but simply doing my best to expose the cause of a few living and pending tragedies. I belong to no political party. And though I warm at the thought of Michael Foot, Neil Kinnock and David Steel, I am also capable of thanking Margaret Thatcher for having brought back some self-respect to Britain. I have some affection for Ronald Reagan and George Bush and I am daily praying that I am justified in the beginning of a smile towards Mikhail Gorbachev. No, I have no Party allegiance; but perhaps that is why I am often regarded as dangerous by quite a few powerful influences. Oh! and I am not inconsistent; but my consistency lies unbroken inside my own head.

Long before that first meeting with Michael Foot and Neil Kinnock; indeed very early in my film-making career (as against my ancient film acting one), I received a communication from the Indian High Commissioner in Britain. I had no connection with India whatsoever apart from boyhood dreams of being a District Commissioner, or more realistically, a private soldier on the North-west Frontier together with a smattering of Rudyard Kipling, which is much the same. 'Mr Griffith, do you know that our Prime Minister, Mrs Indira Gandhi, is coming to Britain to meet your Prime Minister, Mr Edward Heath?'

'Yes, sir.'

'Well, she wonders if you would have a meal with her. . . .'

Imagine how I felt, unaccustomed as I was. And then almost totally unadjusted to my new political involvement. I had just completed my second film effort, which was a life of Cecil Rhodes. In that film I was pointing out, through the terrible life of Rhodes, that all was not well in that part of British Central Africa. It was before we had heard of Robert Mugabe and company. Incidentally, today, I would like to make a film pointing out that all is not well with Mugabe's bit of Central Africa – if I were allowed to go there to do it, which I wouldn't be – how complicated is the thread of a truth if you try to follow it.

I asked the Indian High Commission: 'Why does Mrs Gandhi want to see me?'

'Because, Mr Griffith, she is interested in your work.'

'Oh, thank you.'

The convoluted ways of film and television! I have since discovered that it was probably the late and much missed Marie Seton who had placed my sermon on Rhodes before Indira Gandhi. Marie Seton, friend of Jawaharlal Nehru and of his daughter. Marie Seton who had been a film editor for Sergei Eisenstein and, I believe, his lover.

I was not the only guest invited to that dinner party with Mrs Gandhi and that evening I made friends with James Cameron, Gentleman, and Leonard Cheshire, Victoria Cross. How ever, when the meal was over I was invited into a private room by Marie Seton to talk to the Indian Prime Minister. I was in a highly-strung state. Mrs Gandhi sat on a chaise-longue. There were perhaps two other Indian ladies present; I remember their saris. What was happening to me? In a rather imperious tone Mrs Gandhi launched the conversation: 'Mr Griffith, do you think anything is to be gained by criticising the British Empire?'

I opened my mouth and strove for the truth: 'The only reason that I have hesitated in my reply, Prime Minister, is because *you* have asked the question! Now that I am recovering: Yes! Confession is good for the soul and telling the truth – as I see it – can be a sort of apology.'

I can't remember much about the middle part of our chat except that I continued to be highly strung and I remember the two or three Indian ladies being very amused at my no-doubt astonishing behaviour. But Mrs Gandhi wasn't laughing. However, I was unstoppable: 'I believe, Prime Minister, that you are going to meet Edward Heath tomorrow.'

'Yes, I am.'

'Well be very careful.'
'What do you mean?'
'He's not like other men; he has difficulty in communicating with ordinary people. He seems to be missing on one cylinder.'

Well, I wouldn't have made it in the Diplomatic Corps! Though recently I was in conversation with a distinguished diplomat and, having mentioned my unsuitability for such a career, he quickly rejoined: 'You may be wrong; telling the truth is often effective.'

I recall running and skipping eastward along Piccadilly through the night and repeating to myself: 'I told her! I told her!' I presumed that I was skipping away from India, but I wasn't.

I am very vague about the general details of my life; I mean the sequence of events, the time lapses, the dates and so on. I am liable to say: 'about three years' when in fact it was eight years – or vice versa. I don't lie; such facts have relatively little significance for me. Perhaps judges and juries should bear such anomalies as mine in mind. Anyway, the years rolled by and I led my film-making life around the world: America, Europe, Africa, the Middle East. The subjects varied, but there was always a purpose – a cause, to explain the effect. Occasionally I was able to have a well-paid holiday. I mean occasionally I could find the time simply to act in a cinema film.

After performing in front of the camera for most of the ninety minutes of one of my own films, what a luxury it is to share the burden with many other Thespians and to be paid liberally for the relatively little effort involved. But do not misunderstand me; film acting, like any other job, is not easy to do well. You may have weeks free of work in an exotic location, but you must remain poised to deliver your contribution at even a moment's notice and that piece of the film's jigsaw must be delivered with finesse and professional skill. And it was for such a job that I was brought to India for the first time.

Euan Lloyd, the tenacious, fighting, feature film-maker invited me – and many other actors – to India to act in *The Sea Wolves*, an adventure story of the Second World War. I had acted in Euan's previous robust and highly popular film, *The Wild Geese*; but that was in Africa.

The truth is I didn't want to go and I told Euan so. I had been brought disturbingly low through one of those domestic catastrophes which my flesh is only too commonly heir to and the will was draining away. Still, the dealer of the blow prevailed upon me to go and I went. How strange it was; particularly now in retrospect. I saw the very different people and the exotic images of India through a haze of grief but I was aware that under normal circumstances I would have been consumed with excited curiosity. I recall saying that I was unable to focus on the colour or anything else. Grief is a formidable shroud. However, actors and actresses are a warm-hearted lot and I was not without support, particularly from Bernard Archard, who was also in the film.

We worked mainly in Goa, that old Portuguese colony; a singularly beautiful place. The Portuguese had been there for over four hundred years and the Goans are very different from any other people in India that I have visited – and I have now travelled north, south, east and west. It is a land lighter in spirit. The people seem freer. The Roman Catholic faith still pervades and however the evolving chemistry of mixed cultures has flowed over the centuries the result is, particularly of an evening, exquisitely adorned young women and immaculately slim young men, apparently going to some innocent celebration.

Now, you may properly ask: 'How can you recall such gentle images through that mist of grief?' Well, it was in Goa that I first met my friend, Chiara Peretti, and she was able to make me stand upright again. These days we work together on 'our' films. I then saw India. I saw it with the innocence of a serious passer-by. I saw the vivid colours of India and the astounding physical contours. Chiara and I even penetrated by a hazardous route the very centre of India: the ancient deserted magnificence of Vijayanagar. The city where the primordial Hindu authority suddenly ceased on the sub-continent. As we wandered, astonished, through the square miles of ancient Indian power we didn't even know what the city had once been! We were unaware of its dread significance. I saw India, then, like most tourists see it (not that many tourists, in those days, saw Vijayanagar!). And there were few humans present to ask for information and almost no one who could speak English. Today I know something about that incredible city, but today I am wiser and more battered than I was. And much of this condition has been meted out by what lies beneath the surface of India. Once I stood in the precincts of a Kali temple – way up in the north-east of India – and disturbed, I puzzled the deep reverence paid to the terrifying image, surrounded by human skulls and the representation of human blood. 'Please, sir, can you explain to my European ignorance what is the significance of the goddess Kali?' The sympathetic Indian did his best in the flare-blown night. But I didn't truly comprehend. Today – woe is me! – I have a fairer idea. The reward is memorable but the cost is a shortened life.

Well India, it was 'hello' and 'goodbye'. The Taj Mahal is more beautiful than any Air India poster can convey and it is true that I still contemplate the architectural miracle of that white mausoleum from most possible angles, but now I also lean against the intricate stonework and observe the reactions of visitors and I boggle at the gap between the surface of India and what lies seething beneath or – more charitably – beyond.

I have a long list of potential film subjects in my head and those ideas are backed up by a substantial reference library in my home in Islington, London. Well down on that list was Robert Clive, Clive of India. Again Euan Lloyd intervened in my life. He was visiting me and while browsing through the Asian section he saw the wodge of books on

Clive. 'Clive of India,' he said; 'For so many years I have wanted to make a film about him. Do you know that people are beginning to forget who he was!' There was a moment of nostalgia for the more romantic and ambitious days of cinema. 'But where would you find two hundred battle elephants today?' Euan paused and then to my astonishment: 'Would you make one of your films for me? About Clive?'

Now, in my films, only I appear on the screen and so it is my lonely responsibility to persuade the viewers to imagine that there are two hundred battle elephants. Therefore, such problems as hiring massed elephants don't exist and the cost of one of my sagas is relatively minute.

Euan continued with his customary enthusiasm: 'I know that people throughout the English-speaking world see your work. It will remind them who Clive was and we can use that to build up to a feature film! We'll find the elephants!'

I replied: 'Yes,' as I usually rise to the unexpected, and I like Euan.

'How much do you get for your research and the script?'

I told him and there was a cheque in my pocket. However, soon afterwards Channel Four television also asked me to make a film for them and they financed *Clive of India* and consequently I gave Euan back his money. He was happy; he only wanted the film made.

Among my Indian friends is Admiral Rustam Ghandhi, who is retired from the Indian Navy. I asked him, 'Russie, will you help me make this film – in a professional capacity and guide me through India?'

'My dear Kenneth, I would love to, but I have just become the chairman of the India Shipping Corporation and I therefore can't. But, my dear Kenneth, you are absolutely right in turning to me. You must have an Indian with you who understands our system and who has some authority. Otherwise you will not complete your film. I will ask a friend of mine, also a retired Admiral, Satyindra Singh, if he will do the job. He is now writing the official history of the Indian Navy, but he may get a release for a month or so.

He is a Sikh; and you can count on them!' Admiral Rustam Ghandhi, incidentally, is a Parsee.

When my colleagues and I arrived at Delhi Airport during the early hours of a morning, there was Admiral Satyindra Singh, saluting our arrival and wearing a ship-shape and Bombay fashion sikh turban. Admiral Ghandhi was right; I cannot imagine how we could have made the film without Admiral Singh's assistance. He saw us and our equipment through the then ramshackle airport – no small achievement – and the next day he began to guide me through the unbelievable labyrinth of India's deeply suspicious bureaucracy. We paraded through many offices and before many bureaucrats. I have experienced nothing remotely like it before or since – except when I was to return to India! Not only do you have to receive permission for everything that you have to film from the *Central* Government of India, but also from all of the *State* Governments in whose areas your historical locations may be. The waste of precious time and energy is incalculable. But I quite enjoyed it; observing Setty, as I now called the Admiral, dealing with the living and breathing officials and, no less intriguing for me, watching those officials parrying our innocent well-meaning hopes.

I calculated that Setty cleared each and every request three separate times. He was never content with one permit; he seemed to like three permits for each proposed operation. His briefcase bulged with permissions. At one point, in New Delhi, during the course of one of those pieces of Alice in Wonderland, I turned to my Admiral: 'Oh, come on Setty; leave poor Mr Chatterjee alone – he has assured us that all will be well!' The Admiral swung round at me, stiff and upright. He said nothing but it was quite clear that I had made a grave mistake and that I had spoken out of turn. I have not repeated that sort of interruption with Setty again. His method proved to be correct. Commonly, one or two of our permissions would fall through, but never all three. We did not lose one hour of filming because of the Admiral going wrong. I recall a hiatus before embarking on a boat up the Hooghly River at Calcutta because the sandwiches had not arrived, but sandwiches were not the Admiral's responsibility.

Yes, I had had a foretaste of the visible Curse of India; but we started filming on time, kept to our hard schedule and 'came in under budget'. And, in India, that, I now realise, was a miracle.

One other hurdle on the *Clive of India* film is relevant to record. While wheeling and dealing through those uncountable offices – the ancient machinery of India – I was asked an apparently innocent question; Indians have a habit of mentioning the lethal request 'in passing'. Until recently I have agreed to everything in an astounding spirit of trusting goodwill. Now, very late in the awful game, I have donned my battle dress and I now enter no Indian meeting without being fully armed. Suspicion, I have sadly learnt, can be confronted only with suspicion. The apparently innocent question mentioned above was put to me by some official in the high-powered 'South Block' of New Delhi. 'Mr Griffith, do you mind letting our Council for Historical Research have a look at your script?'

'Certainly,' said I, all helpfulness and that foolish innocence.

I had visualised some passing interest in my script by the Council for Historical Research and that some easy-going official would glance through it and perhaps, with a bit of luck, might chat with me about one or two of my opinions. But oh no! not in India! Admiral Singh was with me and we were ushered into a conference chamber. We were the first to arrive and there was an enormous elongated table, laid with about twelve pads of notepaper, pencils, drinking glasses and water. It was a sinister sight. There was an unspoken tension between Setty and me; the worst was obvious. And then the academics began to enter, each one carrying a photocopy of my script.

Now one of the great advantages that I have had in my life is that I have achieved no academic distinctions whatsoever. No school certificate; nothing. Therefore there has always been a chasm of difference between all academics and me. I have the enormous freedom of never having been in awe of any of them. But we do tend to talk in totally different languages; indeed I often find them incomprehensible.

The chairman of this group of Indian historians was a lean elderly man who behaved throughout as a superior pedant. And disaster was all around him; each of the other learned men represented the various main influences of India: the Congress Party, the Communist, the Muslim, the Hindu and so on. The meeting was called to order and I pitched in straight away. With the oval ball (if I may use a Rugby Football analogy) tucked under one arm, I charged for the opponent's line as soon as the whistle blew. This I suspect was an unorthodox tactic on my part. I think that it was normal play in this Indian game to kick defensively for touch, again and again. I, charging and dodging up the field on the attack, was not playing the Indian game. But they pulled themselves together and brought me to earth. The play became very rough. There was little love or politeness between us and I quickly lost my cool. And then I noticed a significant weakness in the opposition. One man (there were no women present) attacked a comment of mine in the script about some Hindu aspect of the Clive story and before I could refute it another Indian had said: 'Oh, I don't think that that is a serious matter, but,' (and glaring at me), 'what about that!' And he was jabbing at a Muslim-related matter in the script. And he, of course, was a Muslim. They were all arguing only for their vested interests. It was a microcosm of the tragedy of India as a nation.

The Communist shouted abuse at me. I got on to my feet and shouted back: 'I didn't expect this sort of behaviour and attitude here in India! I am an anti-Imperialist. I believe my script demonstrates this fact very clearly. I expect to be attacked in my own country for my beliefs, but not here!'

I remember clearly what went through my head: 'I would

rather go back to Britain immediately than be bullied into a realignment of the script, which is what their onslaught seemed to demand. Still on my feet I looked to my left where Admiral Singh was seated. His turbaned head was in his hands and he looked distressed. So be it, I thought. Then the meeting was over: 'Well, Mr Griffith, we will consider what has been said,' and most of the academics hurried out of the room.

Perhaps two remained and I said to Setty and them: 'Well, they might have had the politeness to say goodbye to me.' 'Oh,' said one of the remaining Indians, 'they may come back.' I was doubtful, but about eight minutes later, while I was sipping a cup of tea, into the room poured my massed adversaries, laughing, happy and very friendly.

'Mr Griffith,' said the foremost, 'we really liked you when you got angry; then we knew that you were sincere!'

And another: 'We don't ask you to change anything.'

And another: 'But perhaps now you will bear in mind our various susceptibilities.'

I was astounded and moved. Nevertheless I rounded on the big Communist: 'You shouted at me!'

He grinned: 'It is the only talent I have!'

What do you do? Indians often drive me to screaming exasperation – and then I have reason to like them. As soon as I got back to my hotel I went through my script very carefully and made a few adjustments which took note of 'our various susceptibilities'.

What do I remember of our filming of *Clive*? Everything! But this is not the right book for all of that. However, certain salient experiences were vital background for my Indian development.

Our very first whirl of the camera was in the grounds of Humayun's Tomb, New Delhi. Robert Clive never went to Delhi, but I wished to begin our film with such an impressive image of Mogul power. We arrived in the ghost-ridden gardens, with the vast mausoleum in the centre. Michel Pearce, the director, and the lads chose their creative pitch and I wandered off to consider in isolation every nuance of what I was soon to communicate into the camera. I always do this; but I remain within hailing distance. What a pleasure it can be too! Fascinating locations and the story is beginning.

This particular morning was beautiful. Cool and clear with the Oriental birds and the flowers. Oh yes, Clive was present and the other myriad ghosts. And then I noticed, for the first time ever, an astounding Indian phenomenon. Several men were striding, individually, across the early morning grass. They tended to be wearing grey flannel trousers, conservative sports jackets, shirts with ties and carrying free wheeling walking sticks. And they had with them a nice domestic dog. My mind left Clive. What an unexpected sight! I am Welsh and therefore the English are a non-stop source of fascination to me. These Indian men were behaving like Englishmen! Nowhere else in the world have I observed men behave like this, except in England. Perhaps it is possible in Central Park in New York by men of English extraction who read the *New Yorker* – but even there, I doubt the robustness of the stride.

Even as I was attempting to reconcentrate on Clive, one of these men accosted me: 'Excuse me, but may I ask what you are doing?'

'Oh!' said I, ever ready for a meaningful chat, 'this very morning we are about to start a film about the life of Robert Clive.'

'Clive of India?'

'Yes – that is our film crew over there.'

'Ah! the British Broadcasting Corporation!'

I didn't bother to contradict him. 'But', I went on, feeling that a couple of passions could be generated, 'I hasten to underline that this is not going to be a jingoistic British film; no Union Jacks are going to be waved here!'

The Indian stared at me sternly and raised a significant finger: 'Now sir! I hope that you are not going to be unfair to the British Empire! You must not forget that the British unified this great sub-continent. They created our remarkable communications services and our bureaucracy [already the thought shot through my mind that no Britisher should want the credit for this Frankenstein] and many other wonderful unifying achievements!'

I stood there, in the middle of northern India, with my mouth open. I had been politely but strictly admonished. I said: 'Yes, sir, I will bear in mind what you have said.'

'Well,' and he gave me a brisk and civilian salute, 'good day to you, sir!' And with a righteous and friendly smile he moved away with the doggy at his heels. But after two or three strides he stopped and turned. Nodding discreetly towards the great Mogul edifice and lowering his voice slightly he added: 'And of course you British saved us from a terrible tyranny.' And I knew then that he was a Hindu. This story is the truth as I remember it and that citizen of India was far from unique, in my now extensive experience, in his memory of the Old Raj. Again I did my best to ease – a teeny bit – the language of my script.

On the old battlefield of Plassey, under an enormous, ancient banyan tree, around which we were filming, was a farmer's house. Chiara Peretti came up to me: 'When you have a chance, ask if you can look inside.' I duly asked the old men who sat watching us and courteously I was escorted within. The exterior of the house was extremely rustic: wood and smoothed mud and thatch. Inside was perhaps the perfect human abode. It was immaculate. The polished mud floors, the sleeping rooms, the cooking area, the granary, the house temple. Everything seemed to be simply and beautifully arranged for human living. It stands in the centre of that awful and dramatic stage where young Clive made the sub-continent of India British. Cockneys – Londoners – were in that battle.

The ramparts of Arcot; the ruins of fabulous Murshidabad. I walked with Syed Mohammed Baquir Ali Meerza, a descendant of Siraj-ud-Daula, the sometime apex of declining Mogul power, who was broken by Clive, through the overgrown ruins of his ancestors' harem. The cobras were plentiful. I asked Ali Meerza, in his white flowing clothes, if he was frightened of being bitten. 'Of course not! I belong to the direct line of the Prophet. No cobra would harm me!' He pointed to the high verdurous wall above us: 'A cobra fell from there, round my head and shoulder. It would not harm me.' I trod warily.

And so the *Clive of India* film was made. The historical locations had taken us to the Dravidian south, as far as Trichinopoly (though it is now called something else; and this is one of the difficulties on the sub-continent: they are for ever changing the names of towns and streets) and to the far Muslim north. Usually I choose my subject, but as you already know, Euan Lloyd had chosen this one. When I choose the subject it is prompted by something on my mind that I feel is worth broadcasting. When, occasionally, someone else has pushed me into the arena with a subject that is not among my priorities, I have to discover quickly what is the maximum value in filming it; what themes should I emphasise, which would be of universal value. And I have found that in anyone's life there is a message of value for all humankind; that is if people care to listen and look at it. My job is to decide what that message of value is and then to present it as entertainingly as possible. How do you present a serious human issue and at the same time discourage the potential viewers from switching off? That is the task.

Every human life is a universal saga. Of course, in the case of Robert Clive and such, who made a big and romantic splash, the saga is more obvious. Which brings us back to those two hundred battle elephants. But the themes in all human lives become clear and meaningful for me after I have peered closely and researched them.

Clive's life (1725–74) personifies the growth of the British way of Empire-making. The young, uncomfortable clerk of the English East India Company turned to part-time soldiering with such audacious success that soon he was commanding the Company's private army. His employers only wanted the profits of trade. Their main European competitors in

India were the French. And Clive was asked if he could finally eliminate those French. The last bastion was a city called Chandernagore (now called Chandra Nagar – or perhaps something else because I cannot now find it on my Indian map!) and Clive asserted that he could, but turning on his business bosses, he warned them: 'If I take Chandernagore from the French, you will not be able to stop your advance there – even if you want to!' Clive was prophetically explaining that if he removed French power from India, the British would become the paramount European influence and would inevitably have to confront the ruling Moguls of India, naked and direct. Businessmen are always in competition. The English East India Company were a little disconcerted by Clive's warning; they were not Imperialists, they were high-handed tradesmen.

But Clive was shrewdly right. Trade led him to the taking of Chandernagore, which led him to the victory over the Muslims and their French allies at Plassey in 1757, which unerringly led us British, via Disraeli, that wily Imperialist, to the 'Brightest Jewel'. But even Disraeli had little choice unless Britain was to retreat from wealth, fame and power for purely ethical reasons. And which human group has ever chosen to do that? Well, not many. That was the main theme of *Clive of India*. Perhaps not exactly as Euan had seen it. But in explaining the thesis there *were* the two hundred battle elephants and the heroic, brilliant Clive, which I do not sniff at. Yes, viewers did see the charging elephants!

During these intervening years between meeting Mrs Gandhi in London and making the Clive film I heard nothing more from the Indian leader, except what I read in the newspapers. Though when I was in Goa, working for Euan Lloyd on *The Sea Wolves*, she was re-elected as Prime Minister after her fall from power. I stood beneath palm trees outside Panjim's government offices as the election news was announced to very excited Goans. However, I had been told that copies of other films that I had been responsible for had been sent to her in New Delhi, presumably at her request, but this was done by other hands and far removed from me. I am always so totally preoccupied with the research, writing and making of the films that there has been no time for anything else. I was once inveigled into the business side of my film work, but soon retired from the wretched battlefield, rather badly wounded.

So it came as another big surprise to me when Mrs Gandhi invited me to her home at Safdarjang Road in New Delhi. I had then recently made a film for the BBC on the life of Thomas Paine, the great eighteenth-century republican, which I provocatively called *The Most Valuable Englishman Ever*. In fact, I had said, early in the film, that Paine was 'a candidate for being the most valuable Englishman ever' and a friend of mine, Edward Proud, learning of this, urged me to go the whole hog and call it *The Most Valuable Englishman Ever*.

Well, Mrs Gandhi – unbeknown to me – received this film in Delhi and after seeing it issued the invitation. Again it was something of a traumatic experience for me. I am well used to living intimately with great statesmen, soldiers and shifters of this world's direction, but always dead ones. I feel very at home with them. Indeed, my third wife, Carole, once made a devastating comment: 'I often wondered when you disappeared into your library for long hours, why you loved those old dead people more than you apparently loved me.' After many years I haven't yet succeeded in mulling this remark through to a reasonable conclusion; perhaps I daren't. But those 'old dead people', whom I know so well and live with daily, are dead and they have finished and completed their deeds; Mrs Gandhi was, on the other hand, alive and well and was then actively steering a course for six hundred and eighty-three million Indians.

I know the exact population of India at that time of meeting Mrs Gandhi because I said to her: 'I suppose, Prime Minister, that you are well accustomed to dealing with people who cannot treat you as an ordinary human being?'

She rather swung on me: 'Please, Mr Griffith, would you explain to me why that is so? I am clearly an ordinary human being.'

'Well,' I replied, struggling with what I thought to be obvious, 'you are at the head of six hundred million people.'

And like a reflex came: 'And eighty three million, Mr Griffith!' The exploding population of India clearly haunted that extraordinary woman daily.

For these films that I am responsible for, there seems to be no neutral reaction from the viewers. Either I suffer the most uninhibited personal attacks, which can only be prompted by nothing less than hatred, or I am overwhelmed by sometimes extravagant praise. All public assessment of my work makes me feel uneasy. It is so unpredictable; I can never be sure if anyone is going to say 'wonderful' or 'terrible'. Certainly the evidence is that the films get at people, which they are meant to do, and from then onwards the reaction is personal and subjective. I do find the hatred and its complex motives the most interesting and, of course, the most unsettling.

Mrs Gandhi, as I have made clear, was one of those who admired the films. She said to me: 'The Tom Paine film is perhaps the most moving and disturbing film that I have ever seen.' Such a remark is a punctuation in one's life. It helps to define an answer to those ever lurking questions: 'Who am I?' and 'What am I?'. Well, Mrs Gandhi had informed me that a woman who daily worried and helped to organise six hundred and eighty three million people held a good opinion of my human effort.

What can you say to yourself? I certainly tried to do my utmost and in this case I had won a soul. And a formidably significant soul. You do your best and you suffer the judgement. Not only the hatred but the respect as well. I find that praise is also painful. Nobody knows better than oneself what one has done or failed to have done. Of course, praise is spoken to you; dislike (to put it mildly) is usually written. Spleen is commonly expressed from a distance.

Mrs Gandhi told me that her son, Rajiv, was also an admirer of my work. And she introduced me to him and his wife, Sonia. Sanjay, her other son, was already dead. Shri Rajiv Gandhi was, to me, a soft-spoken, self-effacing man. I asked him if he missed flying. (He had been a pilot for Indian Airlines until his brother was killed while piloting a single-engined aircraft.) He replied: 'I can't describe to you how much I miss it, Mr Griffith. But circumstances have dictated that I must now help my mother in any way I can – and India if I am wanted.' That was the gist of what he said and I liked him very much.

But the most extraordinary experience for me to come out of that visit – and the reason for this book – was when Mrs Gandhi said: 'Perhaps one day, Mr Griffith, you might make a film – for India – about my father.'

The effect of those words left me bewildered. I did not know much about Jawaharlal Nehru except that he had fought and suffered through the middle of his life to remove us British from India, that he became India's first Prime Minister and that he was at the helm of India for the rest of his life. And now his daughter and his dedicated disciple and the person who was pursuing his mission was hoping that I, a Britisher, should make a film of his life!

She had just paid me the greatest compliment that she could. I pondered the situation. Not in her presence, of course; as far as I remember I was so shocked I made no comment then. It was later that I pondered, and I came to the conclusion that in those words she had demonstrated what a formidable woman she was. Having viewed my work over a period of many years, she had assessed certain facts and she had come to the conclusion that I was good enough to speak for her beloved father and it didn't matter that I wasn't an Indian; it didn't matter if I was Chinese, Russian, American or even British. She had decided that I might be good enough to achieve justice for Jawaharlal Nehru in a film. Few people are big enough to rise above national prejudice in such a way.

As I meandered away from India, I felt that there wasn't the dramatic material in Jawaharlal Nehru's life for one of my sort of films. And then I was very busy, being pulled into other work. And I failed to dig any deeper. I remained in ignorance of Mrs Gandhi's father's life.

The truth is that in my library was a foot or so of books about the obvious famous hero, Mahatma Gandhi. And they had been there for a very long time before I had heard of Sir Richard Attenborough's interest in the subject. Nehru had always seemed to me to be a figure in the shadow of that astounding phenomenon. Today I am better informed. The sum of my feelings about Nehru was that he was a good, decent man, who had led a country after its independence in a spirit of goodwill. India under Nehru was one of those very few countries in the world that no one need fear. A splendid commendation; but where was the big drama that I must have, on which to hang the meaningful information and at the same time to avoid a television switch-off? I remember saying to Mrs Gandhi that from where I was in life, the great Indian idealists, Mahatma Gandhi and 'your father' Jawaharlal Nehru, were more important than the world-shakers, Winston Churchill, Joseph Stalin or even President Roosevelt. Again Mrs Gandhi swung her attention at me, rather like a well-trained gunner: 'Make no mistake about Mahatma Gandhi, Mr Griffith; Gandhi was a very practical politician!' She did not deny or qualify that her father was an idealist. Anyway, that was about the sum of my knowledge of Jawaharlal Nehru.

Chiara Peretti and I were sitting in Zululand, Southern Africa (where I was working on a film, as both writer and actor) when I learnt that my friend, Indira Gandhi, had been brutally and obscenely murdered in her own home at Safdarjang Road in New Delhi. In the home where I had last seen her. Assassinated by two Sikhs whose sworn duty in life was to guard her body. Without going into the merits and demerits of Sikh national extremism, the murder of Mrs Gandhi must be one of the most treacherous acts ever committed by human beings. Immediately before they had emptied their guns into her body, she had placed her hands together, bowed slightly and wished them *Namaskar* (Salutation). I recoil in abhorrence when I think of it.

In Zululand I turned to my friend and said: 'I want to make that film about the life of Jawaharlal Nehru, more than anything else.' It was a purely emotional response, but I meant it with all my heart. However, I did have sufficient common sense to allow my feelings to lie fallow for a while. Practical problems had to be considered and, of course, my wish to serve Mrs Gandhi by carrying out her hope of a film on her father's life would probably have been lost in the avalanche of commiseration that must have been pouring into India.

Mrs Gandhi had said nothing to me about who should finance such a film. Indeed, I had presumed that if I made a life of Nehru I would simply go to one of my backers and say that I wanted to do it, which is my normal procedure. But now as I brooded over how I should go about the next stage, it became obvious in my mind that 'India' should confirm it wanted me to fulfil their dead Prime Minister's wish. At the very least I should secure India's support and approval. And I thought that armed with this certificate, I would then approach one of the companies – foreign or British – for which I had made films previously.

Mrs Gandhi's surviving son, Rajiv, was voted to take her place. And since he had joined his mother in approving of my work and since we had met, I was clearly pointed in the direction of informing him of my feelings. The truth is that Mrs Gandhi had told me that after her son had seen *The Most Valuable Englishman Ever* for the first time, he had stood up and said: 'I wish that man would make a film about Grandfather [Nehru].' And that, together with his gentle, friendly bearing towards me, suggested that he would agree to my proposed project.

In due course I wrote to the new Prime Minister – from South Africa! I felt that it was also essential in this letter to declare my attitude to the White regime there. India never seems to speak or write about South Africa without prefacing the name of the country with 'racist'. I find it extremely difficult to hide anything up my sleeve. If one starts deceiving, no matter how mildly, I believe that one's validity is in jeopardy. I confess everything! Only then can I begin to hope for some peace of mind. My third wife, Carole (and the person who had disturbed me deeply by suggesting that I loved the old dead soldiers more than I loved her), once also told me that I was the most public person she had ever met. Sometimes I confess so that I can survive; so there is, among other elements, selfishness on my part.

Anyway, I had the provocative compulsion to inform Mr Gandhi what I felt about the racial predicament in South Africa. I wrote that in my opinion it was not an unadulterated matter of good and evil, of Good 'Blacks' and Evil 'Whites', and that the information being pumped out to the liberal world against the South African 'Whites' was far from being the whole honest truth.

I have come to the conclusion that 'racist' is not the correct word; 'culturist' is nearer to the truth, Which culture will dominate? That is what imperfect humanity is ever concerned about – all around the world. People are, understandably, very afraid of living under an alien culture.

Of course, I didn't write all of that to Rajiv Gandhi. But I did state that there was more to the South African conflict than met the liberal eye. However, having made that point, I took the precaution of enclosing in my message a photostat of a letter I had just received from the Chief Minister of Zululand, Mangosuthu Buthelezi, stating that a film I had been responsible for about the British Zulu War of 1879 (I had made it for the BBC for the 1979 centenary) was his favourite film and that he and his family and friends had seen it often. In that film I was very properly on the side of the black Zulus and not on the side of white British Imperialism. And I stood four square with the Liberal, Gladstone, and opposed the Tory, Disraeli!

Rajiv Gandhi wrote back to me stating that he had handed the film project to Doordarshan which, after enquiry, I learnt was India's state television monopoly. The Prime Minister also remarked in his letter that he knew how much his Mother had hoped that I would make the film. That was the gist of the epistle.

I wasn't at all sure what was now expected of me. I had been employed in South Africa to write three film scripts of my own choosing, which in due course I was expected to turn into films. Naturally, I was very interested in all the subjects. The big one was a life of Paul Kruger, the great Transvaal President who had stood against the ambition of British commercial Toryism, which act had culminated in the tragic Second British/Boer War of 1899–1902. I had wanted to tell this very important story for a long while. The other two were less grandiose: a life of an 1820 South African settler from Scotland, named Thomas Pringle, who was a fine poet and man of high principles. And, finally, a life of George Rex, a person who many believe was the eldest legitimate son of King George III of Great Britain. He died in South Africa. This was to be an investigative film.

But now I had declared a new and unexpected priority: a life of Jawaharlal Nehru. I was not legally bound to do the filming of the three South African stories, so I explained my predicament to my singularly kindly employers and with goodwill on both sides I returned to Britain. I planned eventually to return to South Africa and complete my work. I had then been in Africa for about one year.

In London I was informed by Ms Pamela Cullen, who virtually seems to run India's international film arrangements, that India, through Doordarshan, wanted me to make the Nehru film for them. They wanted me to depart for India 'as soon as possible' and once there 'to formalise the arrangements'. Ms Cullen, who is very shrewd, efficient and overworked, asked me how much payment I would require for my various responsibilities as executive, producer, researcher, writer and entire cast! I told her and she said, 'Very reasonable'. I also stipulated that Chiara Peretti was to work on the film from beginning to end as my assistant, and as general factotum to the director and also she would undertake other heavy responsibilities such as being in charge of wardrobe and continuity. I said that I would have to have a car with a driver every day. Ms Cullen said that she could foresee no possible objection to any of these conditions.

By this time I had done some intensive reading about Nehru's life. I was observed hurrying around southern England's bookshops, searching and cajoling my many bookseller friends for anything relevant. Never before had I taken on a film project without knowing much about the subject. I had now placed the cart before the horse.

But I was getting the image of Nehru's life. And it was very different from anything that I had contemplated before. His Daddy, Motilal Nehru, a wealthy, extrovert Indian lawyer who admired the British, wanted to make his only beloved son an English gentleman. He sent him to Harrow Public School for elite Britishers, to Cambridge University and to the Inner Temple in London, to study law. Motilal succeeded; Jawaharlal was transformed into an upper middle class English gentleman.

But not quite a typical one! Jawaharlal became particularly interested in the great Emancipators of history. Men like Garibaldi and then with heroes who were battling at that very time: the Irish patriots, Roger Casement, Michael Collins and company. Nehru received the seed of an idea which was to become an unrelenting service: the freeing of his country, India, from the dominance of another country that he also loved, England. And how was he to properly divest himself of his English culture and find – discover – his Indian culture? He was too honest and wise and sensitive to try and tear off that English quality and destroy it. But he was going to search for his ancient Indian heritage and work for its fulfilment. That was an essential main theme, which I recognised very quickly.

My brand of romantic idealism was now operating fully. I said to Pamela Cullen I felt very strongly that every other member of our film team, with the exception of Chiara Peretti (Italian) and me, must be Indian. Ms Cullen, while approving of my proper feelings, added: 'But I do feel that you should have with you one of your film director colleagues, because your style is unique. I myself am still not sure how your films are put together.'

Now this has been said to me before by other highly-experienced professional film-makers. I have been invited to Harvard University and various film seminars in the United States to show my efforts and answer questions about them. The Americans tend to say that they are not documentary films. They are quite different from anything else that has gone before.

For example, I invent no dialogue. Every word that the historical characters speak they actually spoke or wrote. And then we go to enormous trouble to speak those historical words in the precise location where they were uttered. I suppose the most stupendous journey that we have ever made was to the remote island of St Helena, deep in the South Atlantic Ocean. It is a volcanic rock, six miles by ten, between the west coast of Africa and the east coast of South America. No aircraft can land there. One smallish ship arrives every six weeks. Some of us wrested our way there via the West Indies, Ascension Island in mid-Atlantic and then hazardously south to St Helena. We were making a film about the last six years of Napoleon's life on that little island. It had to be told in the house that he lived in there, Longwood, and the other historical sites.

And then the bit about our unique style of film-making, which seems impossible to imagine unless you have seen one of them, is that I become all of the historical characters. I have been as many as four people around a table. I have not heard of any viewer who has been confused. The potential of television is, as yet, virtually undiscovered.

Two last points for clarification – I do not use any make-up, and I never don the precise historical costume. Simply a hint and always some clothes that I would wear myself and indeed do wear in my own life. There must be a minimum of shock disturbance for the viewer. Again all of the many historical characters must be as truthful to their respective spirits as I am capable of comprehending and performing.

This technique is what Ms Cullen was concerned about, so I communicated with my long-time colleague, Michel Pearce, and he said that he would like to do it. It is possible that Michel likes India more than he likes me. . . .

CHAPTER TWO

Preamble to Shooting

The time had come to travel to meet Doordarshan in New Delhi to 'formalise the agreement'. I asked Ms Cullen: 'How long might this take?'

'Oh, two weeks I should think?' I thought how civilised; two days to go over the general pattern of professional needs and a week and a half to wander around India and talk to people.

I took the precaution of arranging with my bank to draw up to £1,000. I was given a tourist's visa for three months, and an 'executive class' return ticket to Delhi. Ms Cullen informed me that I would be met at the airport by Shri Jawaharlal Malhotra (Shri simply means Mister), the head of Public Relations for Doordarshan, and that I would be staying at the Kanishka Hotel, a government establishment rating five Indian stars. Ms Cullen said that first I would meet Shri Sharada Prasad, who had been an official close to Mrs Gandhi and was now close to her son, Rajiv. I was told that probably I would spend a little time with the Prime Minister, perhaps travel with him.

In India, unlike most foreigners, I wear Indian clothes; informally, a cotton kurta (collarless shirt) and cotton trousers with leather chappals (sandals) on my feet and, formally, a Jaipur suit (jacket buttoned up to the neck). I had worn such clothes on previous visits, but now, on this extraordinary assignment, I felt that it was essential. I felt that I must demonstrate a maximum respect for India and particularly for Jawaharlal Nehru. By wearing Indian-style clothes I would be making a constant declaration for all to see and I would be ever reminding myself. I like unequivocal statements. Also, the kurta outfit is the most sensible to wear in the heat of India.

On the morning of my departure from London I wore a Jaipur suit and I boarded an Air India aircraft wearing it. I have not donned European clothes in India from that day; that is, in my private life, as against in front of the camera. On that day, as I flew eastward, I reckoned that the film would be completed and delivered about eight months into the future.

The Indira Gandhi International Airport was a big surprise. The last time that I had seen Delhi's airport, it had been a disastrous mess. Great miscellaneous piles of luggage which, as far as I can recall, were simply dumped there. And people trod on each other to scratch for their pieces. Now it has been transformed into a vast modern area, full of the paraphernalia of modern air travel.

Waiting for me was Shri Malhotra. Jawaharlal of public relations is a thick-set man of slightly less than medium height. He has a nice face; indeed, many months later, someone – Chiara? – was saying what a handsome people the Indians were, and referred to Shri Malhotra as an example. He was solid and friendly and, indeed, reassuring. He escorted me to a car and a driver. I thought that he ordered this man about in a peremptory manner, but this is a common Indian style and I now believe, like so many other relationships there, it is deeply rooted in the ancient caste system. You had better know your place in this Indian world and you will not be given much of a chance to stray.

Of course, my position – my caste position – was ambiguous and detached. I was obviously someone extraordinary and to add to the strong flavour, I was also British, which is, understandably, still a disturbing ingredient on the subcontinent. The Indians and the British have been through a couple of hundred years of colourful experiences together. The blood is certainly still marking the walls.

Once, some years ago, I was sitting on the back of a cart, being pulled by a horse, through the crowded streets of

Jaipur, just at dusk-time. Chiara Peretti was up front with the driver. Out of the exotic massed throng came a young man on a bicycle with a friend on the crossbar. They kept close to me gazing at my confusing appearance – perhaps Europeans in Indian clothes don't usually travel in Jaipur hanging over the back of a horse-drawn vehicle. Finally, the young man had to ask: 'I am a Brahmin; what caste are you?'

'Middle caste,' I replied. And that clever answer of mine seemed to satisfy him. He veered away with a wave and a grin. Clever it may have been, but hardly true; I came from a Working Caste. Once, on some BBC interview programme, I said that I came from peasant roots. Several people from my home town of Tenby in south-west Wales were outraged. They felt that I had insulted my long dead and beloved Grandparents.

That was by the way, but also as a reminder that we British have a similar human social structure to the Indians, but I do declare, not nearly as remorseless.

Jawaharlal Malhotra travelled with me to the Kanishka Hotel and supervised my registration and occupancy of my reasonable accommodation. He asked at what time would I like to see him in the morning and I presumed that 'the formalising of the agreement' would get under way.

The next morning Jawaharlal collected me and off we went to the headquarters of Doordarshan, a national television service which is potentially one of the biggest in the world. Incidentally, Doordarshan means Distant Vision. The building which housed it is called Mandi House, after one of the old princely states. When the British moved their Raj administration from Calcutta, on the north-east coast of India, to the northern centre of India at Delhi, the many princely states, run by their Maharajahs and Nawabs (Hindu and Muslim respectively), hastened to build extra palaces around the British Viceroy's new magnificence. These satellite palaces are very interesting; they each reflect their distant state's character, frozen in an Indian 1920s' style.

Mandi was not one of the major princely states and the building reflects this, but it is still pulsating with an arrested atmosphere from a time that preceded the invention of television. The building, though not ostentatious, has fine, discreetly-carved stonework embedded in it. They are now beginning to demolish the little palace. I have fussed round a bit on behalf of the carved stonework. I have been told that it is to be saved; I hope so.

For a television centre Mandi House was astoundingly ramshackle. Jawaharlal Malhotra's office was in a cluttered open room, off which were partitioned other departments. An air cooler, with a motor sounding like a jet-engine, blasted its air and spits of water across the face of my new friend's desk. Indian glass paperweights kept everything from being swept westward. Across from Jawaharlal was Shri Kamerar. Like everyone and everything in India, it is not easy to discover anyone's or anything's precise, specific function. There is a grading system, but its structure is not as simply direct as ours; it is compounded with an ancient Eastern ritual. And that basically is why it is within a manic scream of us Westerners being unable to function with Indian Easterners. Unless, of course, for the sake of modern commercial progress, Indians have decided to play most of the Western game. When that happens, they can quickly become very Western-efficient and thereby affluent. Cite the Indian communities in the West.

Dare I hazard an opinion that Shri Kamerar was junior in position to Shri Malhotra? Certainly, the latter issued unsmiling orders to the former. Shri Kamerar is also thick-set and has very black hair and dark, dark, penetrating eyes. But then, even after he has heard me shouting extreme, uncontrollable abuse round our film production office, or aimed up at the fifth floor of the newly-constructed Mandi House where the power lies, Shri Kamerar always flashed a warm smile at me on the slightest friendly cue.

And again with me and my uninhibited rages against the impenetrable wall of Indian fudge when action is desperately needed, I have noticed Shri Kamerar's dark eyes staring at me with – what? But one minute later, because of my deep affection for him – I have given him that Indian sideways nod of the head (which does not mean no in India, as it does in our society) and he answers it with his flash of white teeth and, dare I believe it, reciprocal affection?

Jawaharlal Malhotra introduced me to the managers of Doordarshan, including the Director-General, Shri Harish Khanna, to whom I began to communicate my enthusiasm for the great responsibility of what lay ahead of us. Quickly I began to sense that my enthusiasm was not penetrating Shri Khanna's mind. It wasn't that he was exactly impolite; it was more that he had nothing creative or human to share with me. Naturally my first twinge of unease pricked me; he was, presumably, my leader. What blunders can a straightforward innocent like me make as he enters this strange alien Indian culture? I seem to recall that Shri Khanna was continually looking at his watch as I spoke to him about the moving significance of Jawaharlal Nehru's life.

Ah! But now to the heart of my task. I was asked to attend South Block, from where the Prime Minister, Rajiv Gandhi, operated. The disconcerting shambles of Mandi House (even the Director-General's office looked like a poor theatrical set for a soap opera) would be dispelled by the authority of the Big Guns. This must be 'down to business'. First I was to talk to Shri Sharada Prasad.

South Block is part of Sir Edwin Lutyens's magnificent centrepiece, built for the governance of India by the British Raj, and now inherited by the Republic of India. It is valuable to consider carefully this outstanding piece of architecture, designed and put together by the British after the First World War; the significance of the British move to Delhi or rather to New Delhi, New simply because it was built at the southern end of Old Delhi; the political significance of the move to that place in India which had been the centre of the disturbing Mogul Empire with its vast overbearing Red Fort and also of more ancient memories of brutal conquest. I have been aware, as I stood in the ruins of a great mosque, of the ominous shade of monstrous Tamburlaine who visited these places and then returned to Samarkand. Consider the weight and fine detail of architect Lutyens and the Imperial mentality of those who employed him. It is all a very clear statement that the British had no plans whatsoever to leave India. Who could have foretold the Second World War and its revolutionary consequences?

Well here I was at South Block, on my way to the rooms of power. The tragic ritual of super security began and here the formidably armed soldiers were friendly and courteous. In one of my pockets they discovered my little penknife, which they took and gave me a receipt for. The security checks were more extreme than in any other country that I have visited; with the exception of my beloved Israel. No, I am not Jewish.

To Shri Prasad's ante-room. Again the personnel there were quietly efficient and gracious. My confidence in the reality of my strange mission was returning. I was shown into Shri Prasad's large office. He is a man of slightly below average height and I have guessed that he is in his latish fifties. He came from behind his large desk to greet me and then returned to his seat of authority.

Having asked if all was going well for me in India so far, to which I had replied in the affirmative, he began to state the practical arrangements: 'I think, Mr Griffith, that you should first meet some of the people who knew Panditji [Nehru] and perhaps you should talk to some of our historians; they might be able to assist you.'

'Yes, sir. Thank you, sir.'

The telephone sounded and I had the impression that it was the Prime Minister. Shri Prasad glanced up at me with a smile. 'Ah, he is here now.' I understood nothing more and, putting down the telephone, Shri Prasad continued: 'Arrangements will be made for you to meet the best authorities on your subject. And though I am not a historian, I am deeply interested and perhaps I can emphasise certain books which should prove of most value to you.' And then Shri Prasad made it clear to me that he shrewdly understood what elements I would need for my sort of film. He was extremely perceptive about what was required to hold the viewers' attention – always an emphasis on the human element, which would help to communicate the saga.

The Most Valuable Englishman Ever (a life of Thomas Paine) had been sent to India in the diplomatic bag before my arrival and the top officials concerned, who were not already familiar with my unusual style, had studied it. This must have included Shri Prasad. And now I was witnessing not only perception but direct and deep concern for the spirit of Jawaharlal Nehru. I felt that I was with a brother spirit and was reassured that my improbable adventure was going to be all right. After the messy, inexplicable fog of Doordarshan, the sun was upon me again.

As Shri Prasad reached for this volume and that volume from the library in his office, he gave succinct analyses of each of the writers' qualities and points of view; he did not dismiss non-academic works, which comforted me no end. He summed up his own attitude: 'What I would hope to see in your film, above all else, is the man's courage and humanity.'

Just before I left him, Shri Prasad said: 'And, Mr Griffith, I think that it would be best if you talked with the Prime Minister a little later; after you have familiarised yourself with the subject more.' I agreed. I was feeling elated as I checked out of South Block into the heat of a Delhi winter.

Suddenly a well-armed soldier came running after me: 'You've forgotten your pocket knife, sir.'

Doordarshan is not independent, like every other television service I have come across around the world. The organisation is strictly in the deep pocket of India's Ministry of Information and Broadcasting and, of course, the Ministry is part of the Indian Government. And in that unfortunate structure lies Doordarshan's sickness and doom. No one should criticise Doordarshan without bearing in mind this built-in crushing inhibition. All of the hopeless faults that lie within Mandi House are rooted in this destructive fact. At this early stage of my Indian visit I was not aware of the enormity of the fault; I was sensing only the inevitable effect. But the ominous reality for me was that the Prime Minister of India had proposed I should be employed by Doordarshan. This, if it came about, condemned me to be cast into a very dark and deep pit indeed. And from that uncomfortable place I would be expected to make a sophisticated film on the life of India's great leader. But I was still bathed in the light of Shri Prasad's wisdom.

Now I was to meet the Minister of Information and Broadcasting, V. N. Gadgil, and all the heads of the different departments. I got out of my working-day kurta and put on a grey Jaipur suit. When I entered his large office, the Minister was seated behind his sweeping desk and facing him was his entire upper-echelon team. Shri Gadgil is a smallish man and he smiled warmly as I came in. There was a look of admiration in his lively eyes; I felt that this was the first Indian that I had met, on this visit, who appreciated me as an artist first.

As I came forward in my Indian suit, I noted that Shri Gadgil was also wearing one but that all the other nine or ten bureaucrats present were wearing Western clothes. As Shri Gadgil directed me to a chair in the midst of his staff, he remarked on my appearance, with a naughty twinkle, 'It sits very well upon you, Mr Griffith.' I sensed that the others were not so pleased.

I then noticed that the Director-General of Doordarshan, Harish Khanna, was seated in the lengthy line-up, to my right. 'Oh, good morning, Shri Khanna,' said I.

'Good morning, Mr Griffith.'

Shri Khanna always seemed to me to be in a highly-strung state – like me. He looked pleased that I had seen him and had greeted him clearly among the rather forbidding assembly.

The Minister continued to beam at me: 'Mr Griffith, I do

admire your work very much.' Out of all the many, many officials I have had to work and deal with in India, I think that Shri Gadgil has been the most open and direct. I liked and trusted him. Normally, I was learning, Indians hold their cards very close to their chests; it is part of the system to give nothing away. But at that time I didn't know.

Even in this distinguished meeting, to which I had been invited and for which there was little doubt that I was the reason, there was a disconcerting silence. It wasn't the warm, friendly atmosphere that I had perhaps expected. Indeed there seemed to be patches of coldness. Or was it even hostility? Fortunately, the boss-man continued to beam at me.

Both Nature and I cannot abide a vacuum, so I made the running. I launched into the reality of a film on the life of Jawaharlal Nehru. I gave and gave in spirit and received nothing, that I can recall, in return. I told the gentlemen what my last film had cost and how long it had taken to make. I put strong emphasis on my wish to keep the production as Indian as possible. It struck me I was making a heart-felt confession (a practice I am subject to) and that I was at pains to demonstrate there was nothing up my sleeve. One or two cool questions were put to me from unsmiling faces and I answered them clearly and positively.

Nothing was given in my direction. No help. No encouragement. No information. So I pushed on: 'Sir [addressing the Minister], when do you feel that we can, ah, formalise our agreement and begin work?' Shri Gadgil turned to a man near him, 'Oh, I think we could get it settled by Monday.'

'Yes,' replied the man unenthusiastically, 'or Tuesday.'

Well, that was the pattern. Nothing happened on the Monday or the Tuesday. Indeed nothing happened or moved for six solid bloody months. And no one had the common manners to explain anything to me. There were a number of ghastly meetings at the Ministry, always instigated by me and usually presided over by the Chief Secretary,

G. N. Mehra. Shri Mehra is a sharp dresser, sleek, with a thin pencil moustache. I suspect that he was the real generating power there. He was the permanent civil servant at the top. Ministers may come and ministers may go, but Shri Mehra. . . . On a shelf behind him was a sepia photograph of Jawaharlal Nehru. One of his apparently awed heads of department whispered to me, in Shri Mehra's hearing: 'It's a family heirloom!'

And so my days, weeks and months rolled nervously by. I was in an extremely strange and difficult position. I had pushed aside my other film plans to make this Nehru film. I could not have had sounder reason to believe that all must be well: I was here in Delhi at the instigation of India's last two Prime Ministers. The Indian High Commission in London had assured me, everything that I had asked for had been verbally granted and in India I was visited almost daily by Jawaharlal Malhotra, the head of public relations for the Doordarshan organisation.

But the formalising of the agreement that was to have been easily embraced within those two weeks had not happened and everything was enshrouded in – as Chiara Peretti described it – fog. After a while I had spent quite a considerable sum of my own money. Is it surprising that I began to suffer a nervous stomach?

Each day I would ask Shri Malhotra: 'When do you think. . . ?'

'I believe that something should happen by next Monday.'

It didn't.

In the Kanishka Hotel restaurant I carefully scrutinised the menu so that I wouldn't be eating too extravagantly at poor India's expense. And then I began to receive pressing requests from this Government-owned hotel to settle the fast-growing bill. I thundered down to the manager and pointed out that I was the guest of his government and to stop worrying me with such impolite demands. I raised the matter with Shri Malhotra who reassured my fraying nerves that all was well and that 'the bill will be settled soon.' But the bills kept coming to me – into my little room. I stormed down the seven floors again and shouted: 'Give this bloody thing to Rajiv Gandhi and not to me!' Come to think of it, I began to crack up very early in India. Later I was near to being a nut case.

However, the time was not unproductive. Arrangements were made, by whatever tenuous, unknown route, for me to meet a number of distinguished Indian authorities on Jawaharlal Nehru. This was interesting for me, but it was against the background of no contract and the worries that this generated. I couldn't utilise the opportunities to their fullest. The historian who impressed me most formidably was Doctor Bal Ram Nanda, and particularly his perceptive and charming wife.

The Doctor had seen one of my films (*The Most Valuable Englishman Ever*) and was delighted with it. He had assisted Sir Richard Attenborough with his vast Gandhi epic. And he was remarkably enlightened about that film. Though Doctor Nanda is a distinguished academic, he had a full understanding of Sir Richard's task. All that mattered was that Gandhi's spirit was conveyed to many millions of people around the world and that those millions benefited from it. And we both agreed that this had been achieved. And that is all that Doctor Nanda would say publicly on the subject.

And he immediately recognised my very different task. My films are nearer to the doctor's factual obligation. What is said by the respective characters was historically expressed by them. My unavoidable liberty is to carve out a meaningful drama within my employer's prescribed time limit. All of this Doctor Nanda happily supported.

And my other uplifting communication was with Shrimarti Vijaya Lakshmi Pandit, the beloved sister of the protagonist of the proposed film. Her daughter, Shrimarti Rita Dar, arranged the first meeting. Mrs Pandit is now an elderly, bright, good-looking woman. She shares certain unusual qualities with her famous brother. An intelligence that is refreshingly open and direct. On one occasion we went to an enjoyable party together, which was attended almost entirely by Kashmiri Pandits (learned men) and their families. Brahmins from Kashmir, who may have emigrated south to the great plain of India centuries before, know very clearly who they are and they still hold together as a proud and pleasant community. Their food can be deliciously distinctive. Of course, there are many different groupings in India: ethnic, religious and finally crushed into even thousands of recognisable sub-caste systems. Sometimes it is a strength, but more often in this time of human history, it is in conflict with all modern political and moral concepts – whether of the right or the left.

This experience of Kashmiri exiles was an unadulterated pleasure for me. They are valuable cultural fact and I hope that they never conform themselves out of existence. India daily uses an unusual English word – that is, unusual in Britain – communalism. It is a dread word on the subcontinent. What India means by communalism is when these ethnic/religious groups threaten each other and often kill each other. It is like a domestic sort of racism.

India is ever lecturing the Afrikaners of South Africa in the most unrestrained and strident language. India doesn't like to be reminded that its own domestic cultural conflicts are multiple and far more irrational than South Africa's. It doesn't like the two problems – India's and South Africa's – to be equated. But they are both cultural conflicts based on the fear of one culture being overwhelmed and ruled by another.

Of course, India offers universal suffrage to all. But the fear of the Muslim minority of being ruled by the Hindu majority forced the partition of India and about half-a-million murders. There are far more Indians dying in the Punjab and elsewhere at this time than there are Black Africans dying south of the Limpopo River. But to mention gently to a liberal Indian, who may be even aggressively proud of his particular community, that the Afrikaners feel they cannot agree to live under a Black African culture and that that is the reason for their unshiftable stand, and then to equate that predicament with their own relatively insignificant cultural reasons for fear, could easily lead to an explosion. Hypocrisy is often sightless and deaf.

The difference in culture between the White Afrikaners (in spite of their having resided on the African continent for three hundred and fifty years) and the Black Bantu is probably more extreme than that between any other two cultures on this planet. One of many facts to be at least considered in this terrible dilemma is that democracy is anathema to the African mind; enfranchise all adults in the Republic of South Africa and the liberal-thinking world would very soon lose the biggest patch of democracy (limited now to the European White Africans) that presently exists on the African continent. Cite Mugabe and company in today's Zimbabwe or Zambia or. . . .

Perhaps no one short of God Almighty can be just about such human realities. I squirm each day as I hear the blind shallow liberal hypocrisy. Is the dominant culture of a country to be decided by the majority of voting hands, even if that elected majority immediately sets about eliminating the very democracy that gave them the political power? At least let us consider both of the two tragic points of view. But such an argument seems to be too complex for facile liberals. They seem to analyse no deeper than the colour of a person's skin or their mode of dressing or worshipping, whether we are considering the Punjab or the Republic of South Africa.

And are we not to give a sympathetic thought to the Melanesians of Fiji? Is their ancient culture to be subject to an alien Indian way of thinking because Indians tend to breed faster? Of course, we British are to blame for shipping Asians to the Pacific as indentured labour for our own material advantage. The old bully-boy Imperialism is now in some sort of chaotic reverse. All I am writing is that right and wrong cannot always be simply defined by which group has the most voting hands. There are other comprehensible factors. But clean liberals are not tempted to think beyond their 'unctous rectitude' as Cecil Rhodes once called it. No, generally I am not an admirer of Rhodes's ethics.

The above is a lengthy aside, but very early during this visit to India I began to sense heaving inconsistencies and a blinkered vision about their own ethical Indian position – a cultural difference of opinion between us, I suppose.

And so I was trapped in this wasteful limbo. Days, weeks and months with no practical decision whatsoever. Shri Malhotra continued to call on me at the Kanishka Hotel and to reassure me that everything would be settled by 'next Monday'. But a nightmare was now ever edging around me. What the hell was I to do? Occasionally, I saw the Director-General of Doordarshan, Harish Khanna, but he seemed to be heading for a very nervous breakdown and could offer me no advice.

Rajiv Gandhi had sent me a message through his colleague, Shri Prasad: 'Whenever you are stuck, Mr Griffith, please let me know.' But reading daily of his monumental problems, I was extremely reluctant to bother him with my completely negative predicament. And so I suffered the Alice in Wonderland life and applied my thoughts and activities to creative thinking and historical investigation. Though it was not particularly aimed at Jawaharlal Nehru's life; I dabbled with it. There was a psychological impediment against intensive work in the Nehru direction because I was not yet contracted to research and write the film; though once I am committed contractually to a project, it becomes all-consuming, and I was wary of being obsessed about a subject that might mysteriously not come to fruition.

So I began to focus my days on studying the history of my own people, the British in India, with particular emphasis on what we have called The Indian Mutiny of 1857.

I knew that this would deepen my understanding of Nehru's life, when or if I eventually had to deal with it professionally. You see, I was already bathed in doubt. Sometimes I had to wrestle with the disturbing fact that I had disrupted my life, on trust, and perhaps it was all for nothing. All around me was that Indian fog which Chiara Peretti was to describe. Of course, at this juncture of the enterprise I had no European colleagues with me.

Now Delhi was the eventual heart of the Indian Mutiny. In the old city is what was the last centre of Mogul strength: the vast Red Fort. In that fortified palace, in 1857, was the Emperor, Bahadur Shah. He was then an old man, given to composing innocent poetry, who knew that the Moguls' once terrifying power had dwindled to almost nothing; first by their own degeneracy and finally by the ascendancy of the British East India Company.

The origins of The Mutiny are mysteriously complex as only an Eastern complexity can be. After one hundred and thirty years of historical probing, no one is clear about its cause and growth. The most famous reason, which was given to me during my schooldays, was that sepoys (Indian soldiers serving in the British Army) objected to touching animal fat, which was believed to be lubricating the cartridges for their guns. I suspect that this trouble originated among the Muslim sepoys, who believed it was pig fat (the pig is unholy to Islam), and that then the Muslims cleverly informed their Hindu comrades that cow fat was also being used (the cow is holy to the Hindu), and thereby achieved some unanimity of action. I suspect this sequence because there was clearly an intention to rally round the frail old Muslim Emperor Bahadur Shah in Delhi. The Mutiny of the Indian soldiers was fundamentally an attempt to resurrect the defunct Mogul authority. Many Indians today will not approve of this statement. There is some inclination to call 1857 'The First War of Independence' because Indian political nationalists would like to believe that the terrible event was simply a united freedom struggle. I would concede that the Muslims (many by forced conversion from original Hinduism) had become sufficiently assimilated into the Hindustan concept of existence to recognise the British as a far removed, alien culture and that, unlike the old Muslim invaders and rulers, the British had no intention of settling down on the sub-continent and becoming Indians. To that extent there was unity of identification among the Indians. And the officers of the British East India Company were predominantly white. It was clear to all whose culture was in charge.

The Mutiny first exploded in the city of Meerut, which lies to the north-east of Delhi. Legend informs us that the first sepoy to take violent action was a man named Pandey, who must have been a Hindu, which goes against the above argument. But the whole trauma was a foreboding mystery. Among many typical legends is the unexplained appearance of chapatis (bread pancakes) in many villages of north-western India, which was reputed to herald the holocaust. The British have investigated and heart-searched the cause, but have signally failed to find the simple answer. Like every human effort to try and understand a cultural conflict, it would be very funny if it wasn't so ghastly. Certainly, the British, even when they exercised a sincere social concern, misread the Indian psyche again and again, just as I have been unable to come to terms with it over the past two years. The chasm is desperately deep; even when it is approached – as I approached it – with idealism and goodwill. Let the world take deep note of Rudyard Kipling: 'East is east and west is west and never the twain shall meet.' It is no use the jolly clean liberals dreaming otherwise; reality will stare us all in the face. And my new white hairs, acquired recently as West tried to live with East, are the material proof.

And so I visited Meerut. I called at a local police station to enquire about various historical sites connected with the Mutiny and their locations. I received the strong impression that people did not usually voluntarily visit these particular arms-of-the-law. There was a mystified, sinister attitude towards me. But I usually counter such mistrust or hostility or both with an open spirit of innocent bonhomie which often disarms – but not always!

This time I more or less won. I was given a cup of coffee and eventually the uniformed and well-armed senior officer communicated that he would accompany me in the taxi I had hired. Often, because of language difficulties, situations arise which are neither wanted nor understood. This armed officer never smiled once during our, perhaps, two hours together. He registered on his face a perpetual suspicious glower. But he peremptorily ordered my now cowed driver to the places that I wanted to see. He was accompanied by another police officer, in civilian clothes and very hefty but more obviously friendly, who spoke a modicum of English.

They took me first to the Pandey Memorial. This place seemed to be a combination of a religious and nationalist shrine. The big detective tried to explain to me a mystical legend about Sepoy Pandey, which I was forced to digest with a large pinch of salt.

And then to the old British graveyard and the ghost-ridden Garrison Church. These British graveyards of India are always pungently disturbing: the familiar British names, usually of very young people and many, many infants; the Christian messages in an alien land; a sense of an old-time respectable courtesy; all around, the Eastern trees and flowers and different birds; and, above all, the hot sun on the dusty earth.

The police officers departed and for further hours I peered at the names of the British men and their wives. The regiments, the places of birth in England, Ireland, Scotland and my own Wales, and the names of the old countries. I have done much grave-watching in India and I have always felt a reluctance to depart from the remains of my fellow country-people. Meerut's British Cemetery is a beautiful place. I did not see any great evidence of desecration. Indeed, a few Christian Indians are still being interred there. There was an area where some of the victims of the 1857 terror are buried.

And then to the Garrison Church. I knew something of what had happened. I imagined the shouts, the screams and the smoke. I could almost see the horse and trap racing from the church gate in the hope of dear life.

It is a spacious church and, like so many in India, almost dead; but not quite. The Anglo-Saxon and Celtic spirits still roam and the odd Anglo-Indian and Christian Indian; small groups keep a few candles lit. And there are the brass memorials on the walls. A résumé of the British Raj in India. We British came back to Meerut before we finally departed from India round the year 1947. There are more names of parishioners, men, women and children, who died in 1857 and much else besides. Few tourists visit 1857 – Well, why should they?

A vast, sloping and deep balcony surrounds the body of this Church of England. I have never seen anything like it. The great wooden floor is still sturdy and all around are the names of dead military men. Is this where the rank and file of the British soldiers stood and sang lustily? I could hear them for sure.

When I was a young boy, I met and got to know three soldiers who had returned from India. One was a regimental sergeant major, tall, lean and upright. He wore his khaki uniform with a coloured sash diagonally, across his chest. He had a moustache and, strangely, there was an impediment in his speech. Somehow he was related to me and he had just returned from India. I had tea with him. And then there was Major Julian Allen, a gentle inventive soul who was one of the best friends I have ever had, though I was nine years old and he must have been fifty odd. I believe that he and his good wife contemplated adopting me; but it never happened. And I also knew his brother, Colonel Harold Allen, who was quite taciturn and very like the conventional image of a British Indian officer. I have often placed all three of them in my mind's eye in such places as the Garrison Church at Meerut.

Since I visited the city there have been monstrous pogroms in Meerut between Hindus and Muslims. I have read in the Indian press that the local police were not as helpful as they might have been. I think of my suspicious police officers and of racist South Africa and of racist Meerut.

The Mutineers of 1857, having eliminated the British and the ever-expendable Jews of Meerut, rode and marched south-westward to the doddering Mogul Emperor in his Red Fort at Delhi. The great red complex is virtually as it was in 1857 – though now amply looted. British civil officials attended at Bahadur Shah's court. One of them was standing on the north-eastern ramparts when he saw a stream of strangely undisciplined sepoys crossing the Jumna River from the direction of Meerut, along a pontoon bridge. Realising that something was amiss (to describe it mildly), he gave orders for the north-eastern gate to be closed and then he raced for the Lahore Gate, the main entrance to the fort-palace. Now everyone knows the Lahore Gate and the Delhi Gate, but this north-eastern gate was unknown to me; so I began to explore in that direction.

During the British time in Delhi, after 1857, we built army barracks within the Red Fort and they do not compare happily with the sophistication of the Emperor Shah Jehan's architecture of 1638 to 1648. The British structures are pure nineteenth-century Aldershot: stone and those stout wooden criss-crossed balustrades. The Victorians decided what was best and stuck to it, all around the Empire.

Between this presumed hidden gateway and me lay these sometime British barracks, now inhabited by detachments of the Indian Army. Soon after I entered the area, several soldiers hastened towards me shouting: 'Restricted!' Now there are many parts of India where you will see Restricted Area and often there is no sound logical reason. It is frequently part of the Holy Bureaucracy of India, which incidentally is far more powerful and influential on the subcontinent than either Holy Hinduism or Holy Islam. In this case the area was understandably restricted.

However, I now had the compulsion of investigation in my head. 'Please take me to your officer,' I politely requested.

'Restricted! Restricted!' was the only reply.

'Please take me to an officer,' I kept repeating as I continued to walk, 'Take me to your leader!' And gradually the soldiers drifted away from me in the heat. I did wonder if I was about to be shot; but the rest was silence. I also registered to myself that my behaviour was a wee bit naughty. And that self-confession brings a sort of personal absolution.

I clambered up on to the overgrown ramparts. There were British Victorian hoists to lift heavy ammunition. But nothing that could remotely be a military secret. And there was the famous gate! I stood above and heard the rabid threats from the Mutineers below. And a small shaft of horror empathetically touched my soul. I turned back to retrace my steps to the Lahore Gate where the tragedy of Delhi had first struck, over one hundred and thirty years ago.

Through the Lahore Gate stormed the Mutineers, though there was no opposition to assault, and into the Meena Bazaar where Emperor Bahadur Shah's many ladies did their shopping. It is still a bazaar today, but now for less exotic tourists. The rabble of Mutineers met the odd Briton and the odd sword may have been drawn, before the European was pulverised. Above the shops a few British ladies were taking tea with one or two very respectable male compatriots. No doubt they had time to stand up on hearing the commotion below. But there was little time to scream before blood was on the white walls.

I asked the Indian shopmen if they knew anything about what had happened on their premises in the year 1857. There was not a word; not a flicker of recognition from any of them. I asked them about ghosts; but only a blank stare. It is a curious fact that I could find no one in the whole of Delhi who knew any details about the high melodrama that had been enacted within the Red Fort at that bloody time. I asked the Archaeological Department of India, which is housed within the mighty walls. Nothing could I elicit. No one seemed interested. British tourists amble through and dabble with souvenirs and very few can hear anything from the rooms just above their heads.

Old Delhi lies adjacent to New Delhi, but as my important friend Miss Norah Nicholson (a true Delhi wallah) says: 'There is only Delhi and New Delhi.' But then Norah is a purist. Anyway, in Delhi, the main street is called Chandni Chowk and runs from near the Red Fort's Lahore Gate north-westward (I think!). Off Chandni Chowk are the myriad streets and lanes of antiquity, and it was here the mutinous sepoys spread out and murdered almost all the Europeans they could catch – and the Jews, of course. Today these labyrinthine ways still teem with human beings. Though Hindus and Muslims segregate themselves into specific areas. Oh yes, very clearly demarcated ones. A year and a half ago I approached the Jama Masjid, the Great Mosque; I edged my way through formidably-armed, khaki-clad para-military policemen. They didn't stop me; they simply stared.

Suddenly, a man (I presume he was a Hindu) hurried out of a doorway: 'Sir, don't go any further. It is dangerous.'

'Oh, I think I'll be all right.' And on I marched. Around the corner was the Muslim threat. I have already personally suffered the barbarity of the Ayatollah Khomeini's Islam in the city of Shiraz and elsewhere in his good god forsaken land, so I turned round without pause and searched to thank my anonymous Hindu friend: but he had disappeared.

In these lanes of Old Delhi the Mutineers caught some fifty or so European women and children whom they did not kill – immediately. They were transported to Bahadur Shah's palace and, after a nightmarish interval, were publicly hacked to death in the shade of a revered tree, with the Emperor's principal sons enthusiastically watching.

I don't think the old royal man was there. Again I failed to find anyone who could tell me where the site of this atrocity was. Certainly, there is no memorial.

Moving northward through Delhi towards the old British cantonment, I visited the remnants of the pre-Mutiny Christian cemetery. The graveyard is now inhabited by a small community of Indian Christians, where I have always been received most hospitably, particularly by a retired sailor. Just beyond this old cemetery are the gatehouses of the British arsenal. When the Mutineers reached this lethal and significant place, a few Europeans defended it till the situation became untenable and then blew it up, including one or two of themselves.

Close at hand is an obelisk commemorating the men of the British telegraph station, which stood near by. For a short while these men knew that bloody anarchy was approaching and they steadfastly transmitted warnings to other British stations. Eventually, they were overwhelmed and at least one young man died at his place of work. The plaque has not been defaced, but over the past year and a half at least – to my knowledge – bicycle tyres have been rather skilfully hoopla'd round the memorial. I have contemplated cutting them away out of respect for the long dead men, but so far I have found neither the time nor the courage to do it. It is a singularly public Indian place. I'll think about the matter further.

Further north along the main road on the right-hand side is the beautiful St James's Church, which was built by a colourful Anglo-Indian, Colonel Skinner who founded Skinner's Horse, an independent regiment, but always allied to us British. If you rummage round the Skinner family's private cemetery patch you can note the burial of a Skinner child who died in Scotland and whose body was transported back to India, to be buried here. What does that tell us about those often tragic people of part-Indian and part-British blood? Oh yes, cultural prejudice lurks on both sides of the East-West divide! Also within the church grounds is the mass grave of those British bodies that were somehow recovered.

One day I was attending a Sunday service in St James's with my chum Miss Norah Nicholson. The congregation now pursues the modern custom of taking the hand of one's nearest neighbour at some specific point in the ceremony. I turned round and joined hands with a handsome middle-aged man; I later learnt that he was the present Colonel Skinner. The descendant of an exotic, historic family.

Close by and across the road is the Kashmiri Gate that will be ever famous in British Imperial history. It was here that the Brits eventually blasted their bloody path back into Delhi to exercise immediately a staggering revenge on the city. There was no turning the other Christian cheek. And one eye to be exchanged for one lost was not remotely enough. But the Kashmiri Gate with its Victoria Crosses came later in my chronological perambulations.

I walked up on The Ridge to the north-west of the Kashmiri Gate. This area is now an informal park. Here, overlooking Delhi, the British mustered their makeshift military force for the relief of the captured city. But on that first exploratory walk I knew very little about the old events. I came to a strange circular building, which immediately disturbed me. It was Victorian Gothic and I discerned a cross motif in the design. The place was in good repair but formidably locked. I peered through decorative apertures into a stark interior. I asked passing Indians: 'What is this place?'

At last came the reply 'Flagstaff House,' but nothing further. The place made me shiver with unease. Later I was to learn that it was in this building that the last survivors – bloody European women and children – from the horror below, were given shelter. Don't tell me that there are no ghosts.

Here on The Ridge the British soldiers and their loyal Indian allies – Sikhs distinguished themselves – grimly reformed and anxiously pondered their critical chances of a successful battle. The Mutineers made brave attempts to dislodge the British force, but, often in messy hand-to-hand combat, the British battered them back. Epidemics hit the defenders of The Ridge.

On the western extremity of the British position as the hill descends is the Mutiny Memorial giving the nerve-wracking statistics of the British force; as far as I can recall there were about fifty per cent losses. The Memorial, which again is heavily Victorian Gothic, is almost entirely intact, though tropical plants are beginning to grow dangerously from among the stonework and the site is now mainly occupied by body-building Indians with a religious bent.

No, the Indian Government has liberally restrained itself from interfering with what, in truth, is a provocative record of people from a distant, very foreign land, fiercely in conflict with soldiers from India, whether freedom-fighters or Mutineers, call them what we choose. What the Indian authorities have done is to add another marble slab in close proximity to the Mutiny Memorial, stating words to the effect that 'the enemy' mentioned on the British structure were India's brave soldiers fighting for freedom. Though I would question the simple Indian definition given, I feel that a civilised compromise has been achieved. But can't the British War Graves Commission makes itself responsible for the upkeep of these military memories? The memorials also represent part of India's evolvement into the approaching twenty-first century. Pity to bury even mixed blessings.

And now I trudged back to the Kashmiri Gate. Here is the turning point of the Indian Mutiny. The British force up on The Ridge decided to come down and do battle. The commanders decided that they would go for, primarily, the Kashmiri Gate and fairly nearby, the Mori Gate. A blazing focus was projected. The British heavy guns forced their passage very close; the location of our forward artillery was on a slight hill in what is now a neat pleasure garden and from that gentle rise they blasted at the bastions for all they were worth.

The thick stone wall close to the Kashmiri Gate was eaten away by exploding iron and these tall, wrecked city walls have been preserved – probably by the British before they left India in 1947 – as they were after the assault. Unfortunately, the Indian authorities have constructed what appears to be a long, ugly concrete urinal along the foot of the battered battlement, which defaces the historic memory. Though I have very often gazed at this ghastly structure, I have funked entering. The truth is that public urinals are extremely rare in India and only now, with pencil in hand, have I wondered that it might not be what I thought it was. Other men have failed to use it as a urinal; I have witnessed lines of men pissing against its outside wall. Has this any hidden meaning? A rejection of British heroics? Certainly the British soldiers and their loyal Indian comrades charged into bitter gunfire where the urinal now stands.

Volunteers were asked for to get against the great gates which are called Kashmiri. British and Indians stepped forward into probable death. And as Victoria Crosses were earned, these extraordinary men eventually blew the bloody gate apart. And in charged the screaming soldiers. We were back inside Delhi!

The Kashmiri Gate battleground is a very small area and so many soldiers observed the frantic happening that individual details are thoroughly recorded. I walked from square yard to square yard easily reconstructing in my mind's eye the lives and deaths of known men. Not far away an ascetic, noble commander, John Nicholson, was killed. He is known as the Hero of Delhi, which fact touches again on my friend Norah Nicholson.

I spent many hours at the Kashmiri Gate. One day men working for the Archaeological Survey of India (an institution founded by that entertaining snob, Lord Curzon, while he was Viceroy of India) were digging there with their Indian picks-cum-shovels. I watched these labourers for a while and then I began to ask if anyone ever found relics of the fight: 'You know, bullets, cannonballs – whizz! bang!' The labourers were very entertained by my amazing European exhibition. I think that they understood what I was enquiring about; anyway, having discussed it amongst their kind selves, they made regretful negative signs. Not of course our 'Western' shaking of the head from side to side (which in India means 'Yes'), but they made it clear that they had found nothing that had gone 'whizz' or 'bang'. I then asked the labourers if I could look for myself and I clambered into the wide pit and was handed a tool by a bewildered man. But I dug diligently in the Indian sun and soon I was sweating heavily with the best of them. After only five minutes a crowd had assembled to gaze at the unusual sight. I received the impression that they had previously believed that a European was incapable of wielding a pick and shovel. All of the Indians, observers and fellow-workers were very pleased with me but I found nothing.

The Indian in charge of us workers leaned down to speak to me: 'You must speak to Shri Srivastava. He will help you.' 'Who is Shri Srivastava?' 'Archaeological Department. He knows about the battle at the Kashmiri Gate.'

'Where can I find Shri Srivastava?'

'He is coming; we have sent for him.' And he arrived; tall, craggy and warm and smiling. He was a deep Hindu, visably heralded by horizontal coloured marks across his forehead. These very positive Hindu caste symbols have long impressed me, if not intimidated me. In the Christian Church I tend to favour the priest who wears a long black uncompromising gown rather than black leather and even earrings.

He introduced himself: 'My name is Janardan Prasad Srivastava', and with great enthusiasm he described to me how he saw the Battle of the Kashmiri Gate. We instantly became friends for life.

Shri Srivastava asked me: 'Do you know, Shri Griffith, where you British fought your first battle for what you call 'the relief of Delhi'?

'No, sir.'

Janardan escorted me there. It lies about seven and a half miles (a vague estimation) north up the Great Trunk Road, which, if you continue on it, will take you to Afghanistan. The route by which all of the great Muslim invasions travelled southward.

A few men were desultorily working on the ancient caravanserai. All that is left are the two fine gatehouses and between them the extensive sometime camping ground. A large field's distance away north-west is a slight natural elevation and it was from this position that the Gordon Highlanders made their successful charge across open ground and drove the Mutineers back towards Delhi.

The area is now filthy; indeed it is a vast public convenience, if you can bear the monstrous euphemism. I believe the British dead were buried on the mound. There are signs of British graves, cruelly desecrated. And Janardan told me that there were more gravestones to be seen till recently. I was sorry about the ugly shambles, but the soldiers had died with their faces aimed at the enemy and no one can change that fact. And my friend was a cultured, kindly Indian, who regretted the vandalism as much as I. And, anyway, what happened to the Indian dead?

The British Army slaughtered its way through Delhi. The soldiers were fearsomely stoked up by the tales, and evidence, of mutilated European women and children. They mutilated in return. When the British plundered into Delhi through the Kashmiri Gate, Emperor Bahadur Shah evacuated the Red Fort and fumbled his way south, out of the city. With him was his ramshackle retinue of women, children, court officials and several of his despicable sons. They didn't travel far; a mile or two outside the Delhi Gate is the sixteenth-century Emperor Humayun's Tomb, where I had been reprimanded by that Indian citizen on behalf of the virtues of the British Empire, and there Bahadur Shah took, perhaps, symbolic refuge. Humayun's actual tomb is a simple speck embedded in the middle of a vast structure of many chambers. The room where Bahadur Shah miserably lurked is known.

Back at the Red Fort, a tearaway Britisher, Lieutenant Hodson, the founder of Hodson's Horse, decided to pursue the last of the Moguls. Hodson pinned the old man down in his room inside Humayun's Tomb. Hodson offered to spare Bahadur Shah's life if he quietly returned to his palace; the old man agreed and the humiliated entourage retraced their escape route. Hodson kept his word to spare the Emperor's life, but just before reaching the Delhi Gate, at another structure called the Bloody Gate, Hodson killed the royal sons. Hodson explained that the Muslim citizens around him and his detachment of mounted British soldiers had become threatening and so he simplified his expedition by knocking off the lesser royal blood. I don't necessarily believe Hodson's explanation; his behaviour and his life were not unlike those of an Errol Flynn film character.

Later, many months later, Hodson was to die himself while charging in the van of the British relief of Lucknow. I have visited his grave, just as I have lingered in Bahadur Shah's dark chamber inside Humayun's Tomb, and just as I have probed round the Bloody Gate – and all of this exploring while waiting for my strange employers, Doordarshan and the Ministry of Information and Broadcasting, to arrive at some positive decision. So, you can understand that I enjoyed certain valuable benefits as I lived out my eccentric limbo life in Delhi.

We British put Emperor Bahadur Shah on trial in the Red Fort. Day after day the British formalised their anxious enquiries. Painstakingly. Was Bahadur Shah in any way responsible for the Mutiny? Was he a party to the atrocities? And the Indian witnesses and evidence enveloped the court trial in a miasma of Eastern fog – much the same unanswerable fog that I myself was engulfed by. Perhaps the difference between an Indian Ministry today and a Mogul Court is not very great.

The British verdict was probably correct: the old Emperor

barely knew what was happening. He knew that the Mogul game was long over. He was old and all he wanted to do was to jot down poetry and play around with his favourite wife. The British exiled him to Burma where he died. And that left an empty throne for Queen Victoria to sit on – just like an Empress.

What else did I do while I waited those inexplicable six months of Indian indecision? I spent many days exploring the splendid remnants of Mogul autocracy, and of earlier times, which bespatter themselves for miles around Delhi.

Qutab Minar, to the south, is early Pathan. The place is still magnificent. And here you can observe the brutal defacement of the last Hindu Delhi Kingdom by the now Muslim masters. Standing from truly ancient times is a fine iron pillar. Modern scientists are trying to fathom how the Hindus of antiquity were able to produce such pure metal; after two thousand years exposed to the harsh India elements, it has not rusted.

The great ghost city of Tughlukabad, to the east of Qutb Minar, was built during the early fourteenth century and is known as the third city of Delhi – which must give you some idea of what we are talking about. But I believe that this metropolis lasted for only fifteen years before it was abandoned to 'the vultures and the cobras' as someone once wrote. It was a time of gigantic whims.

The grandiloquent Purana Qila city – palace of late Pathan origin and the place where thousands of Muslim refugees sought shelter at the partition of the sub-continent of India in 1947. Where my nascent film subject, Jawaharlal Nehru, and Mahatma Gandhi, walked, exclaiming: 'We hold our heads in shame!'

And the magic Lodi Gardens where that namesake dynasty is interred. The fairly formal gardens were the inspiration of Lady Willingdon, wife of a British Viceroy. The Indians of the street, as against their professional political brothers and sisters, still happily refer to the 'Willingdon Gardens'.

One fond impression of mine is of the Feroz Shah Kotla and in particular its ruined mosque. Here the awesome Tamburlaine prayed. In 1952 I had the privilege to act in the justly famous Tyrone Guthrie production of Christopher Marlowe's saga *Tamburlaine* at the Old Vic Theatre. I played Darius, the King of the Persians. Sir Donald Wolfit, the last of Britain's great actor managers, played Tamburlaine. What a Thespian experience! What excitement! Only Peter O'Toole is left to keep the old pirate flag flying. At the end of the first night when the curtain had closed, Donald Wolfit stood on the stage, raised his shaggy head and prayed, 'Kit Marlowe, we've done yer proud!' And so we had, led by Tyrone, who was always called Tony, and Donald, who was advisedly called 'Sir'. Each time I stood in the mosque of Feroz Shah Kotla, I always wished that Donald Wolfit could have stood there – preferably with me for my pleasure. I know that Donald would have prayed again, marrying the memory of the Terrible Conqueror and the wild multicoloured poet, Marlowe. And I would have also wanted Tony Guthrie to be there to relish the scene fully. How I miss them! But I was a part of those great theatrical days before they dissolved into the well-fed wisps of our contemporary institutional theatres.

I held on to these imaginative explorations, so that my Delhi life should not be wasted by India's miserable bureaucracy. I was torn between the worry of lost time with its accompanying uncertainty and the luxury of so much leisure. And I had that promised car and a driver. The driver's name was Umrau Singh and he was an excellent man, a good driver in a nation of mainly bad ones. He was dependable, straightforward and courteous without being obsequious. He quickly became a true friend.

After some months of this unfathomable official Indian torture, which, as you will have learnt, I had done my utmost to annul with my investigative activities, I began to deteriorate physically. Ever since my poor military efforts during the last World War my hands have shaken when I am under pressure. Now, in Delhi, I had reached the point when I couldn't successfully drink a cup of coffee, even with the help of both hands. Frankly, the strain on my lonely brain was excessive.

So I sat in the Kanishka's coffee shop trying to get food and drink into my mouth. And now I was also vomiting throughout the night.

Shri Malhotra still called on me religiously. He was a friendly soul, but he was simply carrying out some basic instructions. He must have reported my sickening state, but no one else came to my assistance; no one else demonstrated an ounce of concern. I began to digest what I was up against in being associated with the dehumanised Indian system.

The staff of the coffee shop were extremely kind to me. They discreetly ignored my difficulty in feeding myself; they just smilingly wiped up the food that I often dropped. That is an enigma of India; the arrogant dismissal of normal human courtesies by certain sections of their society – almost invariably their Government servants. And then you meet, outside those dying buildings, the tenderest of human concern. Which led me to suffer continuously in India rage and then remorse.

Anyway, in the coffee shop was a very pretty Hindu supervisor. She was rather stand-offish, or so I thought until one day she suddenly approached my table and placed in front of me a bunch of flowers: 'They are from my parents' garden; I would like them to meet you.' Life is packed with astonishments. It had been many years since a pretty lady had postulated, 'I want you to meet my parents.' However my foolish fantasy quickly evaporated when she added: 'You see, Uncle, I think that you would all like each other.'

And so we did. Her mother is Doctor Madhur Singh and her father is Doctor Kartar Singh and there were three other very pretty and enlightened daughters. These people took me under their wings. Doctor Singh introduced me to the Principal of the Delhi University Hospital and each day the daughters escorted me to the hard-pressed clinic for injections and general treatment. My important potential employers did nothing. They simply ignored me.

After a few weeks I was apparently recovering, but one night I was overwhelmed again by uncontrollable shaking and vomiting. I became a little frightened, but out of this emergency was born a significant revolution, which has changed the course of my life. I have always been at pains to keep myself detached from all Establishments, whether they be of the entertainment business or of the Government. It is, I think, because I am a radical Celt and because I want to avoid being subject to anything, except myself, if I can avoid it. I need my independence very much. The result has been that I have viewed the Union Jack and the other British national accoutrements as objectively as possible. The philosophy of 'my country, right or wrong' has always depressed me. Therefore my very own work has tended to be critical of aspects where we British have been morally in the wrong: Ireland, for awful instance. Which has led to the Mrs Thatchers of our British world not liking me very much. Hey ho! But now, in Delhi, my attitude was about to be changed. As I shook and choked in a very foreign land, the British Council appeared on the scene, in the person of their cultural representative, Mr Robin Evans. Like discreet lightning I was whipped off to the delightful hospital within the British High Commission compound. The words were very English: 'I think perhaps, Kenneth, we should look after you.' I was too poorly at the time to register exactly what was happening to this Welsh renegade.

Doctor Tennant, a Scotsman, was in charge. The matron, Ann Meagher, was an Irishwoman and the nursing sisters were Indian. What quiet care I received. I was speedily nursed back to health. At night I would be aware of female Indian faces silently peering to see if I was all right. The food was excellent. I was spoiled.

An interesting fact emerged. During my months in an Indian limbo, I had met perhaps thirteen Africans in Delhi: men, women and children. They were attached to High

Commissions, Embassies and such. Zambia and Kenya predominated. Every single one of these Africans hurried to the hospital to visit me, some several times.

The only members of Doordarshan and the Ministry who came were the ubiquitous Shri Malhotra and his kindly colleague, Shri Saxena – both from middle management. Of course, other Indians, outside of the arid Government stockade, appeared at my bedside. The husband of one of the Indian nursing sisters would visit me most days and we would discuss Indian history.

One morning, while I was luxuriously recuperating in the beautiful walled garden of the hospital, two Indian Admirals advanced on me and both were holding bouquets of flowers and edible delicacies. They were Admirals Rustam Ghandhi and Satyindra Singh; the former had just been appointed Governor of the State of Himachal Pradesh.

After a few weeks Doctor Tennant remarked: 'Well, Mr Griffith, I think that you have recovered.'

'Yes, sir; but I don't want to leave.'

'Well, I don't see why you should; we are not at all busy.' And so I stayed on and it was there that my poor old head began to regain a degree of peace.

And now occurred my conversion. One morning I was sitting in the garden, wearing one of my cotton Indian dressing gowns and reading an edifying book, when I became aware of something floating in the air to my upper left side. It was the Union flag – popularly called 'Jack'. It was gloriously weaving in the air, quite a distance away, high over the main British High Commission building. My eyes didn't leave it; it gracefully wreathed with a slow sensual movement. The old multi-coloured rag that has sometimes arrogantly announced our British arrival around the world. The banner that degenerated on to T-shirts in Carnaby Street in the 1960s. I gazed at it and the truth was inescapable: I was very grateful to be under its care. I muttered to myself: 'Griffith, they have got you!' And with them I remain and I count myself relatively fortunate.

After a couple of extra weeks I left the hospital and, bypassing the inefficient Kanishka Hotel and hybrid New Delhi, I moved northward through Old Delhi, past the Kashmiri Gate to the sometime British Raj hotel, the Maidens: I had stayed there before; six years previously when we were filming *Clive of India*.. It is a grand old place and is now well cared for by the outstanding hotelier, Shri Oberoi.

There I was in the Maidens Oberoi Hotel. I was much happier. As I have implied, I like ghosts. I enjoyed seeing the shades of my old friends: Major Julian and Colonel Harold Allen, walking in and out of the place, long, long ago. And the creator of Pakistan, Mohammed Ali Jinnah, always liked to stay there. And the dark, tragic figure of General Dyer – more of him later – stayed at the Maidens before he was shipped back to England in, perhaps, questionable disgrace. Oh yes, I saw many of them! In my mind's eye.

The hotel suited me fine. The management gave me a spacious suite at a very reasonable rate. While I was filming *Clive of India* I had written a piece about Clive for their glossy house magazine; I was an old friend.

And I like Old Delhi. I do value ghosts and their still-standing haunts. Every day from the Maidens, usually in the relative cool of the evening, I would stroll in every possible direction and I was to learn, on these gentle expeditions, so much about India.

Many of the buildings in that area, which lies between the British Ridge and the Kashmiri Gate, are from our old Imperial days. I would gaze at such buildings and would eventually ask a passing Indian: 'Excuse me; but do you know anything about the history of that building?'

After the reply, the person would almost invariably say: 'Would you please walk with me to my house and take tea?' And in this way I entered many Indian homes and learnt many aspects of a generally warm-hearted people.

For some time during these pleasant peregrinations I had noticed an unusual building with a clock tower above its gatehouse. So, early one evening, I probed a little deeper and walked in. Now, I must remind you, I was wearing a white cotton kurta and matching cotton trousers. I was not a jarring figure in any Hindu, or Muslim for that matter, setting.

Inside was a large courtyard and in it were many young Hindu men. They were all dressed in their own Indian costume and not in our spiritually uncomfortable Western habits, which are now monstrously prevalent. I had hit on an authentic spot; this place was a notable school for studying the ancient Sanskrit language and thereby, inevitably, the root philosophy of five thousand years of Indian civilisation.

The young men spoke very little English, but were quietly courteous. And through a few of them I was able to communicate who I was and what my Indian interests were. They told me that I must meet their sadhu, their learned teacher. I was escorted to a bare stone cell and there was the man, talking to two other religious scholars. I was invited to join them and I sat on a carpet on the floor.

The sadhu began to speak to me in English, but I had never heard English spoken like this before. It was high-pitched and contained many prolonged hisses – particularly when an 's' was involved. I listened very carefully and was able to discern almost everything he said. The curious thing about his manner of enunciation was that his vocabulary was well-above that of the average Britisher, but he had perhaps never before spoken with a native English speaker. His pronunciation was purely academic. He came from Nepal and no doubt his speech was much influenced by his mountain tongue. He was remarkably young for a man who was struggling towards sagehood. Thirty-eight years, as far as I can recall. I was then sixty-five years old, give or take a few months.

The short of it was that he and I became close friends. I would return to his cell to be in his company each week. He hoped that I would help him improve his English. Was it

'Tales from Shakespeare' that I bought for him to follow as I read the text? I did think to myself what strange and profitable situations I get myself into.

The young sadhu and I discussed many of the dilemmas familiar to all human beings. One day he announced to me: 'Griffith, I know that we will love each other for as long as we are on this earth!'

I replied that I also felt that this was an inevitable truth. And then I pondered: 'But what about *after* we have died?'

My friend would sometimes get himself into ecstasies of emotion. At my question he coiled into a ball of inner feeling. 'Dear Griffith, I do not want to be born again! I am so weary of being reborn and reborn! That is why I am working so hard to earn my place in the . . . [did he say 'cosmos'?].'

I plodded along with my Celtic mind and mulled over his Eastern convolutions. Eventually I expressed myself: 'But couldn't we still be loving friends – out there in the cosmos?' This question sent my learned chum into paroxysms of unadulterated delight. Perhaps I had made some sort of philosophical breakthrough. But he never gave me a clear answer.

Months had gone by and little news seeped through from my supposed bureaucratic patrons. Yes, they were paying my expenses and for the car and driver, which had been a condition of my coming to India, who turned up every day and took me wherever I wanted to go in Delhi. And then one day the car didn't appear. There was no warning; it simply didn't come. And it was a difficult day to be car-less.

I had received an invitation from the High Commissioner himself to attend a party at his residence to celebrate Her Majesty the Queen's birthday. Now, for a non-establishment man like me, this was a rare treat, or at least, experience. For such a formal occasion I planned to wear a Jaipur suit, buttoned up to the small, neat collar. But there was no car! I telephoned Shri Malhotra and by some miracle the telephone worked and I informed him.

'No, Kenneth, there is no car for you today.'

'Why?'

Silence.

'Who gave the order!?'

'I don't know.'

'Why wasn't I informed?'

Silence.

'What the bloody hell am I going to do? I'm expected at the British High Commissioner's residence. It's the Queen's birthday!'

'I'll see what I can do, Kenneth.'

I waited anxiously in the foyer of the Maidens Hotel. I had told my good Indian friends, the staff of the hotel, about this most recent treacherous act on the part of Doordarshan and the Ministry. They held their breaths with me. And then the car arrived. The hotel doorman, a friend of mine, said: 'Mr Griffith, I don't think you'll like it.' No, I didn't; it was a decrepit, battered old car with a frantic, slightly ragged driver. Not my smart, excellent friend, Umrau Singh.

You see, I was in an awkward spot. I had chosen to wear an Indian suit for the Queen's Birthday. It was a somewhat provocative gesture on my part. But I felt strongly that I must fly my Indian colours because, supposedly, I was a loyal employee of the Indian Government, engaged by them to perform a very important service for India; that is, to make a film about the life of their great hero, Jawaharlal Nehru. And which film was to be transmitted by them during the centenary of the patriot's birth. And I therefore knew that I would be discreetly but curiously watched by my fellow Brits and other distinguished guests. I felt I could pleasantly carry off the sartorial gesture if I arrived quietly in my unobtrusive but well-kept car, with Umrau Singh efficiently at the wheel. But now, Whooh!

Anyway, in I got, smiled at reassuringly by a large proportion of the hotel staff. But the car wouldn't start. And so everyone, including the immaculate manager, gave the ancient jalopy a push and off we rattled south towards the august assembly. Rattle, rattle. The sweating driver was riding the thing as if it were a recalcitrant horse. I tried very hard to remain cool and dignified. We clanked past the heroic Kashmiri Gate. The poor driver was bent low over the steering wheel. I glanced at my watch; I might not be late. And then, as we were shuddering past the Red Fort, the car lurched and stopped. As a matter of fact I have been told that it never ever moved again – of its own volition.

It was disaster time for me. I was sunk. But, to my astonishment, my poor underprivileged driver leapt into the road, exclaiming: 'No problem!' And quickly he stopped a three-wheeled motorised rickshaw and at the same time he screamed instructions at the even more underprivileged pilot on how to reach the High Commissioner's residence. In a crumble of panic I crawled into the primitive conveyance and gazed in a dazed condition at my wild-eyed saviour. He stood in the middle of the now darkening thoroughfare. His arms were spreadeagled! 'No problem!' he shouted.

'Thank you,' I mumbled. And as we cruelly bounced away from him I thought clearly to myself, that poor sod is worth more than the whole upper management of Doordarshan and the Ministry, put together. And I have never changed that opinion.

I now tried very hard to compose myself to prepare for the surrogate royal reception. But unless you have ridden in a motorised rickshaw, you cannot possibly imagine how difficult such a mental readjustment is. You are exposed to the wind and thick pollution of Delhi as you speed along over often broken roads on what would often seem to be wooden wheels. Well, you have to be fit.

But we were well on our way. And then, unexpectedly, because my mind was not calm and collected, I realised that we were pressed close to the back of a magnificent Rolls Royce, which, in its turn, was queued behind a shining Mercedes Benz, and anxiously glancing round, I saw that we were wedged in the middle of a cavalcade of grandeur. I tried again to take an iron grip on my emotions. I noticed the grubby old towel wound round my chauffeur's head. I tried to flatten my dishevelled hair. I tried to straighten my Jaipur suit. I fumbled in my wallet for a fifty-rupee note (the fare would have been about eight rupees) as we jolted to a halt at the foot of the elegant steps.

And then I witnessed Young England at its very best as a couple of junior diplomats trotted down to greet me: 'What a pleasure to see you, Mr Griffith!' Neither batted an eyelid.

As I handed the unheard-of windfall to my rickshaw man, I also rose to the occasion: 'Keep the change, friend!' I said airily and quite loudly. Mr Kenneth Griffith was announced and there I was being received by His Excellency and His Excellency's – no doubt – good wife.

I suppose those grander Brits took my spectacular arrival as yet another radical demonstration. But they could very easily take the likes of me in their well-brought-up stride. After all, they are trained to deal with the Ayatollah Khomeini and other such dangerous lunatics. However, I have been told by a reliable but discreet source that I was, henceforward, regarded as not fully acceptable. It was whispered to me that my name was scratched out from all lists to meet visiting fellow British artists.

Once inside the birthday celebration I was greeted by the highly civilised head of the British Council in India, John Hanson: 'Good to see you, Kenneth! There are two people you must meet. Do you know the Vice-President of India?' (He is now the President.)

'No.' And Mr Hanson escorted me to a Mogul-like pavilion where the unobtrusive Indian gentleman sat. In all my life I have never experienced anything like it; I tried to chat about reasonably interesting subjects, but it was as if I were talking to a completely empty chair. There was no response whatsoever. I excused myself, not that he apparently noticed. It seemed that I was doomed, at least for this day.

But John Hanson had said two people. 'Have you met Norah Nicholson?'

'No, I don't think so.'

'Then you must; I think you'll like her,' as he led me through the distinguished throng. Norah was sitting at a table with two young British women (one may have been Australian) and an ebullient Indian businessman.

Norah – now my special friend – was lean and tall and no longer young, that is, in years. In spirit she is timeless; indeed, she is girlish in spirit. She wore what appeared to me to be a long, dark velvet dress. She regally rested one hand on an elegant walking stick. She looked like the personification of what the British Raj should be. In fact, she is the personification of what the British Raj should be. I immediately became her devoted follower. Norah Nicholson has served Britain in India for many years. Her last appointment was under Mountbatten. I have glanced at photographs of Norah with Princess Alice. (Norah, also, was a senior Girl Guide.) All of that sort of British thing.

When the midnight hour struck in 1947 and it was time for the British to go back home, Norah was correctly interviewed about the pending repatriation:

BRITISH OFFICIAL: 'Miss Nicholson, where were you born in Britain?'

NORAH: 'I was born in India.'

BRITISH OFFICIAL: 'Where in Britain was your father born?'

NORAH: 'My father was born in India.'

BRITISH OFFICIAL: 'Ah! Where was your mother born?'

NORAH: 'My mother was also born in India.'

BRITISH OFFICIAL: 'Never mind, Miss Nicholson! With your long and distinguished service to the crown, there will be no problems for you whatsoever.'

NORAH: 'Sir if I cannot have my British nationality by simple birthright, I don't want it!'

And so Norah Nicholson elected to become an Indian citizen. The astounding fact is that she is an English patrician lady in every possible respect; in her bearing, her attitude of mind, her sometimes naughty humour, her invincible spirit, and yet she has never even visited Britain. Perhaps the most intriguing fact about my friend is that there is not even a hint of any Indian accent; it is unadulterated, upper-class southern English.

At the birthday celebration, while enquiring about her history, she fished in her handbag and brought out a British Victorian war medal; it had been awarded to her father for service in relieving the British Legation at Peking in China.

I told Norah and the other people at the table about my momentous journey in the rickshaw. Norah said: 'I live a little way beyond the Maidens Hotel, just behind the old British Secretariat. The High Commissioner and his lady have kindly provided me with a chauffeur and a car; I can drop you off.' And so she took me home.

Of course, I arranged to call on Norah the following day. She had warned me: 'You will see, I live roughly but very happily.' I could not have imagined how roughly she lived. Her home was a rambling shack on a piece of wasteland, which Norah pleases to call 'God's garden'. She and her mother once lived in the Government house across the dirt road from her present abode.

After independence came to India, Norah formed a friendship with Indira Gandhi and even helped the two sons, Sanjay and Rajiv, with their English. Mrs Gandhi had warned Norah: 'You had better take some action or they' – the Indian Government – 'will push you out of your house.' And they did just that. Norah took no action, whatever that implied, and so she was evicted and Norah dragged her possessions on to the site of her present home where she constructed the wooden shack.

There are dogs, cats, pigs and peacocks in 'God's garden'. One day, while I was taking tea with her, I noticed a bruised hockey stick: 'Did you play hockey, Norah?'

'Oh, long ago, Kenneth dear. But now the stick is very useful in driving the cobras out.'

I am terrified of all snakes, quite apart from, perhaps, the deadliest of them all. One nip and you're gone! I jumped: 'What! In here?'

'Yes, but don't be alarmed, dear Kenneth. The poor darlings usually come in during the monsoon, to escape the awful wet. We get flooded here, you know. But I couldn't keep the cobras in the house, so I had to whoosh them away with that hockey stick. To tell you the truth, I don't use it any more because of my poor old leg; I use this.' And Norah held up a can of Flit, a squirting substance usually used to combat flies. 'Cobras can't bear Flit. One or two blasts and out they go. Poor darlings.'

You can imagine how I glanced uneasily round me. I never saw a cobra in Norah's home. And I believe that the peacocks in the garden help to discourage them. Peacocks are, so I am told, committed enemies of the cobra.

Norah Nicholson's life revolves around Skinner's St James's Church. Recently that historic place had its one hundred and fiftieth anniversary. Norah said to me: 'I only pray that God will spare me till after the celebrations and then I am very ready to go.' My dear friend has witnessed the event and indeed, perhaps, supervised it and is still with us. In her very real poverty she collected (begged and cajoled) a substantial sum for the great anniversary. Unfortunately, I was obliged to be out of Delhi filming at the time and therefore missed it. Retired officers from the old, romantic, Skinner's Horse travelled even from Britain to be present.

Close to the church the Hero of Delhi, John Nicholson, was killed, retaking the city in the year 1857. Norah is said to be related to him. A short time ago Lord Hailsham, Britain's outstanding former Lord Chancellor, who also has some family ties with John Nicholson, visited India and was, naturally, staying with the British High Commissioner and his wife. 'I believe I have a relative somewhere here in Delhi – a Miss Norah Nicholson.' His Excellency arranged for his Lordship to meet Norah – not at her shack, but at his residence. Norah and Lord Hailsham now correspond with each other. And because I am such a close friend of Norah's I have been made privy to his Lordship's letters. They are charming and moving. In one of them he confessed to Norah that he was a sentimental old thing and that before departing for England he could not resist visiting John Nicholson's grave for a second time and placing two roses on the tomb and a verse of poetry, which he had composed about the gallant General. He enclosed the words for Norah, but I didn't copy them. The poem was about courage and integrity. And so from these two people, Lord Hailsham and Miss Nicholson, I caught a whiff of the old dream of the best people in my country. I have never liked Lord Hailsham more; I probably didn't know him till I read those letters.

To tell you the truth I whizzed round to General Nicholson's grave to see if there were any signs of the roses and poem. As I turned into the cemetery, which is now named after the hero, I saw an Indian inside the railings of the funeral shrine, brushing it up. I was so moved by this act of respect that I slipped the sweeper a very generous ten rupees. There was no sign of the roses or poem, so I was not put to the test of whether I would have removed them to keep as much valued souvenirs. Just as well; I wouldn't have relished Lord Hailsham judging me on such an action. In fact, I am slightly uneasy about my mentioning a snatch from his letter. 'Well, my Lord, I felt that it was done for a good cause.'

Incidentally, when I glanced back at the grave as I was departing, the Indian sweeper had completely disappeared. I suspect that he keeps a look-out for any British Raj type and then hurries to tidy up John Nicholson. It must prove an infallible business.

Norah will not accept any political chicanery. In spite of her rejecting a little condescension from the Brits in 1947, she is deeply shocked about the wholesale corruption in India today, and any uncalled-for slight against Britain prompts her to give a speedy and clear retort: 'We [British] were clean, efficient, honest and as fair-minded as was possible. So don't talk any nonsense to me!' I happen to know that she keeps a Union flag under her mattress. Come on, Mrs Thatcher, what about a little official recognition for our unofficial spokeswoman in India?

The sometime High Commissioner and his wife learnt about Norah and to their good credit have kept an eye on her; hence the chauffeur-driven car from the hut to the Residency and back again. And there has also been a little extra assistance in other directions. Not that Norah would ask or expect even a bar of chocolate.

In spite of these many valuable human experiences in Delhi, I was near to breaking point. I enquired as to who had withdrawn my car and after much evasion of the question I was whispered: 'Shri Mehra'. Mehra was the Secretary to the Ministry of Information and Broadcasting; the one with the signed sepia photograph of Jawaharlal Nehru behind his desk. But to know such a truth, for certain, in India is virtually impossible. Almost everyone is fearful of having a sly black mark put against his or her name and thereby suffering hidden and vindictive victimisation. It is much safer for everyone to see no evil, hear no evil and if you speak it, be sure that it pleases your superiors. The very safest thing to do is absolutely nothing, which has been brought to a remarkably fine art in India. So I can't be sure that the car business was Shri Mehra's doing. It would seem a petty action for a man who was daily manoeuvring quite big problems.

The withdrawn car was important to me for several reasons for, after my hotel bill was paid, there was little money left over to pay for taxis and so on and I had already expended about £800 of my own money. And so I now travelled everywhere in the cheap rickshaws. Remonstrances on my part to Shri Malhotra got me nowhere.

And also the withdrawal of the car was the first clear breach of faith with me on the Indian Government's part.

There were to be many others, but I didn't know that at the time; though, of course, I was already alarmed at their drift from the ethics that I had been accustomed to all of my life in many different parts of this world.

And so I had to go to the top. I still hesitated to take up the Prime Minister's 'Whenever you are stuck, come to me', but I did the next best thing: I communicated with Shri Sharada Prasad, right next door to the Prime Minister. His reply was, as always, 'Come and see me today.'

Shri Prasad is a very interesting man. He always strikes me as a person who has witnessed and striven with most of the problems that political flesh is heir to. He knows about the reality and that he has to deal with nothing less. I know he values ideals. But he knows that an uncompromising pursuit of ideals can break good hearts, as they almost broke Jawaharlal Nehru's good heart.

I believe that Shri Prasad has hoped – even more than I – that things in India were different. But obviously he knows far better than I how impenetrably difficult it is to shift the awful Dinosaur while at the same time remaining a democratic state. Easeful thoughts about the value of totalitarianism creep into my mind in India.

I gave Shri Prasad my gentle spiel in full. At the end of ten minutes, he very quietly said the words that he was always to say to me, 'I will see what I can do. But, Mr Griffith, you will have to be patient for another twenty-four hours.' He also said, 'I am glad that you have not approached the Prime Minister.'

Twenty-four hours later I had my car and driver back. And very soon Shri Saxena, Shri Malhotra's friend, who had visited me in hospital, was instructed to work with me on the draft of my contract. And that was a curious exercise! Shri Saxena and I sat at a table in Old Mandi House in what was a public thoroughfare and talked through my minimum needs. Several strangers sat around and listened. But I didn't object to that. I am an introvert who has had to become an extrovert in order to perform my very public work freely. Many performers have had to pass through this difficult discipline. Sometimes when Shri Saxena and I were debating a contractual point I would happily turn to the miscellaneous group of observers – whatever their caste might be – and appeal to them: 'Don't you agree with me? What I am asking for is only reasonable!' The watching and listening people would be a little disconcerted at being officially, as it were, roped in, but quite enjoyed the fun of it. And so did nice Shri Saxena; I think that he felt that I was no end of a card.

Of course, there were hitches; it was a makeshift agreement. Always before, my lawyer or agent or both had battled through agreements on my behalf. Once or twice I said to Shri Saxena or to Shri Malhotra: 'I really feel that a lawyer or my agent should discuss this contract with you.'

'Oh no, Kenneth; if that happens this business will take years. Anyway you are the honoured guest of our country and everything that is fair will be given to you.' And so, dreading the threat of further delays, I allowed several important matters to be taken lightly and on trust in that agreement. (I and my European colleagues were to suffer, quite seriously, for my rather enforced open trust. But more of that in due course.)

I had approached, as I have already related, my old colleague, Michel Pearce, to direct the film and so he, by name, and Chiara Peretti, were included in my contract. Chiara's specific duties were to handle the continuity of the film, the extensive wardrobe and to be my assistant and general help until the end of the film. In the contract continuity and wardrobe were specified and everything else was covered by Shri Saxena's etcetera. I did remonstrate that this left Chiara's latter duties vague. Shri Saxena reasonably replied that since she was to be paid her salary and her daily expenses up to the end of the film, just as the director and I were to be, etcetera was sufficient. And so I agreed; but in due course the powers that are (not Shri Saxena) reneged on this arrangement and so Chiara suffered a serious financial loss. Such unfortunate attitudes have continued throughout our work in India.

I think it is true to sum up that I entered on this Nehru film project with idealism and complete trust. As I once remonstrated to senior people at the Ministry: 'You must not treat me like a businessman. I am not one! The only way for us to do this job is by holding hands.' They did not hold my hand – not once. And they consistently treated me as a businessman who was bent on cheating them. It is the attitude that the Indian Governmental System has towards their own Indian people. And they were going to make no exception of me. This attack, on my part, against this Indian attitude is mainly on behalf of the hundreds of millions of Indians who have to suffer it all of their lives and not just for two years, as I have had to suffer it.

Each time the contract was given to me for my approval, I would uneasily ask, usually Shri Malhotra, 'Nothing new has been added?'

'Nothing important.'

And then I would notice that some undiscussed clause had been slipped in which, if agreed to, would penalise me or hold me responsible for events which would be outside of my control. In all of my life I have never met such ruthlessly sly behaviour.

Michel Pearce, the director, whose name now appeared in the contract, wrote to me: 'I have the opportunity to direct a feature film [meaning for the cinema] in Australia. Must start Nehru film within two weeks.' I informed my potential employers; it was completely ignored. Two weeks later Michel sent his regrets; he was off to Australia. Again I informed these sad men and this time there was a disconcerted reaction. Michel's name had appeared on the contract and now he would not be directing the film. That fact rang some bureaucratic bell in their heads. Fortunately, I had not yet been asked to sign the contract. I told them that I would find another director who could handle the difficult style of this type of film.

By this time I was continuously being asked by Indians and foreigners, 'What is happening?' For many of the agonising months, I had covered up the situation. But now I began to tell the truth about my predicament. The foreigners – mainly from the Italian, German, Swiss, Canadian and American embassies – gave me sad, old-fashioned looks which implied that they were familiar with my suffering. They said little more than, 'Well, this is India . . .' The Indian private explanations for the incredible delay were never less than alarming. 'They are waiting for the Prime Minister to be overthrown'. 'Perhaps you haven't bribed anyone'; 'There are political people determined to stop your film.' Of course, I couldn't accept such accusations. But the fog had become so thick that I was in danger of some paranoia. The only light relief for me came from a Briton: 'Your situation is very similar to our helicopter problem. We thought we'd sold them to India, then we hadn't; then we had.' It gave me some comfort to be equated with an important arms sale. Once or twice my name cropped up in the Lok Sabha (the Lower House of India's Parliament) and was quoted on television, so I was still officially alive and someone was fishing for any political trouble that could be created by my presence.

I discovered from Indian newspapers and from television that Neil Kinnock, the British Socialist leader of Her Majesty's Opposition, was heading for India to talk to Shri Rajiv Gandhi. I learnt that he was to take lunch with the Prime Minister before the first chat was to take place. Imagine my pleasurable surprise when at 9 a.m. on that very morning, my telephone rang at the Maidens Hotel. Neil Kinnock was free till midday; could he come over to the Maidens to talk with me? Not, mark you, would I travel across dusty Old Delhi to call on him, which he had every reason to request. Mr Kinnock may not thank me for saying so, but the man is clearly a gentleman.

I thought perhaps I should unobtrusively warn the management of the hotel; after all, Mr Kinnock was very much front-page news. A socialist leader of Britain is deeply significant to India. I and the staff of the Maidens were poised in the foyer when there was another message for me: 'Mr Kinnock has been stricken with the dreaded Delhi Belly,' – the scourge of a high proportion of new visitors. His immediate problem was how the hell could he struggle to the Prime Minister's feast!

I was told by a number of friends that on India's television service that evening, Mr Kinnock spoke about me and my film work, which he values. He could not have known that he was reaching out a friendly hand towards a very uneasy compatriot.

Well, the contract to make the Nehru film was eventually signed, with the Director instead of Michel Pearce's name, who by this time had probably finished his Australian film. I had in my mind the choice of four former colleagues whose work I admired. Returning to Britain I quickly learnt that none of them was available at such short notice. And so I went to discuss the problem with my old friend and agent, Dennis Sellinger. Now Mr Sellinger is the star manager of many famous film stars and such. Perhaps there is no one in Europe who understands the film business as thoroughly as he; perhaps anywhere. But his focus is on the international cinema business; my films are for television, are idiosyncratic and require special understanding. Dennis's client-directors would not normally be aiming in my direction. Dennis pondered for me: 'There's a young director I admire very much. I'm looking for the right opportunity for him; I'm convinced that he'll go a long way.' (Dennis meant in the commercial cinema.) 'His name is Alan Birkinshaw. I don't know whether he would want to do it; he wants to do feature films.' Dennis arranged for us to meet. I looked at a little of Mr Birkinshaw's commercial work (advertising films) and he was familiar with my style.

After a brief talk I asked him if he would like to direct the Nehru saga and he promptly said yes. He added that it was important for his career to be involved with a serious subject.

And so Alan Birkinshaw was made my colleague. I was straightforward with him and warned him fully of the extraordinary difficulties of working with the Indian bureaucracy.

Now I began my work in professional earnest. I made my research headquarters at the Nehru Memorial Library, which is within the grounds of Teen Murti House which was Jawaharlal Nehru's last home in Delhi and had previously, in the days of the British Raj, been the Residence of the British Commander-in-Chief.

The director of the library is Professor Ravinder Kumar and I was made a sort of honorary member under his sponsorship. Nevertheless, since it was India, I was called on to fill in a fairly copious form and under the section, academic qualifications, I wrote, 'None whatsoever.' This inscription caused quite a furore. Officials thought that I was facetiously deceiving them; I was questioned closely (not by Professor Kumar, I hasten to underline – he had already accepted my high official credentials and he was above our heads in his learned castle): 'But, Mr Griffith, you must have some!'

'Nothing!'

'But you are the author of two history books!'

'Yes; but no scholastic qualifications; not even a school certificate!' The look of frustrated incredulity never left their faces. But I was made welcome and soon, as a daily student of Jawaharlal Nehru's life, I found the excellent library a happy and profitable refuge from my usual tribulations in the Delhi outside. Also, the hot weather was under way and the library was efficiently air-conditioned.

Now the discovery of Jawaharlal Nehru, through reading, thought and discussion was truly in progress. The process is simple: I read everything available that I can lay my hands on. I make copious notes of everything that seems to me to be a key matter. Gradually, the significant themes become clear: what are the qualities in the subject that are going to be of most use to the present-day viewer and perhaps tomorrow's also? What are the universal elements that will disturb or even shock or provoke the viewer into thinking or rethinking about issues that are of great moment?

I am reading and hearing many people's versions of the same life. As an actor I was always fearful that I might be so impressed by another actor's performance of a character I was being called upon to play (having seen Peter O'Toole as Shylock, for instance) that I would be influenced and plagiarise it; but when undertaking Shylock myself, I found that I was incapable of doing what he had done. I could, of course, have copied him; but that is not within my puritan nature. It is the same with researching and writing about the life of a historical character. You may agree and admire or disagree and dislike other historians' views of the same life or event, but if the facts are truthfully distilled through one's unique self, you finally arrive at your own unique version.

Of course, after a while, you begin to know clearly what exactly it is that you want to communicate through the protagonist's life. I even find myself *searching* for elements. I might say to myself, he *must* have said such a thing or he *must* have done such an act! I already know the character and I need such words or such a deed for my 'play'. Obviously, I can't invent the words as a playwright can and does, even with historical characters. (I was much offended with the words and actions heaped upon Mozart in the play *Amadeus*. I owe Mozart too much to find it acceptable.) My words and actions have to be verifiable in recorded fact. And all of that was my fundamental job in the Nehru Library.

And, naturally, the Nehru Library is peopled by Indian historians and sociologists. It is fair to write that we were a band of mutually interesting brothers and sisters. I met there the Marxist professor who had shouted at me ('It is the only talent I have!') during the meeting of the Council for Historical Research to judge my *Clive of India* script six years earlier. He is now researching and writing a life of Krishna Menon, the indestructible Indian patriot who conducted his freedom fight in the capital of the Imperialists, London. I made friends with a lofty, left-wing young Afghan, who is researching Allah Knows What. I always greeted him with a clenched-fisted salute, which he would return with an Afghan grin, while I demanded loudly: 'And when are you going to chuck the Soviets out?' He would reason with me very quietly and with persistent good humour. He is a very pleasant man and has invited me to his home, 'After the trouble is over'.

And in the Nehru Library I met my now close friend, Doctor Prakash Chandra. He is quite young enough to be my son, but I am perhaps closer to him than to any other Indian. He is a historian and sociologist and an exemplary good man. He has been victimised for his unflinching high principles, as is almost inevitable in India. But Prakash is sufficiently big for martyrdom if it came his way – and it might. I discuss all of my problems with Doctor Chandra. I have never before depended on such a young man. Of course, we often have disagreements, particularly over Indian history and politics, but they are sincere ones. I have learnt so much from him.

And in all of this mixed debate and argument I was discovering Nehru, and even the six months of unpaid waiting was beneficial to my big task. Normally, I could never have afforded so much time to wander among the remains of five thousand years of Indian civilisation or to have spent so much time with Indian men and women. And even the daily agonies with the Indian bureaucracy instructed me about what had gone wrong with Nehru's and Gandhi's great dream. And how I have worried whether the great dream can be put on course again. Drastic action. Revolutionary action, perhaps. Anyway, it was all on the long road to The Discovery of Nehru.

Having completed this stage of my work – about fourteen weeks – I became a little uneasy that I had had almost no communication with the man to whom this proposed film would be most personally important, Rajiv Gandhi. I could comprehend the different stages of his involvement: wanting me to do it because he thought highly of my work and then feeling deeply that his mother's wish should be fulfilled. He also probably felt it was timely for India to be reminded of what Nehru stood for. And then the warning that he must remain detached from the project otherwise he could easily be accused by his vindictive, small-minded political enemies that the film was merely for himself and that if he communicated with me they might accuse him of telling me what to say. So his detachment was wise. But all of this was surmise on my part; but I have never doubted that it was correct.

And so I wrote a letter to the Prime Minister. The main gist was obvious: 'No one has even asked me if I like your Grandfather; well, I hasten to state that I do. Is the film meant to be for Indian or international viewing or both? At the moment I am presuming that it is for international viewing.' The letter was along those lines. I received no reply to these concerns of mine. To write the truth, I have received no reply, in writing, from any Indian official source (with the exception of Shri Sharada Prasad) unless an answer gained them some advantage. But now I was contracted by the Government of India to make an ambitious film about a man who was deeply significant to India, yesterday, today and tomorrow. And there was no colleague at Doordarshan or at the Ministry, with whom I could remotely share my problems on a professional level. So, hey ho! I would plough on quite alone as I have always done; but always in the past, surrounded by more pleasant and supportive colleagues in many different parts of the world.

I wrote to my old friend, Admiral Rustam Ghandhi, who was now Governor of Himachal Pradesh, the mountainous state which has Simla, the British Raj summer centre, as its capital. I wanted a peaceful place to compose my script. My good friend, the Governor, arranged for me to live in the guest suite of the Himachal Pradesh University at Simla. It was a perfect place for me; my rooms jutted out into the great forestland of the Himalayan foothills. Only the birds and the monkeys made a sound.

I travelled to Simla from Delhi by car with Shri Yatendera Singh (who had replaced Shri Umrau Singh) at the wheel. Yatendera was an equally excellent driver as Umrau and again we became very close friends. Yatendera was as immaculate, in every respect, as a man can be. In his general appearance, sartorial and otherwise, he tended to make me look a little scruffy. And though he did me the great honour of inviting me to visit and stay in his Rajput village, he would never allow himself to overstep the demarcation that he established between the driver and the driven. He welcomed our friendship, but disallowed familiarity on his part. I could truly count on him. He, like Neil Kinnock, is a gentleman.

I also took with me Vikram, my houseboy. Vikram was a rather untamed young man from whose native home you can see Mount Everest. He was quite wild in a way and basically hostile to the likes of me. No amount of smiling on my part could change him. The most I could expect was a less ferocious glower than usual; but I liked him and brought him along for a holiday.

On this adventurous journey I suddenly saw an Indian police sergeant attempt to man-handle Yatendera for no reason. I jumped at the sergeant demanding: 'Don't you dare touch my friend!' And the Indian promptly let go. An odd social balance can exist in India.

Of course, Simla is redolent of Nehru's days of struggle with the British rulers. He trotted through Simla, mounted on a white horse, during some spate of political negotiation. Across the rocky track from me was a grand old house in which Mahatma Gandhi stayed when he was in Simla on similar business. I wandered through this curious Anglo-Indian mansion. There was Gandhi's bedroom, his anteroom, his kitchen and so forth, all at the back of the house, overlooking the garden. I find the proximity of Gandhi even a little uncomfortable; his methods of getting his own way were so extraordinary and generally so successful, but so alien that I can dwell on him only as across a deep ravine.

For that reason I felt uneasy; perhaps it had something to do with the contrast between the grandeur of the house and Gandhi's obsessive simplicity; he often lived in such houses. But all of this is probably too subjective and unfair.

What a British ghost-town Simla is! Close to my academic residence was Viceregal Lodge, where the latter-day Viceroys of India lived during the hot half of the year. 'Lodge' is a surprising word to me; the place is a vast, Gothic, Scottish-like pile. Now it is a post-graduate place of study or something of the sort. Like all such places in India, it is rather run-down from its former days of Imperial glory. I thought to myself what a pity this was, but was wise enough to realise the perhaps prohibitive cost of upkeep for a country still struggling to stretch itself economically. The British insignias have been removed and Indian symbols, a shade incongruously, have replaced them, except for one fine piece of royal stone in the back garden (if so mundane a description is permissible). Somehow the British ghosts were very distant; perhaps because their old living prototypes were restrained in such a sometime Imperial power house. Of course, there were viceregal balls and I did hear the ripple of high-bred amusement.

The most extreme decline is in Simla's Christ's Church. It was and is the main point for any distant view of Simla. It is simply an Anglican place of worship stuck on a ridge of the Himalayan foothills. No one compromised. In front of it is Simla's wide parade-ground. The rolling of carriage wheels and the clop-clop of fine horses; both civil and military. The stentorian commands and the slap and crash of rifles. The restrained silence as the Viceroy and Vicereine were received by the Bishop and ushered in.

I was told that during the British times ordinary Indians were not allowed up there. Now the Mall and the square are thronged with them; ninety-five per cent wearing European clothes. Only a few Indian die-hards and me wearing indigenous costumes. This world is truly upside down.

The Church of Simla itself is barely holding on to survival. Several times I paid my lonely respects. A few Indian Christians and their children treated me with cheer and a feeling that I was a welcome thread from the past. And me a poor Welsh Chapel boy! The noble plaques on the wall. Hasn't Rudyard Kipling's artist Dad got a fine piece of stained glass there? And high above the disconcertingly nostalgic church is the very active Hindu temple devoted to Hanuman, the popular monkey god. They say that all good (and bad) things must come to an end.

Chiara Peretti, who is usually close by me when I am at my labours, has a connection with Himachal Pradesh. Her father, Colonel Biagio Peretti, of the Alpine Divisione Julia was made a prisoner-of-war in Ethiopia and was transported to a camp at a place called Yol, also in the foothills of the Himalayan Mountains. The British allowed the Colonel to form a Club Alpine for his fellow prisoners. Chiara commissioned the Simla sculptor, Professor M. C. Saxena, to design and make a bronze plaque to the memory of her father and his comrades. She plans to ask His Excellency, Admiral Rustam Ghandhi, to help us arrange to install the small memorial at Yol Camp.

Each day I did my disciplined quota of writing. It was an idyllic life. Good Himachal food was brought to my room and sometimes the cook would come personally and play traditional music on a flute-like instrument to me. He also invited me to his home in the hillside forest where his wife had prepared an excellent meal. India is packed with fine, loving people. My dislike of the country is confined to the political, bureaucratic element and towards them my dislike is intense. But for the six hundred and ninety-eight million (presuming that there are seven hundred million) Indians that I am not expected to meet, I have nothing but love and gratitude. Let's get that clear!

I also probed north, towards the big mountains, for up to seventy miles. I watched the wild Sutlej River. The valleys were so beautiful. The butterflies made the land an enchanted place. I have a friend, Toni Green (married to the invaluable Benny), who is literally enchanted by butterflies. Butterflies are a motif in her life. How I wished that she could have been with me in that Sutlej Valley – if Benny will be good enough to understand what I mean! Of course, everywhere in India there are endless exotic butterflies. To have such a defined interest as Toni Green, creates a special relationship. Whenever a friend – me or any other – sees a butterfly, that friend cannot escape thinking of Toni. Once I saw a man on a street in New York City selling multi-coloured plastic butterflies perched on the end of thin stems; the butterflies danced. I had to buy a bunch for Toni. Once I saw exquisite butterfly jewellery, but I was forced to resist that gift as they were made from rubies, diamonds and emeralds. But I thought about it!

Also in that Himalayan valley were many snakes and once, as I wandered in paradise, a large dragon-like creature charged away from near my feet. I was told that this creature is a formidable enemy of the snake. And one night, returning to Simla, I came face to face with a large leopard; it stood in the middle of the road and then leapt away into the forest.

However, my most disturbing memory of my leisure time in Simla happened one evening when I had been invited to visit a family, who again lived within the great hill forest. As I approached their house I saw the figure of a man, absolutely still and with arms upraised, gazing at a full moon. I had never seen such a sight before. I also stood still among the trees and watched him. He was a somehow significant image. I must have gazed at him for five minutes and then I quietly moved towards the house I was visiting. After I had been received by my host and his family in an oil-lamp illuminated room, I told them about the extraordinary sight I had just seen:

'What was he doing?'

'Oh, he was praying to the moon.'

'I would like to meet him.'

I was led through the moonlit forest to a small, dark house and at the door my host whispered: 'He's a little mad.'

'Tell him that I am very impressed to see a man praying to the moon.'

My friend went into the unlit room and suddenly the object of my interest appeared in the doorway, looked straight into my eyes, then knelt and touched my feet. This is an Indian custom which expresses homage. I like to believe that the moon-worshipper recognised me as a human being who understood what he was doing, which I think is correct.

And then my friends, the Governor and his wife, known to me as 'Bubbles', would welcome me to official luncheons and such, where I would wear one of my Jaipur suits and there meet many interesting notables of Himachal Pradesh. It is a little disturbing to face a chum you know as 'Russie', who is now 'His Excellency'; anyway, I am not used to it. Mark you, I watched my etiquette and in the presence of other guests no one outdid me for noblesse oblige and all those trimmings.

Writing as a professional actor, I have never doubted that as an actor my friend Rustam Ghandhi would have risen as high as he did in the Indian Navy. He is very handsome, dresses immaculately and positively revels in every duty that he has to perform. To get to the top in any job requires more than skill or academic qualifications to perform the mechanical responsibility. I believe that you must also have the ability to act the part, to show off the part. I never saw Admiral Ghandhi on the bridge of a warship, but I am positive that it was a magnificent sight. And now, as Governor, the performance is one that Laurence Olivier could envy. What panache! And Russie would describe his formal duties to me with such good-hearted enthusiasm. Of course, the performance is not sufficient without the human responsibility. From British times to this day, only top officials are allowed to have their carriages or cars driven along the grand thoroughfare of Simla: the Mall. One of Governor Ghandhi's first decisions was that his car (a splendid, big white thing) would not take advantage of the privilege and thereby disturb the pedestrians. The Governor, for those sorts of reasons, is extremely popular in Himachal Pradesh.

I was also honoured by being invited to dine with the Jimba Lama, a distinguished refugee from Tibet, at his Buddhist Monastery at Sanjouli. This brave Tibetan, among many brave Tibetans, ushered me to his raised dais and personally arranged his cushions for my comfort, while he – high in the Tibetan hierarchy – took a lower seat. He seemed to take upon himself the role of a servant. I presume that this is an aspect of the great Tibetan Buddhist culture, which some crude Marxist Chinese have tried to destroy. The Jimba Lama served and supervised my lunch, and when I left he presented me with the holy white scarf and a Tibetan carpet, both of which I treasure.

I finished my script on Nehru in the Himachal Pradesh University guest house. I hastened copies to the Prime Minister, the Minister for Information and Broadcasting and the Director-General of Doordarshan. Chiara and I returned to Delhi by a very circuitous route. Indeed, instead of heading south we pushed north, through the old princely state of Mandi, on our way to the Kulu Valley, which we had visited while making the *Clive of India* film six years before. It was the very week of the great Kulu Festival, when all of the village gods converge on the palace of the King of Kulu. Rustam Ghandhi had very kindly arranged for us to stay at the guest house of the Tibetan Border Police; a splendid nineteenth-century building with a colourful history, which lies on the steep western side of the valley between Kulu and Manali.

We were most fortunate to be in and around Kulu at that time because out of ignorance we were thrown into the very centre of the ancient and strange events that were beginning to take place. As we drove along the narrow main road that passes through the outskirts of Kulu we spotted a group of men carrying a portable temple, perched on a palanquin, along a residential lane. We guessed that this was one of the village gods on its way to the Royal Palace. And so we left our car and joined the procession. It was a long trudge and climb, but eventually we reached the entrance to an ancient temple where an extravagant pantomime was to take place.

The men carrying the god tried to enter the temple but were prevented by the guardians of that place. The god, propelled by the men who carried it, charged the gateway and was pushed back; this happened many times. The guardians gesticulated in another direction and they were argued against by one of the god's attendants who, though a man, was dressed in a skirt and wept and shouted. As an actor I was impressed by the stream of real tears that ran down the man's face. I began to realise he was in a trance. Later I learnt that through him emitted the voice and spirit of the god. It turned out that every village god – I was told there were a hundred or so of them – had such a spirit-man and I was to note that all of them wore these skirts and that some of the men were remarkable emotional actors – or was it something else, beyond my European comprehension?

Finally, the god and its attendants gave up, turned back and entered a strange, large complex of buildings, which was the King of Kulu's palace. Chiara and I followed and no one objected. Then in the palace courtyard another vociferous altercation took place between the skirted spirit-man and a senior court official. It was ritualistic but the spirit-man undoubtedly suffered great emotional distress. Eventually this god was granted everything that it had asked for and began to ascend the steps into the palace itself. Immediately the spirit-man emerged from his trance and reverted, even casually, to normality. He and his friends chatted together as if nothing extraordinary had happened.

Chiara and I, with discreet cheek, entered the palace with the god, which was placed in the centre of a large sitting room or reception hall. It emerged that this god was supreme among all the village gods and only this one would be allowed to enter the royal interior. Chiara and I sat on large comfortable chairs close to the god and watched privileged

Kulu people make their obeisances to the holy image. No one seemed to object to our unexpected European presence.

Many other gods appeared and argued their precedence. It seemed that it was a special privilege to be allowed to rest on the great verandah outside the main building. The lesser gods were stacked in the courtyard.

Eventually the King of Kulu appeared. To me he looked like a fine British actor of long ago, Donald Calthrop. He was below average height and rather businesslike. He wore a long brocaded gown, which was oddly offset by horn-rimmed spectacles. He authoritatively and patiently suffered all the mysterious remnants of antique ritual with that objective, matter of fact attitude I have observed in some Italian Roman Catholic priests when performing the Mass. When all was completed the gods on their palanquins began to form up and, with the King and his retinue, moved off. I swear to you, reader, that I did not plan or push it, but somehow I found myself walking slightly behind and to the right of the King. It must suffice for my story when I inform you that the fly whisk used to protect the King also protected me!

Now my position was a little over-exposed; people did stare at me with great curiosity. Who could the European be? As usual I was wearing my white cotton kurta and matching trousers. Politicians in India tend to wear this garb; but only the hundred or so gods could have known the answer to the question. I actually replied to the adulation of the people with that grand flutter of the hand that I have learnt from close scrutiny of our Royal Family; one or two people reached out to touch me. I was very forbearing. I learnt it is only the masses' faith that creates a royal personage.

The procession, perhaps a mile long, reached a vast open area and here I lost the King or he lost me. He was more hustled than escorted to a great platform, which had many ropes attached to it. There was an enormous congregation waiting. I found a vantage point. Suddenly, hundreds of men dashed for the ropes and to my astonishment began to pull the crowded platform across the flat ground; the huge dais was on wheels and the King calmly waved to the cheering people of Kulu. I wondered if this spectacular ritual stretched back to the periods of Alexander or Tamburlaine.

At that time, in the town of Kulu, there is also a great annual fair. The tribespeople and the dealers – of many sorts – assemble to enjoy themselves and to make money. Chiara and I were wandering among this exotic throng when I saw, coming towards us, the King – now without his royal raiments – holding the hand of a small boy, just like any good father or grandfather. No one seemed to recognise him. As we came close to each other I placed my hands together and bowed in that gentle Indian salute. The King smiled and bowed his head as we passed; he seemed pleasantly surprised that I had acknowledged him. Well, it was not easy after the opulent contrast of the afternoon.

The Kulu Valley was full of mysterious and wonderful events for us, but I must hasten back to the thud of Delhi. Only one other Kulu adventure will I record here. We were visiting an extremely interesting and unique style of Hindu temple, built of ancient blocks of rock. Music was beaten out on drums and other instruments. We were urged to enter and there, in front of the shrine, a little man was dancing sensually in praise of the god. When he stopped a young Kulu teenager took over the holy dance, but his style was different. As he leapt round he shouted to me: 'Jive for god!'

And then we were back in Delhi to await the reaction and decision on my script. What was going to happen? Reactions and decisions, if they had been made about the film up to now, rarely reached my ears. And to this day, not a single word of assessment has come to me from the Ministry or from Doordarshan. I can only presume that the relevant parties are so terrified of stating anything that might contradict the mogul, whoever he or she is, that nothing is said;

even if it transgresses what would customarily (in our Western world) be regarded as the commonest courtesy.

No, I didn't get a word from the Prime Minister either; but I was summoned to call on Shri Sharada Prasad. Now, by this date, the Director-General of Doordarshan had been changed. The new man was Shri Baskar Ghose and when I first met him I expressed my congratulations, to which he replied, without a flicker: 'Shouldn't you be commiserating with me, Mr Griffith?' I was enormously impressed. Indeed, it was the first remark from Doordarshan that had impressed me. I felt, as I think Mrs Thatcher had said of Comrade Gorbachev: 'I can do business with this man.' And initially this trust bore fruit; but later he disappeared from my life behind that all-pervasive bureaucratic fog. I struck towards the forthrightness of Shri Ghose for a desperate personal need very early: 'Sir, Admiral Satyindra Singh saw me through my filming of *Clive of India* with such authority and skill that we did not lose one single day of film production time. My Doordarshan colleagues, with all due respect and bearing in mind that they have no power (and probably don't want any), are useless. Please may I have Admiral Singh with me to the end of this production, simply so that I can get the film made?'

'Yes, Mr Griffith, you may have Admiral Singh.' And so Setty was hired and we were a partnership again. I thought that all would now be reasonably well – innocent, trusting fool that I was!

I also asked Shri Ghose: 'May I raise the subject of nepotism, sir?'

'You may raise the subject of nepotism, Mr Griffith.'

'I have a son, Jonathan, who is nineteen years old and is a trained still photographer. For no payment beyond his daily expenses [already fixed and settled for the rest of us] could he be our still photographer?'

'Yes, Mr Griffith.'

I also proposed to pay Jonathan's airfare out of my own pocket, but fortunately for me this was forestalled when Air

India offered to give every member of our film crew free air passage. This windfall was achieved through the initiative of my freelance friend, Admiral Singh, and myself.

Admiral Singh came with me to the meeting in Shri Prasad's office. Setty sat to the left of me. Shri Prasad was now somewhat transformed: a touch of the schoolmaster, though ever quiet and according to protocol. He kicked off: 'Mr Griffith, I know that in your covering letter that came with your script, you urged the script should not be shown around [I had emphasised that I was already aware that in India there would be at least seven hundred million different opinions] but we have *had* to discuss it with one or two knowledgeable people. And . . . [a name was mentioned that rang no bell in my head] has said that your script is pro-British!'

I sat there not daring even to glance at my perceptive chum, Admiral Singh. It was a totally new accusation against me. When, some six months later, I was briefly in Britain to do some filming, I told my old friend, sometime colleague and pending boss, David Elstein of Thames Television, this story, and he collapsed into hysterical laughter. When David was able to pull himself together sufficiently, he managed to say: 'Well, you've never been accused of *that* before!' But only in the spirit that confession can be good for the future. Facing David Elstein I thought, Well, you can't win 'em all; or lose 'em all.

I also had the same thought as I sat in front of Shri Prasad. And then the influential man glanced down at a sheet of paper on which was written a longish list of notes: 'On page one, Mr Griffith, you write that Jawaharlal Nehru's mother was a traditional Hindu woman! Why do you have to say that?'

'Say what, sir?'

'*Hindu* woman.'

I could sense that I was edging into trouble. 'But she was, sir – a Hindu woman.'

'Maybe, but why say so?'

It flashed through my mind that it was going to be difficult to make a film about Nehru, which would essentially culminate in the partition of the sub-continent of India and the obscene slaughter of half-a-million Muslims and Hindus, if I was to keep off any seedling definitions of the significance of Hindu and Muslim. Of course, I'm not a fool about Indian politics and I understood what the worry was. Those who supported the cause of Nehru or Mrs Gandhi or her son, Rajiv, did not want any emphasis put on the fact that the Nehru family came from an ancient line of Hindu Brahmins. I understood the problem, but I felt that I was being greatly dropped into 'the fertiliser', as my old friend and distinguished actor, Terry Thomas, used delicately to say.

And so Shri Prasad made his way through the startling list. In all fairness, most of the points that he made were connected with India's communal problems. Those problems where one religion or culture was at another's throat. It is a terrible reality and I am deeply sympathetic. I just wish that the Indians would think a little more perceptively about other cultural problems beyond their borders.

At the end of quite a lengthy lecture and still not daring to look at Admiral Singh, I said: 'I have heard you, sir,' that invaluable Scottish acknowledgement without necessarily agreeing. 'May I have that list of points?' I was not being clever; indeed I was lagging behind the nuances of the situation.

But the penny dropped in my poor old head as Shri Prasad pulled back the list of points with one lightning movement: 'No, Mr Griffith, there are a few typing errors.' It crossed my mind, from my observations in South Block, that the standard of typing in that particular area of Delhi was pretty high; even if it wasn't as high at Doordarshan.

'Then, sir,' and I was feeling my way very uneasily, 'I think that you must nominate someone to remind me of these points.'

'What an excellent idea, Mr Griffith! I will give the

matter careful thought and will be in touch with you shortly.'

I felt like biting my tongue off! What had I just suggested? The image of some political hack standing over my shoulder loomed in my mind. Of course, as I have already explained, I had been given ample reason to fall into a paranoid condition. As Setty and I left South Block I thought to myself how quite a few old colleagues of mine, who had suffered my cockiness over the years, would have enjoyed my comeuppance; or was it? I know that Admiral Singh and I didn't have to debate much; we were both in deep thought about the same threatening issue.

But once again, in my long life of mistakes, I was underrating another human being. Shri Prasad did not nominate a hack; on the contrary he nominated one of India's leading historians: Doctor B. R. Nanda, who was the author of several distinguished books including the well-known family biography *The Nehrus*.

During my lengthy peregrinations of Indian discovery before my contract was signed, I had met Bal Ram Nanda and had enjoyed the experience very much; not least because of the additional civilised treat of meeting Mrs Nanda, a warm, intelligent woman who is a fine painter-artist. When I realised that Doctor Nanda was to discuss the points raised by Shri Prasad, my sigh of relief was very great. But nothing in India is as simple as elsewhere in the world, or at least in the various countries where I have worked. First, Doctor Nanda protested that he had been given no list by Shri Prasad: 'Mr Griffith, I have spent some thirty years studying the subject and I presume that you have been with it, about, two years?'

'Five months' concentrated effort, Doctor.'

'Well, Mr Griffith, all I would like to do is to go through your script with you and if I think that anything is questionable, we can discuss it and, with my long experience of studying Nehru's life, perhaps make an alternative suggestion.'

Well, that sounded very reasonable and valuable to me. And it would be a unique event for me. Never before had any of my scripts been tempered by another person's comments. I believe that the best films are made by reasonable dictators; but this film was being financed and made for a state: the State of India. There was a slight change of emphasis for me; from being an employee of a television production company to being one of a foreign government. But I knew two things very clearly: firstly, the impact of my film efforts relied upon their independent spirit; and, secondly, if that independence was being threatened, I must return home to Britain immediately. And it was clear that wise Doctor Nanda also realised and valued these facts. So we started our astonishing labours; every morning I would arrive at his residence at 10 a.m. and we would work our way, word by word, through the script. Ready to hand, as far as I remember, were two large alternative dictionaries.

I began to make alarming calculations about the sheer cost of these microscopic inspections of my written work. Already a number of us were under contract, which was now based on a weekly salary over an estimated period. Clearly, that period was going to be eroded by these days and weeks of painstaking academic examination. And there was expensive hired equipment lying round – in no way being utilised; the loss of one single day in my past film experience has sickened me. But now I seemed to be the only person worrying. However, my personal responsibility – I have been called 'The Chief Worrier' by my second wife Doria – was being, inevitably, destroyed and there was nothing I could do to control the situation. And no one else was controlling it; the financial cost to India, I had to try and dismiss from my concerned mind.

Though Doctor Nanda had denied any knowledge of Shri Prasad's list, I was never entirely convinced that it had ceased to exist in some form. On page one, the Doctor homed in on 'traditional Hindu woman', except that he questioned – initially – the use of 'traditional', and not of

'Hindu'. Whether this was a slip of the tongue or memory, I cannot be sure. I finally compromised, reasonably I believe, by rewriting it: 'traditional Indian woman'. I felt that as long as I could retain sufficient Hindu and Muslim signals in the pages ahead, I could still maintain a clear comprehension for the foreign lay-viewer of this essential and terrible theme in any proper life of Jawaharlal Nehru.

To tell you the truth, very little was altered; it was often a matter of fine nuance, which made barely any or no difference to what I was battling to communicate. Doctor Nanda said: 'Every day the Prime Minister is worried about the threat of communal trouble, we don't want to add to those problems unnecessarily, do we?'

'No,' I replied and meant it from the bottom of my heart. On the other hand, I thought to myself, I must keep the saga true and clear.

It is valuable to consider a few of the emphases that Doctor Nanda raised. He felt that I was making Mohammed Ali Jinnah, the leader of the Muslim League and the first President of Pakistan, too much of a villain. Now, Doctor Nanda is a good Hindu, so his attitude over Jinnah demonstrates his endeavours for fair play – and perhaps not to upset politically Pakistan sympathisers too much. Not that I failed to see Jinnah's point of view, but he was acerbic and at one point said: 'The Hindu worships the cow; we Muslims eat the cow; what have we got in common?'

It was one of the few quotes about which Doctor Nanda showed signs of being adamant: 'I don't want Jinnah to say that.' And we went through the ritual of a close fight; much as Mr Kampelman (of the United States) and Comrade Vorontsov (of the Soviet Union) must have done during their nuclear disarmament chats.

'But he said it, Doctor.'

'Well, I don't want you to quote him.'

'But it is valuable because it is dramatically gripping.'

'I do appreciate that, Mr Griffith; but it could rekindle dangerous emotions here and there.'

'You know, I sometimes feel that this is a job that I should not have got into.'

'Now, Mr Griffith, you know that you don't mean that!'

There are two versions of this film of the life of Nehru, a two and a quarter hour one for Indian viewing and a one and three-quarter hour one for international viewing. That Jinnah remark is not in the former, but it is in the latter. A civilised compromise, I feel.

The big dangerous discussion between the Doctor and me was, inevitably, – if you understand the emotions of India today – about Jallianwala Bagh. In the year 1919 there was serious political trouble in India, sparked off by, among others, the emerging Mahatma Gandhi. The British feared that the appalling Indian uprising of 1857 might be recurring. Afghanistan, hoping the British fear was correct, began to invade India. The most fearsome threat centred on Amritsar in the Punjab (the place where, ironically, the threat is most apparent today) and the politically-inspired populace took over the city, committing murder and arson. A Britisher, General Dyer, was ordered to restore law and order and, in achieving this, shot dead some four hundred Amritsar citizens who were present at a banned (by Dyer) political meeting in an open area called Jallianwala Bagh. This event was the binding catalyst for Indian independence. Ninety-nine educated Indians out of a hundred, if they mention Britain's capacity for atrocity, mean Jallianwala Bagh. Perhaps it should be noted, to Britain's relative credit, that there isn't anything else to compare with it; no, not in two hundred odd years.

After enjoying a fine exhibition in Delhi, celebrating Jawaharlal Nehru's life, I was asked by the person in charge what I thought of it. 'Excellent; but you shouldn't have misrepresented history in your Jallianwala Bagh exhibit.'

'In which way is it incorrect?'

'Why you have painted your illustration of the event with General Dyer's soldiers (Gurkhas and Baluchis) machine-gunning the people? There were no machine guns.'

For psychological reasons Indians suffer an almost unanimous compulsion to blacken further an already dark event. My anti-Imperialist attitude will not blind me to the whole truth about Jallianwala Bagh or anything else. Perhaps this is what Shri Prasad meant when he said that my script was 'pro-British'. He didn't specify and I, wisely, didn't ask him.

Anyway, Indians, generally and overwhelmingly, have to believe that General Dyer in Amritsar is a straightforward case of unmitigated evil. And in my script I felt obliged to explain General Dyer's historical predicament. And this, as by almost all other Indians I have talked to, was resisted very strongly by Doctor Nanda. He is much too civilised to accuse me of being an Imperialist or of my *approving* of the slaughter; but other Indian friends have.

Over the Jallianwala Bagh issue I had to produce evidence in some detail to prove the basic facts that I had written. The truth is that Indians do not want to know the whole Amritsar truth. I understand why. And also, Doctor Nanda did not want me to link Mahatma Gandhi with the violent Indian emotions in the Punjab. But they were very formidably connected and certainly Gandhi knew it and was appalled at the outcome: the deaths of the many Indians and the few British; he wanted no deaths.

The passing of this episode alone by Doctor Nanda and my very careful adjustments must have taken the best part of a week. But no one was looking at their watches, except me. Alan Birkinshaw in his laconic New Zealand manner would ask: 'How's it going?'

'OK,' I'd boringly reply.

There will be more about Jallianwala Bagh when we get there in the story of the film-making. And I will leave the reasons for Doctor Nanda's and my gentlemanly tussles over Subhas Chandra Bose, an Indian hero with rather stupid Fascist tendencies, till his place in the film chronology turns up. It was during these debates that I found myself saying: 'I will not and cannot be unjust to the British in this film!' Even Mrs Thatcher would have been pleased – if not proud – of me.

And so Doctor Nanda and I came to an agreed text. But Doctor Nanda had been extremely painstaking and at the end of our daily meetings, which had stretched on for many weeks, I liked him more than ever. He called me Kenneth and I called him Bal Ram. At the end of it all, I said: 'They've given you a lousy job and I think you've been brave.' Governments tend to want safe, Establishment-line films and my efforts are always divorced from whatever the Establishment may or may not be working for; I should not even be conscious of what they might want. But Bal Ram Nanda fully understood and sympathised with my particular responsibility. He had worked a little with Sir Richard Attenborough and he sensitively understood the differing professional problems of Sir Richard and me. Doctor Nanda said of Attenborough's *Gandhi*: 'It conveyed the true spirit of the man to many millions of people around the world and that is a very good thing.' Coming from an academic and a highly responsible historian, that was a liberal and enlightened remark. Shri Prasad had made a wise choice.

Doctor Nanda knew Jawaharlal Nehru personally. He told me that when he was writing *The Nehrus*, the Prime Minister refused to see the book till after it was printed; he did not want to interfere or influence. Rather like his grandson, Rajiv, in my case, I suspect. The only criticism Nehru made of Doctor Nanda's book was: 'I feel that there is rather too much about me in it.'

Now what would happen? Doctor Nanda felt that very quickly we would be able to begin filming. But even he could not foresee the full depth of that Indian fog.

One of the great problems of making the sort of film that I am engaged upon is how much screen time should I be allowed? How can you do any, even impressionistic, justice to a human life in one hour? I am usually given one hour and a half. With my preceding effort, a life of the great Israeli leader, David Ben Gurion, which was really meant to be Israel's case through Ben Gurion's experience, I snatched two hours. Jeremy Isaacs, the then head of Channel Four, which had pre-bought the film, said to a mutual friend (so I have been told): 'What am I to do with two hours?' Of course, I, a Welsh non-conformist, felt that Israel was fully justified in getting two hours in the teeth of fairly non-stop Palestine Liberation Organisation propaganda, but Mr Isaacs apparently didn't agree. But many mysterious psychological obstructions creep into people's motives. I am not at all sure that I even want to understand them.

Now, in India, the screen-time problem was being pushed at me in the opposite direction. 'They' (whoever they were) wanted me to retain elements in Nehru's life which I felt were properly expendable in order to hold the screen-time to even the prolonged two hours. How much time will millions of television viewers give to a life of Ben Gurion or Nehru, even if I am prepared to stand on my head or to expose my undressed person, to hold their attention on an important subject? How do you make essentially prolonged screen-time sufficiently entertaining for intelligent viewers? That is the big question. Finally, the television mogul (intelligent or otherwise) is faced with the painful ultimate: 'Dare I be socially responsible and intelligent for just a minute?' A minute? Well, yes.

I had already written, in my original script, what the powers that be now wanted – in terms of detail. But my procedure is judiciously to cut and cut and trim and trim – finally even single words, until the screen-time (by a word count) plus, say, fifteen minutes to be trimmed in the cutting room (the film editor's domain) gets us down to the required length. I warned Doctor Nanda, who was my only contact, that such extensions of content would make the film unacceptable to potential international television markets. Well, they wanted a fuller treatment *and* international acceptance. 'In that case,' I said, 'you will require two films: one for Indian viewing plus an international version that must not exceed two hours' screen-time.' 'So this is what it must be!'

You cannot just cut wodges out. The alternative cutting points must be clearly understood by all concerned before filming starts. I therefore began to mark the film script accordingly. In practice we had to improvise most of these potential cuts as we went along, filming. Alan Birkinshaw is a thorough professional and the onus rested mainly on his shoulders – with occasional sniping questions from Venu Gopal, our cameraman, and me.

Well, all of this necessitated a big shift in every arrangement. We were now going to make two separate films instead of one and with the extra editing and technical work towards the end of the production, our contracts and our time in India and elsewhere would have to be greatly extended. We again entered a long, expensive period with our Indian government employers during which apparently nothing was happening – except my nearly daily rages and Alan Birkinshaw's dogged pursuit of Indian phantoms. By this time I did not give a damn about the waste of India's money; no Indian seemed to care and the whole sick system was eroding my health. Alan and Chiara urged me to keep out of the Indian mess and I recognised that it was beyond my control and that Alan was better suited to cope with the Alice in Wonderland nonsense that is India's official style of doing almost anything.

We had been given a production office that had no telephone and no typewriter and was full of old rubbish and debris. After shouting and ranting – mainly on my part – a telephone was installed and a typewriter appeared; but no typist. After more daily insults, again hurled primarily by me, though Alan banged out many, many memos to those who purported to be running the show called Doordarshan, a series of incompetent young people – one at a time – appeared, some of them apparently learning to type. For a few minutes each morning a frail old Untouchable (as far as the Hindus were concerned) turned up and with fast-fading strength vaguely whisked at the accumulated mess, moving, perhaps, some thick dust from one side of the 'office' to another. This effort on the old man's part was the signal for our Indian assistants to go outside the building; not that this delayed anything, because they were at pains to do next to nothing while they were inside. It was a long period that was as close to hell as anything that I have experienced.

However, Alan, Chiara and I had one escape route to professional sanity. While watching Indian television in my various hotel rooms I had seen one weekly offering that was outstanding. It was a serious but entertaining 'magazine' programme; each week the producers presented a main theme of important human interest: Delhi's courageous blind people; a non-privileged family who were training to be international swimmers and who were pleading to repair and refill an ancient, holy water tank; and a wider story about a few Indian soldiers who had just sailed around the world in a small, second-hand, British-made boat, which put particular focus on one of the soldiers because he had lost a leg. The programmes were collectively called *India Alive* and they were produced by a husband and wife partnership: Jalabala and Gopal Sharman and also by Jalabala's remarkable daughter, Anasuya. These weekly programmes were high above anything else I saw on Doordarshan; every one of them always lifted my battered spirit.

People who knew why I was in India would frequently ask me 'What do you think of Indian television?' to which I would reply by praising *India Alive*. My opinion reached the ears of the Sharman family and they got in touch with me. This proved to be a great boon not only to me, but to Chiara and Alan as well. The Sharmans always offered us their high technical expertise, which was not available within Doordarshan, and their warm, generous human support, which was also not forthcoming from Doordarshan.

This family – is it fair to write 'led by Gopal'? – had carefully built up a fine production organisation inside their own property in Delhi, the Akshara Theatre. It had cameras, editing facilities, sound equipment; everything of the best and carefully maintained. The Sharmans were a self-contained island of excellence, protecting their standards from the incompetence and corruption that reigned outside. We, that is us three Europeans, continuously turned to them for advice and technical support. When matters were desperate we even used their telephone to contact Britain. Their telephone worked more efficiently than Doordarshan's, which anyway had a lock on it and the key was never given to us; 'us' being the producer, the director and the general assistant!

During this period Chiara received a telephone call from Italy with the dreadful news that her only and beloved brother, Paulo, a pilot with Alitalia, had received mortal injuries in an accident in the Alps and was in a coma. I rushed her to Delhi Airport and the representatives of Alitalia there overrode every difficulty to fly her immediately to the Swiss hospital. Alan, my son Jonathan and I held a meeting and divided among our three European selves Chiara's varied responsibilities until she was able to return. Chiara remained for four weeks until her brother died and had been buried and then she flew back to Delhi. We were not surprised that her employers, Doordarshan and the Ministry, did not offer to pay her air fare, but we were surprised when they promptly stopped her salary and her Indian expenses for the period of her absence. Chiara, of course, had to continue paying her Delhi rent and other ongoing costs. But these Indian people were adamant. In fairness to Indians generally, most of them who learnt of this inhumanity felt ashamed. For my part, my hatred for Doordarshan and the Ministry deepened.

In his dealings with these people, Alan displayed a flint-like attitude and it was he who negotiated the terms and duration of our new contract, which now extended to the last day of February, 1988. I believe that under normal circumstances I would have remonstrated with Alan about the long period that he was demanding before completion, but bearing in mind my exasperation with our employers and their incredible capacity for destruction and delay, I acquiesced: 'Whatever you want, Alan, you have my support.' We duly signed our contracts but we were both surprised that Chiara's was not included. The original agreement stipulated that all three of us were to be employed up to the final delivery date of the film. 'Oh,' it was said of Chiara's new agreement, 'hers will be separate.' They claimed that she had requested this, which was an untruth. For whatever reason Doordarshan was apparently planning to penalise her even further. I have been told that it is the mentality of sharks to attack the weaker bodies. However, we registered our unease, tightened our faith and prepared to begin filming.

Jawaharlal Nehru, a few days before he died, copied four lines of poetry by the American, Robert Frost. The words were found on the table by his deathbed.

> The woods are lovely, dark and deep,
> But I have promises to keep,
> And miles to go before I sleep,
> And miles to go before I sleep.

I believe that when Jawaharlal read those words he recognised they summed up his fading life. He loved the countryside passionately, but he had promised to emancipate India from Imperialism and that was still so much to be achieved for India before he died. What he didn't know, as he copied Frost's words on to the scrap of paper, was that the 'miles' of his journey through life had virtually run out. I titled the film: *But I have Promises to Keep; A Life of Jawaharlal Nehru*. I also had inscribed on the front of the film-script: 'Jawaharlal Nehru said to the staff of his newspaper, *The National Herald*: "Whatever you might write, never write out of fear!"' This latter text was aimed at my employers who were, virtually, the Government of India. So, earlyish in this production, I was calling upon Jawaharlal Nehru to protect me from any sleight of political manipulation that his inheritors might try inflicting on me. But as you already know, they didn't – well, not much.

CHAPTER THREE

Making the Film

I will tell you the story of our filming in the chronological order of Jawaharlal Nehru's life and not, neccessarily, in the order of our location filming. This will enable you to follow the man's extraordinary saga and also to understand exactly what I was aiming to achieve with the film. And it will be a summation of how far I had got in my discovery of Nehru.

Our film-crew travelled to that north-western enlarged tip of India, Kashmir. And there I spoke the opening words : 'Jawaharlal Nehru's ancestors came from the fabulously beautiful Kashmiri Valley. They were Brahmins, aristocrats of the Hindu religion, and the males carried the title Pandit, man of learning. It is believed that during the early eighteenth century a forebear travelled to Delhi and served within the mighty Moguls' orbit. After the Indian Mutiny of 1857 – known to some as the First War of Independence – and its crushing by the British Army, the Nehru family retreated to famed Agra and in due course to Allahabad, where Motilal Nehru, the father of our hero, Jawaharlal Nehru, became a highly successful lawyer.'

You may notice from the above passage that a different style of writing is required to the writing of this book. A shorthand of language has to be employed and yet every fact has to be as clear as possible. The viewer, as against the reader, cannot go back and check what has been stated, unless the viewer has a video recorder, but I am not aiming to cater for such dedicated sophisticates. And, of course, the shorthand is dictated by that strictly limited screen-time factor.

As I wrote the above opening film sequence, I visualised

it being spoken (by me) against the famous and spectacular image of Kashmir's exotic lakes. But Alan Birkinshaw and Venu Gopal had sped off on a lightning reconnaissance and had chosen somewhere far to the north and close to the summer snow line.

I decided, long ago, and at least in my sort of films, that if I approve of my colleagues, I must delegate a full creative responsibility to them. I research the subject, I write the subject, I produce (get the whole team together) and finally, heavy burden!, I am continuously in front of the camera. Therefore, the routine on *But I Have Promises to Keep* was that Alan, Venu, Chiara and I, plus our Indian producer, Surendra Dhir, all flew ahead, while the rest of our crew, including Jonathan, travelled by coach, with our equipment, often over long distances. The drill then was that Alan and Venu would select our specific locations, while Surendra Dhir attended to local bureaucratic arrangements and Chiara and I tended to focus on the script and its interpretation at our location base.

So when Alan unexpectedly argued for this isolated northern valley, I questioned him closely, pointing out the world-famous, immediately recognisable impact of the Kashmiri lakes. Alan explained that though the lakes were undoubtedly beautiful and well known, it was more than likely that we wouldn't get the spectacular opening shot the film required with our limited schedule. David Lean and Stanley Kubrick have the financial muscle to wait for weeks, if necessary. Alan stated that in this northern valley he was certain of the opening shot. In such an argument, Venu Gopal wisely stood on the sidelines. Anyway, with a mildly threatening: 'Well, you're the director. . . .' from me, off we all trekked north. And I mean trekked; after we had wound our way up the main route towards outlandish Ladakh, through wonderful mountain scenery and past ominous glaciers that touched our road even though it was high summer, we eventually took to ponies and entered Alan's Shangri-la. And perched on a pony which delicately selected the boulders to avoid, on a track above a hurtling river, I decently acknowledged that Alan and silent Venu were right. The place was magic and it looks so on the screen. I simply changed my script words from 'fabulously beautiful Kashmiri Valley' to 'fabulously beautiful Kashmiri valleys'. As long as one has an answer for the nit-picking critic, all is reasonably well. Valley singular clearly implies the great lakes Valley. Such is the way we worked.

I should emphasise here that working with our Indian film colleagues, as against the nightmare of our Indian bureaucratic ones, was a happy experience. Alan, Chiara and I had for a long period been trying to bolster our spirits by telling each other that as soon as we were working with film people our troubles would evaporate. That proved correct to a point but, of course, our headquarters were inevitably at Doordarshan and the awful Ministry and they would continue to trouble us to the bitter end.

Surendra Dhir bore most of the bureaucratic threat. Every minute expenditure, spread among thirty or so personnel, had to be accounted for. Ask a Kashmiri helper, who speaks – let alone writes – neither English nor Hindi, for a receipt for twelve rupees, and you're in deep trouble. No Indian in government service is to be trusted, for one second, by another government servant. Neither did anyone trust us Europeans for that matter. Dear Surendra Dhir would often say when he returned to the sticklers at Mandi House: 'I am facing worse than ruin, but all that matters is completing the film!'

I would say: 'I'll stand by you, Surendra!' and he would give me what can only be described as an old-fashioned Hindu look.

Incidentally, by this time I had lost my invaluable Admiral Satyindra Singh. He could no longer bear the insulting inefficiency at Mandi House or Doordarshan's failure to pay their debts to him and others, so he resigned. I could not persuade him to change his mind. He always referred to the bureaucrats as 'the bastards' and I couldn't argue with him about that. My friend Setty even got cross with me once (the first and only time) when, feeling deep outrage, I roared: 'I've had enough of this Indian shit!' If I had roared: 'I've had enough of this Indian bureaucratic shit!', he would not have taken exception. I would pray in the Golden Temple itself that he forgives me.

In Kashmir we based ourselves in the lake city of Srinagar and Chiara and I lived on a houseboat. I have been told that in the old days of independent princely Kashmir, foreigners – the British! – were not allowed to own land. Now, Kashmir for the British Raj had many enormous attractions, particularly in the summer. It was relatively cool, it was fabulously beautiful and the hunting and fishing were good. One of the ancient rulers said of it: 'If there is paradise on earth, this is it, this is it!' So what did the Brits do? Being well-educated or at least privilege-educated, they had visited the Victorian-style houseboats on the rivers of Oxford and Cambridge and they began to have facsimiles built at Srinagar and moored them there on the lakes. The Maharajah, apparently, did not object to foreigners floating on his lake.

Today to live on a houseboat is the thing to do and for us it was a very happy experience. There are hundreds of them ranging from magnificent opulence with crystal chandeliers to relatively humble jobs. We chose a middle-range houseboat, which nevertheless did not inhibit the owner from calling it the 'Taj Mahal'. There is something reminiscent of a gipsy caravan about these houseboat interiors. Ours was charmingly and slightly rundown. If I am fortunate enough to return to Srinagar I would like to stay again on the 'Taj Mahal'. What more can you write? Our host was Shri Shafi, a true Kashmiri who, like all citizens of the Kashmir state I have met, was incredibly skilled at extracting the last legitimate rupee out of all visitors. But as he got to know me and, I pride myself, like me, he became merciful, indeed financially generous towards me. His 'table servant', Abdul, was a joy in himself. His white waiter's uniform was much too large for him. But I want nothing changed; the combination of Raj pretensions and homely reality made us all very happy.

Shri Shafi courageously and even foolhardily supervised two firework displays that we held; one was to celebrate Jonathan's birthday, the other America's Independence Day. Chiara inspired those pyrotechnic displays; she has a great weakness for fireworks. We also found the time to float around the lakes in a *shikara*, which is not unlike a poor man's Venetian gondola and the boatman might also sing for you sad Kashmiri love songs.

And then to Allahabad, which was the Nehru family home: 'Motilal Nehru [Jawaharlal's father] was a colourful [I had originally written extravagant, which he certainly was, but I had been asked to change it] extrovert, who enjoyed wealth and found much to admire and emulate in the British way of life, represented by the élite of the British Raj. However, his wife, Swarup Rani, the mother of Jawaharlal, was a deeply traditional Indian woman and thereby, between these two contrasting parents, lies the enigma of Jawaharlal's astounding life.' This sequence was covered by still photographs.

And we filmed at Harrow School, where suddenly I was speaking while holding the essential umbrella as the English rain poured down: 'When Jawaharlal was fifteen years old, he was taken by his father to England to receive the finest education that could be imagined – at Harrow; where, of course, Winston Churchill had recently attended. These two Harrovians, later in life, would become formidable adversaries.'

The probable accident of rain at Harrow was good for us in its contrast to the preceding sun of India. Not only are the words quoted in these films carefully accurate but also we have always crossed the world to the specific location where the event took place, if it still exists. This is all part of a ploy to convince the viewer that I am speaking the truth. The rain dramatically emphasises the shift from one continent to another.

Motilal Nehru communicated with his son very regularly by letter. Here we took creative licence and I appeared on the stern of a ship, dressed in a British tweed suit, collar and tie: 'I am going back to India with the firm conviction that I have sown the seed of your future greatness. You must bear in mind that in you we are leaving the dearest treasure we have in this world, and perhaps in other worlds to come.'

I gave Motilal a rather deep voice, which with an Indian portentousness, made him sound like one or two Welsh characters that I have played. But no one else has mentioned it, so perhaps I would be wise to erase these two sentences. 'Jawaharlal replied: "I have no doubt whatever that my coming to Harrow is the right thing. But sometimes I feel rather lonely. . . ."'

This spoken by me, wearing a single-breasted, light grey suit, in a study at Harrow School. The whole scheme is to encapsulate my understanding of each character's spirit. A search for the true spirit of the characters is nearly everything.

'Jawaharlal's housemaster, the Reverend Edgar Stogdon, reported: "A very nice boy; quiet and very refined. He is not demonstrative but one feels that there is great strength of character. . . ."'

For the Reverend Stogdon I daringly wore an academic gown and, for the following words, I was placed in the centre of the six hundred plus Harrow schoolboys in their historic Assembly Hall and with the school orchestra poised: 'I know that young Nehru very specially likes the Harrow school songs.'

And the six hundred plus burst into splendid voice. It is one of the fortunate perquisites of working on these films that not only do you have to skip about this astonishing world but that wherever you film you have to become part of the location; you are not just a tourist or a visitor; you temporarily become part of the work force. You briefly become, or should, integrated. What a constant privilege. At Harrow School (writing as an ex-pupil of the Tenby Council School and then of the Greenhill Grammar School), I was much impressed by the pupils of Harrow. In Britain today you can easily receive the idea that our youths have become ill-mannered, badly educated hooligans. The good human courtesy expressed by the boys of Harrow came to me as a big surprise. I will give you an example. One of the many Harrow school songs is called 'Five Hundred Faces'; the solo is traditionally sung by a new boy before his voice has broken, because the song is about such a one having to face the other five hundred boys on his first day at school. It is a delightful and moving song; I wanted it to be a constant theme throughout our film, but Alan found the idea difficult. When it was sung for us in the Assembly Hall of Harrow, a small boy rose among the massed ranks to sing it for the very first time. He sang it beautifully and the moment he had finished the now 'Six Hundred Faces' spontaneously applauded the newcomer loudly and for a prolonged period. There was no other sound except the clapping. It was a unanimous expression by the young men of admiration for the boy's hard-won skill and courage. I was very reassured and moved by the experience. We cannot have too many gentlemen (or ladies) whether they come from Harrow or Tenby.

In those days, before I was *completely* disillusioned about my employers in India, I worked very hard to save the Government of India from paying facility fees for the right to film. Harrow School was the only location where I failed. I urged upon the pleasant bursar that India was a relatively poor country and that our film was in no way a commercial venture; it was a factual account of the life of a Harrow old boy – but for once I did not win. I was told that the school is now a relatively small part of a big business and a substantial sum of our limited Indian budget was handed over.

Cambridge gave us the relevant facilities and waived all charges: 'In 1907, Jawaharlal moved to Trinity College, Cambridge: "I feel elated at being an undergraduate with a great deal of freedom," but soon he was saying: "I feel a foreigner – an intruder." East is East and West is West and it is extremely difficult – even via Harrow and Trinity – for the twain to truly meet.'

In such a shot I slipped from myself to Nehru and back again without a film cut. The basic method, apart from assuming Nehru's character when quoting him, is to speak my own subjective words into the lens and Nehru's words away from the camera. It requires some dexterity.

I had planned the following piece to be my voice, over film archive material of the so-called Irish Trouble, as such material does exist. But Alan wanted me to speak almost the entire film in synchronisation; that is, to be filmed speaking it in front of the camera; dare I write, perform it? And then Alan decided to choose what archive material he would blend in at the editing stage; a luxury that had never been allowed on one of 'my' films before; but under our Indian circumstances 'What the hell!'

'During holiday time Jawaharlal Nehru twice visited rebellious Ireland and he was deeply moved by the efforts of Sinn Fein, the Irish freedom party, to emancipate their hard-pressed island from British domination. And after the Irish Rebellion of 1916 Nehru asked himself a significant question: "But was that not true courage, which mocked at almost certain failure, and proclaimed to the world that no physical might could crush the invincible spirit of a nation?" Already his course in life was emerging. Jawaharlal Nehru was beginning to apply that noble Irish question to his own country – India.'

Of course, I was happy that I could quote and comment on the above. Any opportunity to communicate the Irish republican cause is a happy opportunity for me. But I unexpectedly met with a degree of resistance from the Indians on this point. They tend not to like the idea that Nehru was inspired by freedom movements in Europe and instead persuade themselves that he was inspired by the ancient traditions of India; but that angle on his driving emotions came much later in his life and is most clearly illustrated in his book, *The Discovery of India*. Young Nehru, in Britain, was also moved and fascinated by Garibaldi's saga for Italian independence. But I do not mention Garibaldi in the film; you must keep the story as simple as is historically acceptable. But where does acceptability begin and end?

And then to London: 'From Cambridge University he moved to the Inner Temple in London to become a lawyer like his father.'

And back to Allahabad. 'Meanwhile, here in India, Motilal Nehru was dabbling in politics. He had joined the Indian National Congress, at that time a moderate, conservative political movement, aiming respectfully to advance Indians within the British Imperial structure, and Motilal made a speech: "John Bull means well; it is not in his nature to mean ill."'

Cut back to London. Jawaharlal in his London lodgings: 'When the son, here in London, heard, he was not pleased: "As regards John Bull's good faith, I have not as much confidence in him as you have." And when Motilal embraced the British Raj to the extent of accepting an invitation to King George V's Royal Durbar in Delhi, it all became too much for the uneasy Jawaharlal. He had already dared to rebuke his loving father: "The British Government must be feeling very pleased with you at your attitude."'

Cut to India: 'Motilal was badly stung: "I do not, of course, approve of your politics. However, my love for you knows no bounds and I do not see how that love can be affected." Jawaharlal swallowed his radical pride and communicated to his father: "I have ordered the court dress at Poole's; I suppose you want the ordinary levee dress with sword and everything complete. . . ."'

Yes, you may assume that the historical words were spoken on the historical location. I strolled into Poole's in Savile Row in London and after our filming was over the civilised manager of the establishment kindly showed me the old order book with Jawaharlal Nehru's name inscribed.

'Motilal changed the subject to sex and an arranged marriage: "You must not confuse real love with a passing passion. You know the arguments against Indians marrying English women." So it has to be noted that cultural preference is not a one-way traffic.' (This subjective remark was also lightly questioned by Doctor Nanda. I have found in recent years an astonishing touchiness about human facts if there is any hint, no matter how slight, of unfavourable comment about non-European people.) 'Motilal searched and came up with a suitable potential bride – or so he thought.'

'Jawaharlal remonstrated: "As regards the Delhi girl, surely she is too young for me." [She was at that time twelve years old.] "I am nearly ten years her senior."'

'But Hindu custom overrode British fashion and the young man, having passed his law examinations, dutifully returned to India and in due course married Kamala Kaul, of good Kashmiri Brahmin stock. He was to remark, years later, "I was a most unsatisfactory person to marry."'

For the wedding sequence in Delhi, I was responsible for a wardrobe error which, when I realised it, I felt was disastrous. The Hindu marriage ceremony was conducted by a distinguished sadhu (holy man) and his son. I donned my basic Nehru Indian costume for the occasion: a white cotton kurta and matching trousers, plus an Indian waistcoat. Now I had planned, in my head, to save this dramatic transformation from European to Indian clothes for the scene immediately following Nehru's first encounter with Gandhi in Lucknow. Many months later I was looking at the assembled film (virtually Alan's and Reena Mohan's fine cut) for the first time and saw my mistake. I barely fought off hysteria and kept repeating, 'It's entirely my fault.' Soon I accepted my mistake and I have now convinced myself that the transformation into Indian clothes at Nehru's wedding is equally effective.

An Indian friend recently told me a story about a small but confident boy going up to Sir Winston Churchill and asking him: 'Sir, what is the best advice you can give me for my future life?' And the reply came without pause: 'Keep a sense of proportion.'

'Jawaharlal Nehru was already the man between two vastly different cultures and he had been painstakingly placed there by his loving [I had originally written "doting", changed at Doctor Nanda's request] father. Young Nehru agonised over his predicament: "To some extent I come to India via the West, and look at my country as a friendly European might have done."'

This remark of Nehru's is an important recurring theme in the film; it is the first quote which demonstrates Jawaharlal's lifelong schizoid predicament: his eventual commitment to the emancipation of India away from his conditioned English culture. He reiterated this personal tussle throughout his life and he was always too introspectively honest to deny the truth. No, not even for purposes of political expediency. It is one of the qualities that make Nehru a hero in my mind.

And so we had completed our sequences in England and I immediately startled my film team – both European and Indian – by announcing that I was not returning to India – until we were all paid. I personally had been engaged on this Nehru project for about a year and the Indians had failed to pay me anything at all. I told Chiara that we would travel to Italy and visit her aged mother. And I informed the Indian High Commission in London that I would be in daily touch with them and would return to London within twenty-four hours when I had heard from my bank and colleagues that everyone had been paid. The debt was resolved after nine costly weeks.

En route to Italy, Chiara and I stopped in Paris for one weekend with friends. The weather was damp and grey but in the evening I went for a walk on my own and I began talking to myself. The thoughts that I addressed to myself could not have been made if I had not spent that agonizing year in India. France has long been Britain's traditional enemy – in spite of the *entente cordiale*. I muttered: 'What a beautiful city. Oh, it's good to be *home*!'

It was the first *European* sentiment that I had ever

uttered. My hand went to my mouth as I realised what I had said, I stood still on the wet pavement and I digested the significance of the realisation of our shared European culture. India had reminded me that I was relatively at home in France. It was a momentous discovery for me.

And then we were filming in the haunted city of Lucknow: 'For four years Jawaharlal Nehru wandered somewhat aimlessly in the imposing shadow of his dynamic father and then, in this city of Lucknow, he saw the little man for the very first time. He saw Mahatma Gandhi.'

Lucknow was a sometime opulent and undoubtedly, finally, morally degenerate Muslim kingdom. Well, morally degenerate from an early British Victorian point of view. It may not have been from an Indian Muslim vision of behaviour. Anyway, Lucknow is full of strange Indian Baroque palaces and Alan had selected one of these crumbling wonders for me to deliver the above paragraph from. He had arranged that I should walk along an exotic balcony, quite high up; which vantage point would disclose an eerie, romantic panorama of old Lucknow as the tracking (mobile) camera moved with me. Fine! I retreated to study the words to be spoken and their implication. After a while Alan appeared in my Mogul-period room: 'Ken, bit of a problem.'

'It's a wonderful shot; hate to lose it, but the sunlight has edged away from the balcony. No light on your face.'

'Well?'

'If you could climb over the balustrade on to the outer ledge, everything would be fine. The ledge is a good foot wide.'

'Ah, and you are proposing that I stroll in a relaxed manner, on this ledge, as I deliver the words effectively?'

'Yes; look, you don't *have* to do it, if you think it's too risky.'

'Show me.'

Now I knew, but nobody else on the film did, that Lucknow's architectural convolutions are notorious for their fast crumbling plaster. I glanced at the precarious, proposed pathway and noted the formidable cracks.

'Look, I'll try it out first,' said Alan sportingly.

'Be very careful,' said I, as Alan clambered over. I sensed that my director was poised to grab the ancient balustrade if anything collapsed. And anyway he is the sort of bloke who has broken wild horses in Australia during his life's experience. But I, who have never successfully ridden a tame horse, must look very confident and casual.

'OK,' said I as I groaned over the balustrade; 'look, lads, get it right *first* time – whatever happens to me.' This command is always extremely unfair on one's co-operating colleagues. Venu Gopal gave me one of those dark, piercing, southern Indian looks. But he decided that I was worth a small nod of sympathy. We did the shot. 'Was that all right, Venu?' I asked in a tone that challenged even a hint of failure.

'Fine!' replied Venu.

'All right, Alan?'

'Excellent for me.'

'Thank you, lads; let's get another one for safety.' We liked to have two acceptable shots for every scene. Normally Alan would order the second safety shot. But I spared him that ordeal. Like most human beings I can be quite a decent chap as well as a bit of a shit. We got the second acceptable take. The proposed millions of viewers around the world won't appreciate the full achievement of the scene, because they won't know. Except you, privileged readers.

'The Mahatma said: "No amount of speeches will ever make us fit for self-government. It is only our conduct that will fit us for self-government."'

The time had arrived for me to speak Gandhi's words – as Gandhi! I had known all along that if I was to have a Waterloo on this film, my Gandhi would be it. Gandhi is such a strange and powerful image, which these days is reinforced by Mr Ben Kingsley's memorable performance. The whole world knew! And I mustn't use make-up or wear Gandhi's authentic costume. I had long puzzled the pending problem of clothes. I had decided to wear, as with Nehru, a plain white cotton kurta (which Gandhi did not wear), but, of course, I would not wear a waistcoat, as Nehru did. I thought and thought about it. 'Do up all of the kurta buttons, Griffith,' I told myself. (Nehru was casual about such matters: several buttons were almost invariably left undone.) And then it was legitimate (in my mind) to wear my own glasses, which happen to be steel-rimmed. That was all – except the most vital element that was at my disposal: the mind and spirit of Gandhi, as far and as deep as I was able to understand it. And so we filmed the scene, on one of those atmospheric Indian outdoor platforms, bedecked with white sheets and cushions and a plenitude of invaluable Indian bunting.

What was my Gandhi like? Alan was pleased. All I knew was that I had done my utmost. And when you have achieved that, any failure is an honourable one. The television viewers will be the ultimate judges and, inevitably, they will all have views as varied as fingerprints. But opinions have already seeped to me and I will relate them in their due place.

'Jawaharlal stated: . . . [the voice was quiet and low, and yet it could be heard above the shouting of the multitude, there seemed to be steel hidden away somewhere].

'Gandhi explained his very simple belief: "England [I never know whether to be pleased or displeased when such inaccuracies are uttered about our British Imperialism, 'Britain' would have been correct, 'England' was loose thinking on Gandhi's part. It is a common error.] holds India in bondage because Indians co-operate with the Englishmen [there were Welshmen, Scotsmen and Irishmen present] and thereby strengthen British rule. Withdraw that Indian co-operation and the fabric of foreign rule collapses." Gandhi was talking simple mathematical common sense: there were under two hundred thousand Britons, both civil and military, ruling the three hundred and fifty million Indians.

'Young Nehru recognised a prophet when he saw one:

"He was obviously not of this world's ordinary coinage – and the unknown stared at us through his eyes."

'Motilal on the other hand was a hard-headed [requested to change from my "hard-bitten"] lawyer – and though he was impressed by the Mahatma's quiet powerful truth, he remained a professional sceptic: "I have heard of saints and supermen but I have never had the pleasure of meeting one."

'But no one ever successfully upstaged Gandhi – he was among other things a great humorist [with this word I was beaten from comic to comedian and finally to humorist. Nothing serious!] and he disarmed the Motilals of this world: "What I am saying may all sound nonsensical; well India is a country of nonsense – where nonsensical men could solve India's problems."'

And I think that in that statement, Gandhi expresses, humorously, his mysterious, ambiguous skill, which confounded many Britishers and at times was even to infuriate Nehru. What did Gandhi mean? How can you pin him down?

While working in Lucknow I found time to visit the ruins of the old British Residency. Before 1857, during the days of the East India Company, we British rapidly took over various Indian kingdoms which were ruled – at least nominally – under the fast-fading Mogul Empire but after 1857 we installed Residents, senior British officers, who diplomatically oversaw the indigenous behaviour. If that behaviour seriously transgressed a minimum (British) standard, we would remove the offending prince and replace him with an Indian theoretically more capable of meeting Victorian interests and susceptibilities. We did this to the King of Oudh (of which kingdom, Lucknow was the royal capital). The King was a self-indulgent playboy on a monumental scale. The British assumed that the King's removal would please the local hoi polloi, but for many complex reasons, that British action in Oudh was one of the elusive causes of the Indian Mutiny of 1857. And the British Resident of Lucknow and his formidable staff, and human adjuncts, were physically trapped by the Mutineer forces. The British lived in a grand, concentrated village in the middle of the city and that area was, and is, known simply as The Residency.

In the country round Lucknow, and most notoriously at Cawnpore, murder of British men, women and children was inflicted by the Mutineers on a horrific scale. And so the besieged Britons and their few Indian allies were defending themselves from fates that could easily be worse than quick death. The Residency was pounded stone by stone by the mutinous gunfire. The death rate was frighteningly high. But the remnant of survivors held out until a British relief column finally slaughtered its way into Lucknow. Among those British killed while coming to the rescue was Lieutenant Hodson, who had captured the Mogul Emperor, Bahadur Shah, in Delhi. He is buried where he fell on the outskirts of Lucknow. I visited his grave.

The Residency itself was deliberately left by the British exactly as it was at the end of the siege, as a memorial. The Indian Government has not disturbed the haunted patch. Except that until we British handed over power to India in 1947, the Union Jack always flew over the ruins as it did during the terrible conflict; now it has gone. And just beyond The Residency boundary, the Indians have built a tall martyrs' column, to remember the Indians who died while fighting the British. Strangely, that relatively recent cenotaph is also falling into disrepair. Again, in The Residency, I could sense the spirits of those who had suffered so extremely there. And as I wandered about the famous ruins there were the drums and singing of Muslim devotees, which I was able to watch and listen to for a long time.

In Lucknow I met a charming, fascinating young man who is a physicist, I think, and a descendant of one of the old princely lines of Oudh. We met late at night and there was too little time. He had been working on research outside India – in the Soviet Union! He had discarded all sentiment for the old feudal Indian grandeur. But, on pressing him, he confessed that he occasionally visits the site where his great-great-uncle was killed while fighting to throw back the advancing British during 1857. And I glimpsed the nobility of his ancestor. I would have liked to have got to know the young man better.

Close to where Hodson was killed – perhaps in combat with my Indian friend's ancestor – is one of the astounding wonders of this world: La Martinière College, which was founded by a Frenchman who did business with the royalty of old Oudh on a highly profitable scale. His creation, La Martinière (named after him), is packed with architectural entertainment and wonderfully wild decoration. Monsieur Martinière stipulated that the place was to be a Christian school and so it still is. One of the many unbelievable aspects of La Martinière is that the distinguished entertainer, Cliff Richard, was educated there. I wonder if Mr Richard's admirable Christian stand in life has its roots in Lucknow? The present Principal of La Martinière, T. W. Phillips, and his wife entertained us in a most gentle spirit. Down in the bosom of the building is the tomb of its astonishing founder. On a wall I saw a beautiful Zoffany painting of the Frenchman's slim Indian woman protégée.

'Under Gandhi's leadership the smooth flow of British Imperial order became disrupted. But prior to this, Indian political terrorism had erupted and the British replied by enacting a hard set of laws based on the report of Mr Justice Rowlatt. These laws did not dilly-dally. "Religious political conspiracies are to be put down by trial without juries and there is to be preventive detention for some without any trial at all." It was a policy of repression not unlike Britain's recent methods in north-eastern Ireland.'

And with the above paragraph I was beginning to enter the choppy Indian water, which culminates with the raging storm of the four hundred or so dead at Jallianwala Bagh. The basic disagreement between several of my Indian colleagues and me was because, as I have already touched upon before, they somehow have to believe that the British actions during this period were simply evil and that if I so much as gave an historical *reason* for the British behaviour, I was perpetrating the unforgivable: I was condoning Jallianwala Bagh etcetera. Of course, as a Britisher, I do not suffer the Indian psychological need to *force* this significant watershed on the road to Indian emancipation from British rule. And I have always (since a child) undercut such problems; I have consistently opposed any hint of Imperialism. Though I understand, very well, the inevitable steps of the British Imperial advance across the sub-continent of India. And though I can even admire the struggles of the old British administration in India to be socially responsible to their Indian subjects. And despite the fact that I admire the British capacity to abjure corruption and Britain's astounding skill in running the vast place so efficiently, I have always revolted against our fundamental British Imperial role. Once a culture has undertaken to rule an alien one, or in India's case, a multiplicity of alien ones (welded together primarily by the British themselves), that Raj culture can maintain itself only by a discreet backing of force. The British could preach till they were very red in the face, as they interminably did: 'Let us be friends; let us – Britons and Indians – pull together for the future welfare of India.'

But when Indians stopped agreeing and co-operating with that concept (ironically because it was part of British policy to educate the Indians to understand the European version of liberal democracy) the bonhomie façade was cracked and the British Imperialists had to call urgently on the services of Mr Justice Rowlatt and General Dyer. I submit that both Rowlatt and Dyer were simply carrying out their duties – and very efficiently. If there are proper heroes and villains in such a human story, India has homed in on the wrong men; they should have ignored Rowlatt and Dyer and gone for the throats of their political, Imperial masters; no one less notorious in this case than Winston Churchill. General Dyer, in particular, was quickly indicted by the Indian Nationalists and then he was speedily transformed into the grand scapegoat by those British Imperial politicians who had the gall to find their good and faithful servant expendable.

Of course, if India honestly faced these historical facts in depth and then truly abhorred the compulsion to conquer and rule a territory, contrary to the wishes of the majority of that territory's population and irrespective of India's strategic military needs, India might feel morally compelled to withdraw from certain areas – like Kashmir, Goa and even from the curious arrangement in Sri Lanka. And I could quietly add to this list. But India's capacity for hypocritical self-deception (a universal human weakness) is boundless.

The above Rowlatt passage and what was to follow in my film text were painfully debated and examined by Doctor Nanda and me. The general Indian inclination is to present Rowlatt and Dyer as unadulterated wrong-doers and to give no historical explanation about why they, as professional Imperialists, had to do what they did. And if they hadn't acted positively Britain might have been faced with an even greater disaster than India has on its hands at this moment in Amritsar, which is in the Punjab. Should the irony get lost?

'Jawaharlal stated [of the Rowlatt laws]: "One might almost think that the object of the British measure is to create trouble."

'The Mahatma was asked: "What can we do?"

'"Do? Once the Rowlatt bills become law, we offer non-violent resistance!"

'The light was emerging. Jawaharlal Nehru exclaimed: "Here at last is a method of action which is straight and open."

'The Mahatma proclaimed the 6th April, 1919 as the day to begin his campaign of non-violent resistance with a hartal – a national strike. The strike proved to be astonishingly successful and peaceful. However, three days later, on the 9th April, Gandhi was arrested by the British and immediately there was Indian violence in Bombay and other places in western India.'

Also, on Doctor Nanda's part, there was a painstaking effort to divorce Gandhi from any of the pending murderous events in Amritsar. In fact, Gandhi was preparing to visit Amritsar when he was arrested which I do not mention in my film script. Of course, his incipient arrival was enough to generate massed excitement; but Doctor Nanda did not want to confess even this. Perhaps over this omission on my part I can be described as lily-livered. But the going with my friend Bal Ram Nanda was fairly intense and he was also accommodating some of my revisionist arguments. Judge for yourself. Anyway, the *Mahatma* was hiding nothing.

'Gandhi, with his awesome capacity for the truth, blamed not only the British administration for "excesses", but also his fellow Indians for their violence. And, of course, he blamed himself: "I have made a Himalayan miscalculation . . . We Indians have burnt buildings, forcibly captured weapons and killed innocent people . . . A rapier run through my body could hardly have pained me more."'

And then our film crew was in Amritsar. The city is under great tension because of Sikh terrorists who are murdering for an independent state of Khalistan. Foreigners are not normally permitted to visit, but we were given special dispensation in order to film the vital, historic sequences that took place there. Suffice it to note that our film-crew was accompanied everywhere by some thirty odd para-military police plus their officers. And that one morning, as we were leaving our hotel, a man was shot dead just behind us.

'Meanwhile, in this ever volatile city of Amritsar in the Punjab, a placard had appeared on the Central Clock Tower: "Prepare to die and kill others" [a sentiment very similar to today's political anarchy], and elsewhere: "Kick out the European monkeys". [Today, of course, it is kick out all who are not extremist Sikhs.] and so on the 10th April, the British arrested the two main Indian political leaders in Amritsar [very mild compared to what the Indian Government is doing today] and immediately a far from peaceful

Indian demonstration, which was estimated at 40,000 strong, advanced northward, threatening the British residential area. Ironically, there were shouts of: "Gandhi Ki-Jai" – "Hail Gandhi". The British police, fearing the worst, opened gunfire and several Indians were shot.'

The first part of this section we filmed from the roof of a deserted, gun-shattered hotel which overlooks the now notorious Golden Temple. It was a spectacular vantage point, with the whole sinister panorama to be seen behind me. I noticed that our armed guard kept a wary eye on the landscape. The second portion was spoken from the railway bridge where the 40,000 advanced on the British cantonment. And all of my words in the script had been tightly questioned by Doctor Nanda. What patriotically and politically interested Indians want is that it should be believed that this 40,000 gathering was a peaceful deputation to request the release of the two political activists! Well, such Indian wishful thinking is startlingly incorrect. Not only do British official accounts refute all claims of Gandhian gentle persuasion on this occasion, but I have talked to Indian men who were, as youngsters, in Amritsar in those dangerous days: 'I can still see my father armed with a big stick'; 'The shouting and the excitement was frightening'.

Also, what I did not say in the film was that the Indian aggressive spirit was so extreme that the chief British administrator in Amritsar had a nervous break-down, which was one of the reasons that General Dyer was hurried to the beleaguered city. And British police officers confronted the mob (if I dare use such a word; but the more popular Indian expression, freedom fighters, is proving difficult for me to inscribe in this context) and ordered them to retire. Stones were thrown and the police fired.

'The massed demonstration enraged by the shootings retreated to the city centre and ran amok, looting banks and burning Amritsar's railway station. Four Europeans were trapped and were promptly killed – and a British woman missionary was also left for dead, though she recovered.

'General Dyer, a British soldier, was ordered to Amritsar to restore Imperial law; but he pointed out that he hadn't got the military man power to achieve it. However, on the 12th April, he personally paraded through Amritsar with a detachment of soldiers, and issued a proclamation that all political assemblies were prohibited until law and order were restored. On the following day, General Dyer was informed that such a meeting, a very large one – 20,000 people has been said – was being held within a walled area called the Jallianwala Bagh. General Dyer, with ninety Gurkha and Baluchi soldiers, marched towards this massed assembly. General Dyer immediately commanded his men to open fire and when he marched his soldiers away, they left behind them some 379 dead and 1,200 wounded.'

This sequence we filmed in the Jallianwala Bagh site. The place is now an Indian national shrine with monuments, photographs and a large mural painting of the awful event and some of the bullet marks on the walls are carefully preserved. For the period of our filming the whole area was cleared of people and our thirty plus armed escort kept an eye on the surrounding roof tops and windows. There were two arguments put forward by Amritsar people about the possible significance of our presence in the city; one was that the terrorists were hungry for publicity and that if they could knock one of us over, it would be of sufficient interest to go into print around the world. The other was that the terrorists wanted sympathy from foreign countries and therefore they were unlikely to have a go at us. Neither argument reassured me. I could not be convinced by the terrorists' toll of innocent non-political people that any such subtle or fine thought was going on in their heads. And certainly the full focus of advertisement was on our curious activities.

The warden of Jallianwala Bagh belongs to a famous family of Indian patriots and he lives within the area. He treated us with kindly formality and it was he who gave me my first jackfruit to eat. Did it taste like delicious custard? What a mixture of circumstances and emotions I have found myself subjected to! I, a member of General Dyer's race, being treated like an honoured brother and only about ten yards from the clearly marked spot where General Dyer – and I – barked: 'Open fire!'

But my simple, well-authenticated explanation of the cause of the terrible effect at Jallianwala Bagh made the hackles rise of even Indian friends. This culminated for me when our cameraman and my friend, Venu Gopal, said: 'I don't need you to tell me what happened!' I replied that I had been invited by his government to communicate the story and that once I had signed the contract, I had to do it. The trouble was that I was disturbing the Indian fairy story of bad Europeans and good Indians. Mahatma Gandhi could have a go at the truth; but not me. I was in a difficult position.

'The British Governor of the Punjab, Sir Michael O'Dwyer [who was not likely to have a nervous breakdown], and the British authorities generally, had feared that the haunting Indian uprising of 1857 – known to them as "The Indian Mutiny" – might be recurring. General Dyer summed up his own attitude: "For me the battlefield of Amritsar or the battlefield of Flanders is the same."'

That statement by Dyer carries a chilling message: a soldier who has just survived the massive blood-letting of the First World War has little left except to get the awful jobs that are a soldier's lot done. I remember seeing on television newsreel the Indian General in command at the Golden Temple assault; he was in, apparently, a shocked condition as he explained that he had done what he had to do. General Dyer was a much more war-weary man.

'Five days later, on the 18th April, 1919, Mahatma Gandhi cancelled his civil disobedience campaign.'

And then we were in London among the old Imperial halls and I had to become Winston Churchill, the best of the big Imperialists. Again I was faced with a world-famous image. The mentality of Churchill, I believed, I had a fair grasp of. And it is interesting to contemplate that from an assumption of a state of mind emerge, the visible and vocal mannerisms. But what clothes should I wear that also lodged in my own personal wardrobe? I had a black single-breasted suit. (Winston's trousers would have had fine, light-coloured stripes.) Dare I wear a bow tie? Well, I occasionally – very occasionally – wear a bow tie; so why not? And that was it.

'In the House of Commons, here in London, the greatest and most uncompromising of Imperialists, Winston Churchill, stood up and shifted the responsibility away from himself and his political ilk, towards the military man: "However we may dwell upon the difficulties of General Dyer . . . upon the critical situation in the Punjab, upon the danger to Europeans throughout the province . . . one tremendous fact stands out . . . I mean the slaughter of nearly four hundred persons. That is an episode without parallel in the modern history of the British Empire. We have to make it absolutely clear that this is not the British way of doing business!"'

Churchill was not in the habit of molly-coddling Indian sentiments. This was a rare piece of sensitivity on his part towards India. Did Churchill foresee what Jallianwala Bagh could do to the British Raj's standing in India? Did Churchill foresee that this one-off tragedy could unify the disparate Indian nationalist sentiments? And what about 'the difficulties of General Dyer . . . upon the critical situation in the Punjab, upon the danger to Europeans throughout the province'? What would have happened if General Dyer had allowed the political meeting at Jallianwala Bagh to continue uninterrupted, which was contrary to his military order, thoroughly posted up on the preceding day? Might it have been 1857 again? What would have happened to British Imperial law and order? Churchill gave no answer that I know of to these questions. What I do know is that General Dyer's merciless action was the sudden end of bloody insurrection in the Punjab and elsewhere in India. And I can see no end to bloody insurrection in the Punjab today. Political military reality is never a pleasant business.

'General Dyer was removed from his command and, not long afterwards, a broken man, and only a few days before his death, he turned to his wife (he also spoke it to his sister) and said: "I long to meet my God so that I may ask whether as a soldier I did right or wrong in Amritsar."

'The question occurs to me: "Who was the truly guilty man at Jallianwala Bagh – the uncompromising Imperialist, personified by Winston Churchill, or the professional soldier, General Dyer, who had been ordered to pacify an explosive Punjab?"

'But the massacre of Jallianwala Bagh sealed the political unity and strength of the Indian Congress Movement. The political moderates led by Motilal Nehru moved closer to Jawaharlal Nehru's way of thinking and in close support of Gandhi's peaceful, activist policy. Jawaharlal expressed all of their feelings: "I realise now how brutal and immoral Imperialism is and how it has eaten into the souls of the British upper classes."'

And then our film crew were in Allahabad, at the old family home of the Nehrus. And once again I cursed Doordarshan and the Ministry because of their crass inefficiency and total insensitivity; they had finally produced their farcical but holy 'sanction', as they term it, to commence the film, just as the raw hot weather of the north Indian plains exploded. Of course, there was not one word of consultation with us, either about the hazards to our health or the disappearance of so much of Indian floral colour (more valuable to a film than their imaginations could possibly grasp). Those very small but ridiculously arrogant people fumbled out those sanctions to begin filming and there we were.

The first film-shot at Allahabad was on the roof of Anand Bhawan, the Nehru home; the temperature was established as 47°C (117°F) in the shade. And we were not in the shade; we were in the direct glare of the sun. As you will see from the text, it is a lengthy passage and while I spoke it I had to move round the area between Indian cupolas. The scene took perhaps a couple of hours. I seriously considered that I might expire on that roof; many have been killed by a less intense heat:

'The most astounding visual metamorphosis movingly came from Motilal Nehru. The lover of the most expensive way of life, the man who lived in a famous mansion, Anand Bhawan meaning Abode of Happiness, with its indoor swimming pool and endless high-living, suddenly gave it all up, and virtually overnight, put aside his finely-cut London clothes – indeed he burnt four cartloads of them – and he began to wear traditional Indian styles, woven from hand-spun cotton. And very soon he gave that great house, Anand Bhawan, to the Indian nation.'

We moved ourselves to the banks of the famed Jumna River, not far from Allahabad: 'The ordinary, hard-pressed people of India – the undiscovered millions – have a capacity for recognising human goodness, and already they were beginning to look towards young Jawaharlal. Several hundred desperate peasants asked him to consider their exploited plight. Here on the banks of the Jumna River, the young man from Harrow and Cambridge faced them and listened to them intently for the first time in his life: "Looking at these people and their misery and overflowing gratitude, I was filled with shame; shame at my own comfortable life and our petty politics of the city. A new picture of India seemed to rise before me, and filled me with a new responsibility that frightened me." Jawaharlal Nehru, the man who was to lead India to independence, had finally found his true self.'

And then we moved to more remote rural country where a significant episode occurred on Nehru's revolutionary journey: 'As Jawaharlal Nehru identified himself more and more deeply with the most underprivileged of India, so his significance grew. During January 1921, there was a confrontation between peasants and police in this Rae Bareli district and he appeared on the scene while the shooting was in progress. A deputy commissioner [me, of course] ordered:

"Pandit Nehru, your presence in this district is not desired."

'Nehru [also me, of course!]: "And what of these poor down-trodden men and women? What of them? Their blood now lies on the banks of the river. Yet not a word of sympathy comes from the British Governor. He sits in his palace, well looked after. The British peace must be preserved even though the peace it gives is the peace of the grave."

'His father, Motilal, with a mixture of pride and unease, remarked: "If you go to jail, I have to follow?"'

Strangely and sickeningly, all around where we were filming the above sequence, the ground was littered with human remains: skulls, bones and a few fairly complete skeletons. This sight was a big shock to us few Europeans. Who had these humans been? What were their remains doing there? Our Indian colleagues were far less disturbed: 'Oh, there is a cremation area just up that hill [above a river where we were filming].'

'But,' said I, 'there is no sign of burning, of charring.'

'Well,' said Venu Gopal, 'there are many people so poor that no one can find the money to buy the wood to cremate them.'

Someone, unobserved, took a photograph of Venu, kneeling by the side of one of these skeletons and peering down at it. Venu has deep hidden passions, though they occasionally – well, quite occasionally – pop up in ardent temperaments. None of us reported the human remains to the police; I was made to feel that if I had insisted upon it, we would have looked foolish. Anyway for one reason and a hundred others, I no longer felt that I was in command of the film. I simply fought to concentrate on my own story-telling responsibilities.

We travelled to Bombay on the west coast of India to film at the famous Gate of India: 'The British Government then tried to cheer things up a bit by sending the Prince of Wales (later and briefly, King Edward VIII) on a royal tour of

India. Promptly, Gandhi called a boycott of the visit and His Royal Highness motored through fairly silent streets, apart from the very distant sound of gunfire. Jawaharlal and his father Motilal worked hard to make the Prince's visit a fiasco and on the 4th December, 1921, they were both arrested at their house, in Allahabad.'

The story had now reached a date in history where such events as the Prince of Wales's visit had been filmed for the cinema newsreels. And we began to acquire such material to edit into our film. And then we were all in the Old Courthouse at Allahabad: 'Before being sentenced to six months each, Jawaharlal stated: "I go to jail with the greatest pleasure and with the fullest conviction that in doing so lies the achievement of our goal."

'His Dad said: "It is now my high privilege to serve the Motherland of India by going to jail with my only son."' [As Motilal I was now wearing a dark-grey cotton kurta instead of a well-cut European suit.]

'Strangely, in Motilal's arms, in the courtroom, he was cuddling his four-year-old grand-daughter, Indira, later to become Indira Gandhi, Prime Minister of India.'

We began to film in Indian prisons and for me it was an interesting but traumatic experience. I had a strong feeling that the hard-pressed prisoners were no different from me except that they had been less fortunate in their journeys from the womb en route to the grave; certainly my sympathy reached out to them. We found Indian jails varied a great deal; the one we entered now appeared to be the hardest of all that we saw:

'In this Lucknow Jail, Jawaharlal Nehru continued to be a servant of the emancipation cause. He conducted reading classes for illiterate fellow political prisoners, he carried out Gandhi's instructions to spin Indian cotton each day, and he swept, worked and washed his beloved father's clothes.

'Motilal stated, "I wish there were many fathers to boast of such sons."

'But the conditioned dichotomy between England and

India continued to function in Jawaharlal's mind and was expressed by his introspective honesty: "In spite of everything I am a great admirer of the English, and in many things I feel even now that an Englishman can understand me better than the average Indian."

'And then a tragedy occurred which brutally destroyed the Mahatma's edict for non-violence: a crowd of Indian demonstrators attacked a police station at a place called Chauri Chaura and burnt to death twenty-two policemen. And again Gandhi immediately called off his civil disobedience action. Jawaharlal, still in prison, was hurt and shocked: "Are a mob of excited peasants going to be allowed to put an end to our national struggle for freedom?"'

Yes, Lucknow Jail was a hard place. I don't mean that the jailers were rougher than they need have been; I cannot judge that. The prison felt to me as if it was short of reasonable facilities. It felt as if it was being run down from more formidable times and that the present inmates – both prisoners and jailers – were being somewhat neglected. I wandered off on my own, close under the curving inside of the high wall. I came to a large, stone-walled enclosure and peeped through the locked wooden gate. There was the execution scaffold; indeed, as far as I could tell, there was not one scaffold, but four – side by side in the open air. It is not simply morbid to empathise with the human horror that had been enacted there. I do not want to ignore and deceive myself about reality if I can help it. There, but for the mystery of fortune's selection, went I.

As a matter of fact the chief jailers whom I met at Lucknow were more intelligent, perceptive and indeed sensitive than I would expect to meet on an average day. I was invited by the head jailer into his office and he talked, in answer to my probings, about the sometime non-alignment between law and justice with kindly compassion. But the heat and dust added to everyone's discomfort; particularly the discomfort of the poor prisoners.

And as I was leaving Lucknow Jail for the last time, I

experienced a memorable meeting. The Assistant Jailer asked me if I would take some refreshment in his home. 'Oh,' I said, 'I am very tired and I should get back to my hotel.' But always feeling I would be unwise to reject a well-meant invitation in this life, I asked: 'Is your house close by?'

'It is here,' said my new friend. 'Just outside the prison gates.' As I entered his small home he told me that he was a poet. His wife greeted me with spontaneous warmth. In the small living room I could not fail to see a large glass-fronted cabinet full of magnificent dolls representing Indian deities. And then I was introduced to two of the daughters of the house (I think that there was a third who was absent). The elder of the two was beautiful and charmingly grave. The younger one I will never forget for as long as I have a memory. She seemed to me to be about sixteen years old and she was also beautiful, but the unforgettable quality was something else: she light-heartedly gazed at the strange European visitor with total loving innocence. I have never experienced such apparent unadulterated goodness. It shone or rather danced around her. 'The dolls are beautiful,' I commented.

'Choose which one you would like to keep,' said the young woman.

'No, no,' said I, 'I enjoy seeing them, but I wouldn't dream of taking one!'

'Yes,' she persisted, 'take the one you like best!'

'Certainly not!' I reiterated. 'Where did they come from?'

'We made them,' said the older sister. 'And you must accept one of them; the one you like best.'

The dolls were about a foot and a half tall and were exquisitely made.

'Then I will choose one for you!' said the younger sister and, without hesitation, presented me with a beautiful female figure, holding a stringed musical instrument. I asked her to write down the name of the goddess for me. She wrote 'Misra Bai' in English and in Indian characters. After two years in India and having acquired many Indian treasures, it is that goddess of Music that I personally and carefully carried on to the aircraft with me. The aircraft that was bound for Britain. I know that I was briefly in the company of a human being who somehow was more elevated than most of us. I asked her parents if they were aware that their daughters were 'different'; they only smiled in reply. The Assistant Jailer, the father, showed me some of his carefully inscribed poems; I could not read them because they were in a script which I did not understand.

'To Jawaharlal's question in Lucknow Jail, Gandhi replied: "I know that this drastic reversal [cancelling 'civil disobedience' after the murders at Chauri Chaura] of our aggressive programme may be politically unsound, but there is no doubt that it is religiously sound. I have listened to the still small voice."'

We filmed this piece of classic Gandhiism at the ashram of Sevagram where he often lived. Chiara and I were invited to live in the ashram, which still operates as it did during the Mahatma's time. For Chiara and me it was a blessed, peaceful interlude, though we continued to work hard there; from early morning till late at night. The spiritual efficacy of the place certainly embraced us. Several of the people who lived and worked at the ashram had been there during Gandhi's time, including his daughter-in-law. I was very anxious to talk to these people so that I might draw a little closer, in understanding, to the genius. 'Where did you first meet him?' I asked one disciple, who was now about my age.

'Here at Sevagram.'

'What was the circumstance of your first meeting?'

'Oh, he asked me what work I did and I told him that I taught the young children and then he looked straight at me and said: "In that case, why don't you do all of your buttons up?" I felt dreadful that he had seen this fault in me.'

I noticed that all of my new friend's buttons were done up on that morning in 1987. I also felt enormously satisfied with myself that one of the small voices had whispered to me, before I recorded my image of Gandhi for the first time in the film, to fasten all of *my* buttons. Gandhi is one of those powerful spirits who can rebuke a potential error from beyond this life.

Early each evening we stopped filming for about one hour while the members of the ashram held their religious service. It was held in a large area in the centre of the ashram. Mats would be laid out on the ground in long straight lines and finally one single place was prepared in front of all the others and a wooden panel was put there as a back-rest. This was directly under a great tree which the Mahatma had planted. As we assembled (Chiara and I chose to join in the ceremony) I always saw Gandhi take his place under the tree; I found it impossible to see merely an unoccupied place.

The service would begin without formality. One or two musicians – there was a simple, stringed instrument – would begin to play and the congregation would sing in the relatively cool evening air. I could recognise a Hindu prayer and then a Muslim prayer and then, spoken with strong Indian accents but in the English language: 'Our Father which art in Heaven, Hallowed be Thy name. . . .' For me it was deeply meaningful and I always had to mop the tears and to suppress the snuffles.

At Sevagram I was introduced to a compatriot – not Welsh but certainly British – Marjorie Sykes. Ms Sykes is not the sort of woman who will object to my describing her as elderly. She was very slim and dynamic in every fibre of her body. I was told that she had been in India for many, many years and that she had just arrived in Sevagram to interview some of the long-established disciples for 'a work' which she had been asked to undertake. 'Ms Sykes,' I said, 'I would so like to have a talk with you.'

'Well, Mr Griffith, I am sure that that can be arranged before I leave. For the moment I have so much to do. But I will be in touch with you before I depart.'

'Thank you, Ms Sykes.'

And in due course (several days later): 'Well, Mr Griffith, I'm now free to have that talk; are you?'

I questioned Ms Sykes about her near lifetime in India. 'Did you sympathise with India's struggle for independence?'

'Certainly; but my forte is not politics; I am a teacher. I stuck to my teaching.'

'Do you manage to get back to England?'

'Oh yes; every two years or so. To work of course.'

'A-ha,' said I as I angled towards the very sensitive question: 'Do you like England?'

'Oh, most certainly, Mr Griffith! England is so beautiful, so beautiful; so green. In the spring; the early summer. . . .'

And then I uttered the all-important (to me) question. And I asked it with all of the gentleness that is in me: 'Ms Sykes, do you get homesick?'

'Well, Mr Griffith,' and she gazed round her at the sun-baked earth, 'I must confess, that after I have been in England for, say, two months, I do get very homesick for – India.'

'Jawaharlal tried to swallow his bitter disappointment [at what the Still Small Voice had whispered to the Mahatma] as he always did towards Gandhi: "He is delightfully vague, but we all feel that he is a great man and a glorious leader." It was the first intimation that these two towering Indian patriots would diverge in method: Gandhi, the devout man of God; and Nehru, the honest agnostic.

'The British Government decided that this was the time to tighten its discipline over India and, having warily restrained themselves for so long, they suddenly arrested Gandhi. Jawaharlal, who had been released from jail, hastened to the great man's trial. [And for this I was hurrying up the marble steps of the courthouse and into the court itself. Here the Indian officials had kindly and liberally unearthed the original huge royal coat of arms and had replaced it for us on the courtroom wall, behind the judge's dais.] Gandhi stated from the dock: "I believe that I have rendered a service to India and England by showing, in non-co-operation, the way out of the unnatural state in which both India and England are living. In my opinion non-co-operation with evil is as much a duty as co-operation with good."

'Mr Justice Broomfield, who was judging, replied: "It is impossible to ignore the fact that you are in a different category from any person I have ever tried – I should like to say that if the course of events in India should make it possible for the British Government to release you, no one will be better pleased than I."'

On either side of me (as Mr Justice Broomfield) were two splendidly-dressed court functionaries wielding hand-held punkahs to persuade the heavy, hot air to move. This is again a judgement point in our style of filming. Since this entertaining custom is still in operation, we, very happily, used the colourful dressing. Such a scene hovers, humorously and properly, between our hard factual method and conventional theatricality.

'The Mahatma was given six years and he confidently marched off to this Yerawade Prison, carrying five books – which included Jesus Christ's "Sermon on the Mount".'

While filming at Yerawade Prison we stayed at Poona or, as the Indians now call it, 'Pune'. And having some hours of spare time I set off on my usual city-exploring expedition. First the old British Raj Anglican Church. 'Poona' to Britons of my generation was synonymous with a British-Indian crusty colonel; why this joke arose I don't know; probably via the music halls. Anyway, Poona's Anglican Church is no joke; it is now a stern, near deserted, grey stone monument. More than any other such British building that I have visited in India, I found it cold and violated. Not even the mysterious remnants of recent life that were said to have been found on the *Marie Celeste*. I paid my tiptoed respect and walked out into the foreign glare feeling like the last deserter. And then, in the far distance, I saw another tall spire and I headed towards that. I hoped to myself that this second obvious church would be warmer in its hauntings.

I followed the tall spire reaching above the house-tops and then, drawing near, I learnt that it was not a Christian church but a Jewish synagogue. I had never seen a synagogue remotely like this one; it seemed to me to emulate clearly the Anglican Christian style. Sitting on a chair close to the main entrance was a tall, lean, ascetic man wearing a Jewish skullcap. He quietly wished me well and I asked if I might enter the synagogue: 'Of course, you may.'

It was a fine interior and immaculately clean. I returned to the sitting man and he told me that once Poona had possessed a large Jewish community but now it was small. He was waiting to conduct the evening prayer. A husband and wife arrived and so did another lady, on her own. It was a happy Jewish occasion. That unique Jewish humour pervaded our talk; I believe that this quality has evolved indomitably in the torment of the past two thousand years. The Jews scattered across the face of this earth could either give up and die or tell a funny story. They are not going to give up!

I was invited to join the ceremony and, donning a Jewish 'calvaria' cap, the five of us entered the synagogue and the ancient ritual began. I remember the myrtle leaves. I felt most privileged to be part of that small gathering.

The lady who was on her own, Diana Elijah, a widow, asked me if I would like to take coffee with her in her home. She and her late husband had been involved in much progressive social work in India. She missed him deeply and yet her strong good humour lifted me up. She told me an extraordinary fact; in Poona there were two separate Jewish groups: the White Jews (in whose synagogue we had prayed) and the Black Jews, to which Mrs Elijah belonged. And she told me that when she was a young woman, she, as a Black Jew, would not have been allowed into the White Synagogue, 'But now there are so few of us left, I am, as you saw, made welcome.'

It was confusing for me; apparently the White Jews claimed a European connection and the Black Jews an ancient

Indian connection. So even within an ever threatened Jewish community they had separated along ethnic, caste lines. Yet Mrs Elijah had a very fair complexion and I said to her: 'You could be taken for a Russian.'

'Would you like to visit our Black Synagogue?' And so we left her house at 1 Synagogue Street, Poona, and travelled to the second place of worship. The atmosphere there was very different; there were many more people, including children, and it was not unlike an informal party. There was a strong, even noisy, family atmosphere. But again the friendship was warm and again I was deeply moved. I have often wondered if I have Jewish blood intermingled with the Welsh. There was the ritual with the myrtle leaves there as well. My valuable new friend, Mrs Elijah, dreamt about returning to the antique homeland, Israel. In my own way I pray for her.

The next day I took Chiara to meet the husband and wife from the White Synagogue, Mr and Mrs Levi Naji, at 28 Mahatma Gandhi Road, Poona. The Jewish Diaspora is the most overwhelming human drama in the world for me.

'Jawaharlal was rejuvenated as he grasped Gandhi's banner of freedom: "We have shaken off the sloth of centuries. Today India is respected where yesterday we were despised as slaves." And again he was arrested: "Jail has indeed become for us a holy place of pilgrimage . . . To serve India in the battle of freedom is honour enough. To serve her under a leader like Mahatma Gandhi is doubly fortunate."

'The British gave him twenty-one months and the conditions inside Lucknow Jail were made harder. The Viceroy stated: "We have no intention of converting their imprisonment into a comfortable lodging."'

This was the first of several Viceroys that I 'became'; it was filmed in the appropriate Viceregal setting.

'In prison, Nehru heard an Indian patriot being whipped and each time the lash hit his body he shouted: "Mahatma Gandhi, Ki-Jai!" – "Hail Gandhi!"

'And Jawaharlal said of himself: "Prison is making a man of me."

'But when he eventually came out of jail he found the freedom movement exhausted and, turning to Gandhi, he found the Mahatma's very personal philosophy unhelpful. Gandhi said: "Freedom is an impossibility until we have boycotted British cloth." And the Mahatma perceptively said of his young friend: "Jawaharlal is one of the loneliest young men of my acquaintance."

'For the first time in their lives together, Jawaharlal Nehru found the time to consider closely his wife, Kamala, and his daughter, Indira: "My wife wants to play her own part in the national struggle and not to be merely a shadow of me. I have been far too busy to see beneath the surface."

'But now Kamala had contracted tuberculosis and Jawaharlal decided to take her to a sanatorium in Switzerland and with them went their schoolgirl daughter, Indira.'

Behind me were the high snowy mountains. Relevant contrasts are dramatically invaluable in our films.

'As Kamala's health improved, Jawaharlal began to explore Europe. He went to Russia and peered at the results of their awesome revolution: "I found the vast political and cultural changes going on in Europe and America a fascinating study . . . Soviet Russia, despite certain unpleasant aspects, seems to hold forth a message of hope to the world." The dedicated, unorthodox internationalist was clearly forming. And Kamala having apparently recovered, Jawaharlal hastened back to India, carrying with him his broader vision of the world.'

Over the above words about the growing Soviet Union we injected relevant archive film of that period. All these different elements must be blended into a creative whole. A criticism of one of my films (I think it was *Clive of India*) that pleased me very much was: 'The film is seamless'; that, of course, was a compliment to our entire film unit.

'Now there was no holding Jawaharlal back and the British promptly provided him with a notable "Aunt Sally". The

British Tory Government sent Sir John Simon and six other Britishers to India to investigate possible constitutional advances for the sub-continent; but no Indians were included in the Commission. Jawaharlal called them: "The seven uninvited gentlemen from England."

'Dominion status for India was discreetly whispered. Gandhi was to say: "We need not worry if freedom is spelt dominion status or independence."

'Jawaharlal was outraged at the suggested compromise on total independence: "It passes my comprehension how a national organisation can have as its goal dominion status!"

'But the Mahatma knew how to control his idealistic protégé when necessary: "The differences between you and me appear to be so vast that there seems to be no meeting ground between us. I cannot conceal from you my grief that I should lose a comrade so valiant, so faithful and so honest. . . ."

'Jawaharlal quickly climbed down: "No one has moved me and inspired me more than you. And am I not your child in politics – though perhaps a truant and errant child?"

'Gandhi: "Well, it is now your duty to devote your whole energy to national unity and to boycott the Simon Commission."

'Here in this city of Lucknow, Nehru warned: "We cannot rest, for rest is a betrayal of the millions who never eat." '

And it was at this point that Doordarshan in Delhi dealt us another formidable blow. I should emphasise here that throughout our caravanning around India we met with continuous organisational problems. Though Doordarshan had been given a very unusual amount of time to arrange filming at the widely spread locations, we were almost invariably met with – from local officials – 'We have been given no instructions about this matter.' And, of course, Indian officialdom will not move one inch without permits in triplicate. The officials will take no risks whatsoever for fear of that ever-present vindictiveness from their colleagues.

However, somehow, in spite of Doordarshan's unbelievable ineptness, we usually muddled through. But now this Lucknow episode was to be very different and there was nothing that we film people could do to save the situation.

As I have already written, our film crew had expanded from my original dictum for a maximum of nine persons (the maximum I have always used) to thirty-five (most of them grossly underworked and underpaid), and nearly two weeks before our arrival in Lucknow we noted that our supply of cans of compressed air was running low. After every single film-take in India we blew compressed air into the lens of the camera to remove any very prevalent dust, hairs and so on. And so we informed the Deputy Director-General of Doordarshan, Shri M. P. Lele, who was also our Doordarshan top colleague, of our approaching need. Nothing happened. We telephoned again; this telephoning had now become Alan Birkinshaw's additional burden. Nothing. Phone, telegraph; nothing. Eventually, Alan reported to me that Shri Lele had laughed good humouredly on the telephone and had told him: 'But I haven't got sanction for compressed air.' Whether this was meant as an Indian joke I don't know.

Then, at the end of those two weeks, while filming in front of Lucknow's railway station, the last of the compressed air was expended. We all stood there in the blazing heat with our own thoughts about the Indian system. We retreated to our hotels. The next morning – good news, in the nick of time! – a large carton arrived! It was not compressed air but some cans of liquid for polishing lenses. If we had squirted that stuff into the lens the whole camera would have had to be returned to God knows where for a major overhaul. Back in Delhi, apparently, they could not even discover what the compressed air was, let alone what it was meant for or where to get it from. And so the whole thirty-five of us had no alternative but to wend our way back to Delhi, and it was some weeks before we returned to Lucknow; at considerable cost to the Indian people.

I feel that I have been a degree unjust to Shri Lele by naming him. My opinion is that no one at Doordarshan could have improved on his action. The system is sick from top to bottom. Oh! – the cans of compressed air? Alan telephoned London and a crate of them was expressed to us in Delhi. So we eventually journeyed back to Lucknow and picked our story up:

'And it was here [in Lucknow] that Jawaharlal personally marched towards the stick-wielding British repression: "The bodily pain I felt was quite forgotten in a feeling of exhilaration that I was physically strong enough to bear the blows!" And the following day, as Sir John Simon and his British Commission arrived at this Lucknow railway station, Nehru faced, totally unarmed, charging, mounted British police: "I thought how easy it would be to pull down a police officer from his horse. But I did not raise a hand, except to protect my face. Besides, I knew well enough that any aggression on our part would result in the shooting down of large numbers of our men!"

'Wherever Sir John Simon went, thousands of Indians chanted: "Simon go back!"

'The Commission, having heard the endlessly repeated words day after day, arrived at this Western Hotel in New Delhi. In the middle of the night, Sir John had had enough: "They might give us some peace at night!"

'Secretary: "Those are not demonstrators, sir. They are jackals, sir!" New Delhi, the famed British concoction, had not long been transformed from wild bushland.

'The Indian National Congress was about to vote for a new President. Apart from the Mahatma and Nehru, there was a wide range of outstanding leaders available: Sardar Patel, Rajendra Prasad, Rajagopalachari, Sarojini Naidu and Maulana Azad. [I originally did not mention the last four characters, but Shri Prasad, through Doctor Nanda, insisted that I did. All five of these Indians were very important in the struggle for independence, but they are virtually unknown to the world's television public and unknown names that have no other part in a television story are a cue for the dreaded mass switch-off. Of course, from an Indian point of view those names are essential; every thinking Indian knows exactly who they are and has a clear view of their historical significance. And so the names will be heard in the Indian version of the film but not in the international one. Those five names are an interesting example of the critical condition of telling a responsible programme on television and managing to hold the attention of as many viewers as possible. Is an interest in human nature as against an interest in, say, the micro chip becoming lesser or greater? For the sake of our descendants it had better be greater.] There were three nominations: Gandhi, Sardar Patel, the iron man who supported Gandhi uncompromisingly, and Jawaharlal Nehru – Gandhi's "truant and errant child". Gandhi declined the leadership, bypassed Patel, and turned to the agnostic internationalist: "Jawaharlal, do you feel strong enough to bear the weight?"

'Jawaharlal [obviously, such names are not spoken in the film; they are superfluous because you cut to Nehru and the viewer knows who he is]: "If it is thrust upon me, I hope I shall not wince." He was now forty years old.

'And the Mahatma, of course, had the influence to make Jawaharlal President of the Indian Congress. Gandhi said: "For bravery he is not to be surpassed. Who can excel him in the love of India? He is pure as crystal . . . he is truthful beyond suspicion . . . The nation is safe in his hands."

'Jawaharlal's very strong father, Motilal, who had suffered endless disagreements with his son, simply stated: "The one thing I am proudest of is that I am Jawaharlal's father."

'And Gandhi whispered to the new President a near Christian text: "It never was to be a crown of roses. Let it be all thorns now."

'The Viceroy of India, Lord Irwin, carefully murmured: "I desire that the utterances of Jawaharlal Nehru should be watched carefully."

'Lord Irwin was right – from the British point of view. Jawaharlal Nehru stood up at the Lahore Indian Congress: "I am a socialist and a republican and I am no believer in kings or in the order which produces the modern kings of industry, who have even greater power over the lives and fortunes of men and women than even the kings of old. . . .

"The Indian Congress has not the training for organised violence, and violence is a confession of despair. But if only methods of violence will rid us of slavery then I have no doubt that I will adopt them. Violence is bad, but slavery is far worse. Independence for us means complete freedom from British Imperialism."'

And then we were on the river bank and I can remember that we were there later than we had planned and the light was going with the setting sun; time was precious. And in front of startled Indians and beneath the old Congress flag, I yelled: 'The flag of independence was unfurled here on the bank of this Ravi River and thousands roared: *"Inquilab Zindabad"* or "Long live the revolution."'

I am always uneasy about such circumstances; I had not had the time to weigh up in minute detail the sequence in the overall orchestration of the film. Its context. Clearly, this revolutionary piece with the flag was a climax, but where exactly should it be pitched? And then there were the onlookers. We didn't have a big organisation (in spite of the thirty-five bodies, who generally attended only to their often small responsibility) to control outsiders. And as usual Doordarshan had failed to co-ordinate with the local police. And so I had to try and dominate or influence the strangers who gawped. In I dashed and under the high-flying flag: '*Inquilab Zindabad!* Has the light gone, Venu?'

'Not quite!'

'Inquilab Zindabad!' It looks acceptable on the screen though it was a shade hit or miss. I went round the onlookers *Namaskaring* and saying in English, 'Thank you for being so good.'

Lord Irwin, the Viceroy, was undoubtedly a decent Christian gentleman who had been thrust into a rough period. I liked being Lord Irwin and he was very useful in our saga, which after all was not over-endowed with laughs, as touching light relief. Indeed, he and Gandhi were two great comedians; with different styles, of course.

'Lord Irwin, His Majesty's Viceroy in India, was definitely unnerved and he declared: "The Indian Congress Working Committee is illegal." But he also tried to reassure the rebelling Indians: "Now, the natural issue of India's constitutional progress . . . is the attainment of dominion status." And then, adding to his military secretary [while mopping the sweat from his face with a white handkerchief], "We are in India, my dear chap, to keep our tempers." '

This latter statement by Lord Irwin became obsessively important to me. I tried so hard to remember it as good advice. Because in Delhi or anywhere near the sly, stupid face of Indian bureaucracy, I lost my temper continuously. I had lost my temper more often in India than during my entire life before. I could not cope with the flat-faced destructiveness. Poor Irwin! And Field Marshal Lord Roberts of Kandahar and his autobiography, *Forty-one Years in India*, though the military were largely self-contained; they had to set their own practical rules and they had to insist that those rules were kept. But I began to wonder about that old British Raj and I began to be in awe of their unbelievable achievement. A relative handful holding together the vast disparate sub-continent in relative peace and with a minimum of corruption.

'But Winston Churchill wasn't unnerved. He addressed Lord Irwin: "Dominion status can certainly not be attained while India is prey to fierce racial and religious dissensions. It cannot be attained while the political classes of India represent only an insignificant fraction of the millions for whose welfare we British are responsible."

'Lord Irwin replied: "Please don't think, Winston, that I am ever likely to forget the point of view that you are putting, or indeed that I differ from it . . . Half the problems in India are psychological and a case of hurt feelings." '

This scene we filmed in the celebrated Travellers' Club in Pall Mall, London, on a Sunday. The management were extremely helpful. I remember that day with great pleasure; they lit a fire and fed us. Our Nehru journey wasn't all hardship. Of course, Lord Irwin's words are sensitively perceptive; over many hundreds of years India had been subjected to multiple conquests, culminating with the British Raj – a bruised psyche and the attendant reaction were inevitable. Not that Winston was sympathetic to such psychological niceties.

And then the film switches back to Anand Bhawan, the old Nehru home in Allahabad. The house is a huge rambling place; at one time luxurious but now, after the revolutionary transformation, rather sparsely furnished: 'Jawaharlal Nehru became the beloved of India and he was referred to as "the Jewel of India", but his introspective honesty could not accept the adulation easily: "My reputation as a hero is entirely a bogus one."

'And his family didn't encourage the extravagance; at breakfast his young daughter, Indira, would say: "O Jewel of India, pass me the butter."'

Of course, we filmed that scene, in the dining room of Anand Bhawan around the very table. A pursuit of ghosts.

'However, Jawaharlal had called the millions of India to heroic action and therefore he was once again a little disconcerted when the Mahatma addressed an apparently mild letter to the poor Viceroy, Lord Irwin: "Dear Friend, My ambition is no less than to convert the British people, through non-violence, and thus make them see the wrong they have done to India . . . On the eleventh day of this month I shall proceed to disregard the salt laws."

'The British Government monopolised the production of salt and they had placed a tax on this essential need of every poverty-stricken Indian. Gandhi planned to walk some 240 miles to the seaside village of Dandi and there illegally collect a few pieces of non-Government salt.

'Thousands of Indians walked with the Mahatma and details of the carefully planned journey echoed and re-echoed around the world.'

This Dandi Salt March episode we filmed at the sea's edge. What an adventure! What a privilege to speak this story while paddling up to my knees in the sea at historic Dandi. I believe that I performed the scene with a degree of proper abandon. I like myself at Dandi.

'Jawaharlal and his indomitable old father, Motilal, joined the Mahatma briefly and then hurried away to spread the simple idea, particularly to India's youth: "The pilgrim marches onward. Will you be mere onlookers in this glorious struggle and simply watch your best and bravest face the might of the great British Empire, which has crushed your country? Who lives if India dies? Who dies if India lives?"

'The Indian nation, with the Mahatma, broke the British salt law. Jawaharlal said: "It seemed as though a spring had been suddenly released." And something over 60,000 Indians were jailed.

'Winston Churchill didn't underrate the threat of apparently innocent salt or anything else: "Gandhiism and all it stands for will, sooner or later, have to be grappled and finally crushed. It is no use trying to satisfy a tiger by feeding him with cat's meat."

'The Viceroy, Lord Irwin, was in a tizz and he had the temerity to advise the terrible bulldog: "Please, Winston, update your views on India by talking to some members of the Indian Congress."

'Churchill: "I am quite satisfied with my views on India, and I don't want them disturbed by any bloody Indians."'

I found it significant to contrast the above remark with Churchill's words used to appease publicly political Indians by sacrificing General Dyer over Jallianwala Bagh.

'And so the British began to whack – and very hard. Jawaharlal and his Dad were arrested for breaking the salt laws and put into this Naini Central Jail – and Motilal was not displeased: "Now we are together again!" And on the 5th May, 1930, Gandhi was arrested near Dandi – while still making handfuls of salt, presumably.

'Jawaharlal's frail, ailing wife went out into the streets and actively demonstrated against the British and was arrested: "I am happy beyond measure and proud to follow in the footsteps of my husband."

'And what of young Indira? The truth is that Jawaharlal was still putting his country, India, before all else. But he loved his daughter deeply: "Meanwhile you sit in Anand Bhawan and Mummy sits in Malacca Jail and I here in Naini Prison – and we miss each other sometimes rather badly, do we not? But think of the day when we shall all three meet again; the thought of that will lighten and cheer up my heart."'

Naini Central Prison is the most memorable of Nehru's places of incarceration. His cell, or rather his small complex of cells, is within a high, round wall inside the greater prison. It is today a place of veneration to the memory of Nehru. On his prison bed and on his little table are symbolic lines and patterns of flowers, picked and arranged freshly each day, and a light burns. Because of the circular perimeter of the high wall, I was reminded of Oscar Wilde's: 'Upon that little tent of blue/Which prisoners call the sky.' In the garden area, outside Nehru's cell, is still a bed which is chained to a tree, to prevent it being used upended in any escape bid.

Helping us with our film work within the Nehru area were several life prisoners. Again I felt this particular affinity with them. One of the qualities I have, that make me suitable for the work I do, is an abnormal capacity for empathy and therefore I could not avoid understanding and sharing, to some extent, the fate that had led these prisoners to do what they had done – murder – and then the awful punishment of lengthy imprisonment. I find it disturbing that I am free and they are not.

The life prisoners wore bright yellow scarves and, of course, like all Indians, they wore them with amazing style. Give a poor Indian an old towel and he will drape it or wind it round his head as if he were a prince. And even within these walls of despair, the yellow scarves were used with a natural sartorial elegance that would shame the ridiculous couturiers of Paris.

Two of these life prisoners affected me deeply. Both had killed during land disputes. The farmers of India live very personally and closely to the earth that they own and disputes over ownership or encroachment can become life and death matters. One of these men was near the expiry of his sentence, I think. Because of language and general cultural difficulties, the truth is often and mysteriously hard to pin down. Anyway, he was the most elegant man that I have ever seen in my life, even in his prison clothes. He carried a long stick, which he sometimes leaned on like a classic dancer. He conveyed a feeling of unaccountable repose, and yet I knew that he was aware of every moment. It was in no way uncomfortable, but his eyes very rarely left me, whether I was studying the script or simply surviving the hard heat. Was his concentrated and quiet attention stimulated because I was portraying Nehru or because he knew that I suffered compassion for his comrades and him? I believe it was the latter.

The other man was again very intelligent, though more orthodox in his general behaviour. He had committed murder when he was sixteen years old, but because he was so advanced academically he had been allowed to continue his studies. He achieved his Master of Arts degree and became a gold medallist from Benaras Hindu University, and only then did he begin his sentence. He has a wife who is also a Master of Arts and a Doctor of Philosophy. I asked him for the details of his predicament and they are in front of me now. I said to him: 'It is possible that I might meet the Prime Minister again before I leave India; if I do I will give him these facts and I will tell him that I met you in his grandfather's cell. I won't forget.'

My prisoner friend did not say thank you as Indians often ignore such formalities. He smiled and said: 'No, don't forget. It is my life.'

I haven't seen the Prime Minister yet but if it is the only act that I do before I finally sever all contact with India it will be to attend to this matter.

While saying goodbye to one prisoner I performed what

was probably an illegal act. But no names, no pack drill. I left, in the palm of his hand, a hundred rupee bank note. He disappeared and returned with one of the yellow scarves. It is now at my right-hand side, just above my head. As our film cavalcade finally left Naini Central Jail my immaculate prisoner friend was leaning on his long stick and he raised a hand in farewell.

'The British prayed that the trouble would end, but it didn't, and the two Nehrus were in and out of prison like a game of musical chairs. The strain on Motilal, the virile sometime high-liver, became unbearable. Gandhi strove to give Motilal strength: "We shall surely win freedom if you survive this crisis."

'Motilal: "I am going soon, Mahatmaji, and I shall not be here to see freedom. But I know that you have won it." Shortly afterwards he died in his sleep with Jawaharlal sitting by the bedside.

'They wrapped Motilal's body in the tri-coloured Indian Congress flag. Jawaharlal remembered: "As evening fell on the banks of the River Ganges, the great flames leapt up and consumed that body which had meant so much to us. Gandhi said a few words to the multitude, the stars were out shining brightly when we returned lonely and desolate."

'The Mahatma also said: "Motilal's love for India was derived from his love for his son – Jawaharlal."'

For this scene we lit a cremation pyre on the banks of the great river and we filmed it at dusk. Sometimes our unpretentious reconstructions reflected clearly the old memory. It was for us, also, a melancholy evening.

'And then, on the 17th February, 1931, the British agreed to a momentous shift in their attitude to India. Lord Irwin invited Mahatma Gandhi to "forget the past and look to the future," here in the Viceroy's palace in Delhi.

'The Mahatma accepted. Winston Churchill recognised the thin end of the wedge and exploded: 'It is alarming and also nauseating to see Mr Gandhi, a seditious Middle Temple lawyer, now posing as a fakir . . . striding half-naked up the steps of the Viceregal Palace . . ."

'On the other hand, Lord Irwin was at his Christian best: "Mr Gandhi, we must drink each other's health. In tea!"

'Gandhi: "But I shall drink the toast in water – and a pinch of illegal salt."'

It has been reported that the Mahatma, before saying 'illegal salt', fished in his dhoti and pulled out an old envelope which contained the illegal mineral.

'And as the Indian was leaving, the Britisher said: "Good-night, Mr Gandhi, and my prayers go with you."

'Gandhi: "*Namaskar*."

'Aide: "Excuse me, Your Excellency – Mr Gandhi's shawl!"

'Irwin: "Oh! Mr Gandhi, here's your shawl. You haven't so much on, you know, that you can afford to leave this behind!"

'And the Mahatma began his four-mile walk home, through the night, to report to Nehru and the other Congress leaders."'

Yes, I represented Lord Irwin, Mahatma Gandhi and the Aide, in the little kerfuffle at the top of the great flight of steps belonging to the Viceregal Palace, which is today the President's House. And it was a curious actor's experience as I walked down them and across the vast courtyard; very simply representing Mahatma Gandhi.

'At the end of these meetings between Gandhi and Irwin a compromise was agreed; civil disobedience was called off, political prisoners were released and the making of salt was allowed on the coast. And the Mahatma agreed to attend an Imperial Round Table Conference in London to discuss India's constitutional advances. It was called the Irwin-Gandhi Pact. The representatives of the two nations had negotiated together, face to face, for the first time.

'Again Jawaharlal was decidedly unhappy with Gandhi's compromise: "What frightens me is your way of springing surprises on us . . . There is something unknown about you which I cannot understand."

'Gandhi: "Yes; I admit the presence of this unknown element and I confess that I myself cannot answer for it or foretell where it might lead. But believe me: no loss of principle is involved."

'Gandhi stated: "Jawaharlal says he does not understand my language. But language is no bar to a union of hearts. And I know this: when I am gone he will speak my language."'

Basically, that was a true prophesy.

'The Chinese philosopher, Lin Yutang, put it in a nutshell: "The people listen to Nehru; Nehru listens to Gandhi; and Gandhi listens to God."

'In 1931 a new Viceroy was appointed by the British Government, Lord Willingdon, and he was considerably less sympathetic than Irwin. Soon nearly seventy thousand Indians were politically detained, including, of course, Jawaharlal Nehru; this time the British gave him a sentence of two years – again, here, in Naini Jail. And the Mahatma was arrested. And Jawaharlal's two sisters were arrested and imprisoned. And all of this was eagerly accepted. But, suddenly, the unacceptable occurred: Swarup Rani, Nehru's old, deeply-revered mother, was beaten on the head by the British police and badly injured. Yes, she too was demonstrating. Trapped in jail, Jawaharlal now suffered torments: "The thought of my frail old mother lying bleeding on the dusty road obsesses me and I wonder how I would have behaved if I had been there. How far would my non-violence have carried me? Not very far, I fear."

'In prison, Jawaharlal began writing a series of letters to his daughter, Indira. The first was written on her thirteenth birthday: "You have been in the habit of receiving presents and good wishes. Good wishes you will still have in full measure; but what present can I give you from Naini Prison? My presents cannot be material or solid. They can only be of the mind and spirit, such as a good fairy might have bestowed on you; something that even the high walls of prison cannot stop." And in this prison Jawaharlal also kept a diary and in it he stuck pictures of Harrow in England and he made a list of great men who had gone to Harrow School – with particular emphasis on Lord Byron. He read the great Hindu epics, the *Ramayana* and the *Gita*, and the English poets, Keats, Shelley, and, of course, Byron.'

Here is one of the film's main themes: the love that Nehru always held for Britain; the country that Imperially ruled his country, India. This love for Britain even persisted while he suffered in a series of British prisons.

'And later in jail, Jawaharlal digested the seriousness of his wife's, Kamala's, illness. To shield himself from the pain, he began to write his autobiography; but it was not easy: "The thought that Kamala might die has become an intolerable obsession." It was suggested to Nehru, by the British, that if he gave up politics for the period that remained of his sentence, he would be released. When Kamala heard: "What is this about your giving an assurance to the British Government? Do not give it!" He didn't.

'Kamala, now desperately ill, was flown to a sanatorium in Germany. Under pressure from liberal spirits in Britain and in India, the British released Jawaharlal and he hastened out of India to be with her. Kamala said: "Death is better than such a life, but even death is frightened of me."

'Jawaharlal said: "Sometimes, looking into her eyes, I found a stranger peeping out at me."

'Their daughter, Indira, was sitting at the bedside with her father, as Kamala died. The mother's last words were: "Someone is calling me," and she gestured towards a shape in the room.'

'The body was cremated and Jawaharlal took the ashes back to India.

'During 1937 words were printed in an Indian journal: "Jawaharlal Nehru cannot become a Fascist. And yet he has all the makings of a dictator in him: vast popularity, pride, hardness, and yet, with all of his love of the crowd, a certain contempt for the weak and inefficient. Therein lies the danger for Jawaharlal – and India." Unquote. The article was signed "Chanakya", but eventually it became known that the lonely, introspective Nehru had written it himself.

'The Indian National Congress was now the supreme organisation working for Indian independence and Jawaharlal was its President. But there were dangerous religious divisions within the country. Part of the Muslim element, as against the vast Hindu majority, was led by an eminent lawyer, Mohammed Ali Jinnah. Jinnah had once been a formidable champion of a united Indian nationalism, but various political factors were transforming him into an unbending advocate of a separate Muslim state.

'Jawaharlal Nehru described Jinnah's dangerous bitterness: "He felt completely out of his element in the home-spun clad crowd, who were demanding speeches in Hindustan."

'Of course, that other Old Harrovian, Winston Churchill, thoroughly understood how a relative handful of Britons had kept hundreds of millions of Indians in check: emphasise India's indigenous religious divisions and thereby rule them. Divide and rule. Some little while before, Hindus and Muslims had run amok and had killed, obscenely, about three hundred of each other. Churchill said: "This massacre at Cawnpore is a portent. Because it is believed, by some, that we British are about to leave India, the struggle for power is now beginning between the Muslims and Hindus . . . British troops are even now pacifying the terrified and infuriated populace. But this present Muslim-Hindu feud is only at its beginning." And that Machiavellian provocative prophecy certainly helped the awesome concept that was beginning to live in Mohammed Ali Jinnah's mind.

'The very limited concessions which the Congress Party had wrested from the British were put into operation and some provincial powers were extended to the Indians. But Nehru was still deeply depressed by any compromise over complete independence and so he began to travel through India, urging Indians to give further political support to the Congress Party; but while doing so, he was also delving for his Indian roots. He travelled for 130 days, he covered 65,000 miles and he saw and spoke to about 20,000,000 people – and they saw and heard him.

'"Sometimes as I was passing along a country road or through a village, I started with surprise on seeing a fine type of man, or a beautiful woman, who reminded me of some fresco of ancient Indian times. India is a myth and an idea, a dream and a vision, and yet very real and pervasive. There are terrifying glimpses of dark corridors which seem to lead back to primeval night. But she is also very lovable and none of her children can forget her. . . .

'"What is the secret of this strength? There seems to be something unique about the continuity of a cultural tradition through five thousand years of history; a tradition widespread among the masses and powerfully influencing them. That vision gives me a new perspective and the burden of the present seems to grow lighter. . . ."'

This momentous journey undertaken by Nehru gave us a chance to spread our film across great Indian images. Alan chose to film me walking through western coast Indian fishing villages, through the unbelievably rich ruins of Vijayanagar – the centre of the last great Hindu Empire before the Moguls annihilated it, and down and around the deep, opulent grandeur of Hindu Khajuraho.

Perhaps Alan has fixed the camera on me as a storyteller more than has been done before! I had hoped that as Nehru passed 'along a country road or through a village', the camera would have seen 'a fine type of man, or a beautiful woman' and I had hoped that we would have also seen 'some fresco of ancient Indian times.' But these story-telling films tend to carry dictates of their own. And Alan and Venu Gopal chose to give the film as grand and unbroken a sweep as possible. And my discipline is not to fight the director's vision. Gently influence, but never fight; unless a red light blinks. And I saw no serious red light blink on the Nehru film.

'But early in 1938, Jawaharlal's mother died and he sank deeper as he brooded on the condition of India and of the troubled world. He said to Gandhi: "I want to freshen up my tired and puzzled mind."

'Nehru, near to breaking, hastened to the woods and foothills of the vast Himalayan Mountains; but there was no peace: "I heard the tramp of barbarian feet over the pleasant garden of Vienna."

'Jawaharlal left India, speeding compulsively to the festering centres of the impending European holocaust. First he visited the Republican forces in Spain, which were being assaulted by Franco, who was being assisted by Nazi Germany and Fascist Italy. With him was his new friend, Krishna Menon, the hard-working, unsung Indian patriot. Then to Czechoslovakia, which was undergoing the process of betrayal to Hitler by Britain and France. And Jawaharlal began to speak as a brave international statesman: "We Indians have long experience of promises broken by the British Government. Yet it is well that this new Czechoslovakian betrayal has come to our attention also – lest we forget."

'And then, on the 3rd September, 1939, Lord Linlithgow, the current Viceroy of India, made a shattering announcement to the Indian people: "I hereby proclaim that war has broken out between His Majesty and Germany."

'Jawaharlal Nehru stated: "One man, and he a foreigner, has just plunged four hundred million Indians into war without the slightest reference to them."

'Lord Linlithgow invited the Indian leaders: "for full and frank discussion."

'Jawaharlal asked His Excellency the significant question: "How can Indians, who are not free and who have been denied democracy, be expected to fight for freedom and democracy?"

'Linlithgow: "A little more slowly, Mr Nehru – my slow

Anglo-Saxon mind [surely Lord Linlithgow was misinforming Nehru; he was a Scot] cannot keep pace with your quick intellect!"

'But Lord Linlithgow was quick enough to reject Nehru's plea and Jawaharlal responded: "I am sorry for, in spite of my hostility to British Imperialism, I have loved much that is England, and I should have liked to have preserved the silken bonds of the spirit between India and England."

'Well, the silken bonds were being bitterly stretched and thirty thousand Indians were arrested, including Nehru. During his trial he said: "There are very few persons in India, whether they are Indians or Englishmen, who have for years so consistently raised their voices against Fascism and Nazism as I have done. . . .

"And I am convinced that the large majority of the people of Britain are weary of Empire and hunger for a real new democratic order for India and for all of Britain's colonies. But we have to deal not with the British people but with their Government and we have no doubt as to what that Government aims at. We have therefore decided to be no party to this imposed war and to declare this to the world.

"It is not me that you are seeking to judge and condemn, but rather the hundreds of millions of the people of India, and that is a large task even for a proud Empire. Perhaps it may be that though I am standing before you on my trial, it is the British Empire itself that is on its trial before the bar of the world. . . ."

'Nehru ended: "I thank you, sir, for your courtesy."

'The judge sentenced Nehru to "Four years' rigorous imprisonment."

'And then Japan plunged into the war. The dilemma for Nehru and the Indian National Congress was now most extreme. Jawaharlal stated: "We are not going to surrender to the Japanese invader. In spite of all that has happened we are not going to embarrass the British war effort in India."

'However, that opinion was not unanimous. Among the

distinguished Indian independence leaders who thought differently was Subhas Chandra Bose.'

And with the arrival of Bose in our film I again suffered a little pressure from Doctor Nanda to remove certain quotes from the script for what can only be explained as political reasons. Subhas Chandra Bose had very clear Fascist tendencies. One of his statements, which was originally in my script, was: 'We, in Bengal [north-eastern India] represent the real revolutionary force. Jawaharlal Nehru only talks. [Not true, even apart from spending nine years in British jails.] We act! I am an extremist and my principle is: all or none!'

Of course, Nehru concurred with my opinion of Bose, though being a freedom-fighting politician, he had to tread warily:

'Jawaharlal had already confronted Bose: ". . . you hold different views from mine and you do not wholly approve of our condemnation of Nazi Germany or of Fascist Italy . . . I do not at all fancy the direction in which, apparently, you want to go."

'Bose: "I was astounded when you produced a resolution seeking to make India an asylum for the Jews. [Again Nehru, like me, had a deep sympathy for the indescribable Jewish predicament. I mention this because as Nehru's advocate, as it were, I had no disagreement or shortage of sympathy with him.] It is no use condemning countries like Germany and Italy on the one hand and on the other giving a certificate of good conduct to British and French Imperialism."

And then I, originally, quoted Bose again:

'And Bose gave his opinion of the Mahatma Gandhi: "He is an old, useless piece of furniture. It is time for new leadership."

'Jawaharlal: "The freedom struggle without Gandhiji's active leadership is not likely to be an effective one."'

This piece about Gandhi was never filmed. Again it was a very firm 'request' through Doctor Nanda. The political problem today is that Bose is a popular hero in India and very particularly in Bengal where he hailed from and, though Nehru suffered some revulsion against Bose's mentality and Bose insulted the great work of Gandhi, any unpleasant truths about Bose could lose millions of contemporary votes. Well, I am still able to make it clear in the film how much Bose disgusts me; though not as clearly and firmly as I would have wished.

'And then, incredibly, Subhas Chandra Bose began to make his way northward through Afghanistan, then westward to Nazi Germany, eventually ending up in Imperial Japan, where he began to recruit Indian prisoners of war, captured by the Japanese, for a force called the Indian National Army, which was meant to invade India with the hoped-for all-conquering Japanese and thereby liberate India from British rule.'

I think it is time the Indian supporters of Bose digested the fact that if the Japanese had succeeded in being all-conquering invaders of India and had not been stopped by the British and their Indian soldier comrades up in the Chindwin country, Japanese forces would probably still be knocking the shit out of the citizens of Calcutta today!

The psychological truth about many Indians is that, in spite of the noble success of 'passive resistance' to the British Raj, there is a macho Indian yearning that if only they had won freedom on the battlefield it would have been more satisfactory. And as pathetic and stupid as Subhas Chandra Bose's activities were, he and his turncoat men, the Indian National Army, came nearer to fitting that dream of glory than anything else. Painful, but true. As Napoleon once said: 'It is only the truth that hurts.'

'Nehru was asked, in Calcutta, a lethal question: "What would your attitude be if Subhas Chandra Bose leads an Indian contingent of liberation against India?"

'Nehru: "I will oppose him and fight him because he would be coming under Japanese auspices and a Japanese invasion of India would be more for the advantage of Japan than for India."

'But at this juncture Gandhi overrode Nehru's troubled reticence to harm the fighting democracies, led by Britain. The Mahatma issued an unequivocal ultimatum to the British: "Grant us Indians full democracy or quit India!" And then the Mahatma added: "Jawaharlal has almost forgotten his old quarrel with the British Imperialists."

"Well, of course, that was not true, and Jawaharlal Nehru continued openly, though painfully, to lead the Indian people into civil disobedience. He said: "It is better to jump into the uncharted seas of action and do something rather than to be the tame object of a malign fate."

'During 1942, the British began to defeat the Nazis in North Africa and Churchill roared at India like the arrogant Imperial lion that he was: "Let me make this clear, lest there should be any doubts about it in any quarter, we mean to hold our own. I have not become the King's First Minister in order to preside over the liquidation of the British Empire." The iron fist was raised and there was to be no more parley – at least while threatening war lasted. The leaders of the Indian Congress, including Mahatma Gandhi and Jawaharlal, were once again arrested. There was no trial this time. Nehru was incarcerated in this Ahmednagar Fort. And he remained here for nearly three years.'

Ahmednagar Fort is of great personal interest to me. And I cannot resist digressing from the main purpose of this book. I have a fairly well-known obsession: the very detailed history of the Second British-Boer War, which began on the 11th October, 1899, and was waged for almost three years, between the British and Boers, known as Afrikaners today; the white non-British citizens of Africa south of the Limpopo River. They were, and no doubt still are, formidable and heroic fighters. The Boers held the armies of the British Empire at bay for that great length of time in spite of the fact that the British pitched against them a final total of some four hundred and fifty thousand Imperial troops to be compared to the forty-five thousand old men, men in their prime and young boys that they were able to muster against us. The British forced the Boers to surrender unconditionally only by burning their farms and herding their women and children into what we unfortunately called concentration camps; where about twenty-six thousand of these women and children speedily died.

The fighting Boers that we British captured were despatched to prisoner-of-war camps all over the Empire: Bermuda, St Helena, Ceylon and India. And in India many of these brave white Afrikaners were held in Ahmednagar Fort. They were imprisoned elsewhere in India as well.

In my house in London I can produce letters and envelopes written by Boers from Ahmednagar Fort. Perhaps it is difficult for an uninfected person to imagine with what interest I peered into the cells and old buildings, sensing the ghosts of the old South African patriots as well as the nearer presence of Jawaharlal Nehru. I have visited a number of old prisons in India which housed thousands of these Boer prisoners of war. But no Indian official that I have questioned, civil or military, has ever heard of these astounding visitors.

'Inside the prison Jawaharlal wrote a book, *The Discovery of India*. It was not less than his ultimate attempt to escape from Harrow School and Cambridge University. Jawaharlal sat in this very room and considered once again the significance that Indians, five thousand years earlier, had been sophisticated enough to debate their human place in the cosmos. And Nehru asked: "Of our millions of people, how few get any education at all; how many live on the verge of starvation. If life opened its gates to them, how many among these millions would become eminent scientists, educationists, industrialists and artists, hoping to build a new India and a new world?"

'Outside the prison sixty-thousand freedom-fighting Indians were being arrested and some ten thousand were being killed. As Winston Churchill reported it: "The disturbances have been crushed with all the weight of the Government. Large British reinforcements have reached India and the number of white troops in that country is larger than at any time in the British connection."

'The atomic bomb exploded across the face of this earth and Jawaharlal Nehru, unlike many others, saw and heard it very clearly: "Peace seems a dream that has faded, and mankind apparently marches ahead to its doom. For though the atom bomb has come to blast the world, no bomb has yet touched the minds of the world's men of authority."

'Finally, Britain, with its allies, won the war and here, on this old Atlantic island, a very quiet revolution took place: the majority of the returning soldiers and the British people generally, voted for a Socialist Government. The Indian political prisoners were speedily released, including Nehru. He had spent nine years in prison, spread across nine different jails.

'But some Indian military prisoners were still retained and they were under sentence of death. These were the Indian officers and men who, having been captured by the Japanese, had then volunteered to fight for the astonishing Subhas Chandra Bose alongside the Japanese, against the British. Lord Louis Mountbatten, while Supreme Commander in south-east Asia, had already warned Nehru: "The so-called Indian National Army are not politically conscious heroes fighting for their country."'

And then I had continued Mountbatten's warning to Nehru: '"But cowards and traitors who betrayed their loyal friends,"' and I was asked to remove this from the script and it was not filmed. Again I had to make a judgement between hitting Subhas Chandra Bose and his questionable followers and the very real political problem in India today of holding the country together. Several times in Doctor Nanda's study I opened my mouth to say I felt that I should return to Britain forthwith. But it was never that serious a matter. I saw India's problems and I judged such mild censorings of the truth reasonable. There! I've written it. Confessed it!

Also I feel that Mountbatten's stricture 'cowards and traitors' is harder than I could have mouthed. But then Mountbatten was a better warrior than me. Some months ago I was visiting a book exhibition in Delhi and, while fingering through a pictorial history of the Second World War, I came across a photograph of Japanese soldiers performing bayonet practice on living Indian prisoners of war. I picked the book up and stuck it under the noses of the Indian organisers of the exhibition, demanding rather loudly, 'What are you going to do about Subhas Chandra Bose?'

Indian prisoners of the Japanese, having observed the inhuman conduct of their fellow Asians – and a Japanese conduct which was being bayoneted at them – cannot be lightly blamed for joining the Japanese in order to escape themselves from such horrible attentions. I suspect that I can be remarkably brave till some awful person seriously says to me: 'And now I'm going to pull your fingernails out.' But up to this time of writing I can't think of any excuse for Subhas Chandra Bose himself. He was not less than a ridiculous creep. But so many Indians still cheer his name that I was seriously advised to refer to him in the film as 'Netaji' or 'The Leader' – 'The *Führer*'. Personally, the thought of that makes me want to vomit.

Anyway, Mountbatten continued: '"The people who will serve you well in your national army of the future are those soldiers who were loyal – even to their British Indian oath."

'The accused men of the Indian National Army were put on trial, here, in this great Mogul Red Fort, in Delhi. For the last time in his life, Jawaharlal Nehru donned his lawyer's robe and walked to their defence. He said: "These men of the Indian National Army have put themselves on the wrong side and were functioning under the Japanese auspices . . . I do not wish to complain to the British for their strict military rule. But there can be little doubt of the patriotic motives of these men."'

One of the curious stylistic methods which we use in our films is me listening to and watching one of the characters that I am 'presenting'. In this case I, Kenneth Griffith, am seen gazing doubtfully at myself as Nehru as he speaks the last sentence above.

'"As an Indian and as one representing the views of almost all Indians, I would say that it would be a supreme tragedy if these officers and men are liquidated by way of punishment." The British prosecutors were outraged.'

Here again I was asked to cut a quotation, made by one of the British prosecutors: 'But those Indian National Army men, still held by us, are guilty of brutal crimes against civilians!' Atrocities. And the quotation was erased from the film. Once more the wretched Bose was being whitewashed.

And so the script continued: 'But the British Government saw the value of political expediency and released the Indian National Army prisoners.'

So, sadly, we all, sometimes, see the value of expediency. As an old puritan I may decide to call myself 'Expediency Griffith' in future.

We filmed the trial of the Indian National Army people inside the Red Fort. Cheek by jowl with the faded and looted grandeur of the Mogul Palace is the British Victorian barracks. No one in Delhi seemed to know where exactly the trial took place; few Indians are touched by such historical imaginings, unless a god is said to have been born there. So we made a shrewd guess and certainly it was a place redolent of long-ago British spit and polish. Now not so much spat upon or polished; though still inhabited by simple, friendly soldiers – of the Indian Army.

'The Socialist Prime Minister, Clement Attlee, spoke his unadorned truth: "Britain will quit India by a date not later than June 1948 . . . transferring power . . . in the best interests of the Indian people. India must choose what will be her future constitution . . . I hope that the Indian people may elect to remain within the British Commonwealth."

'Well, and predictably, Winston Churchill didn't recognise India's right to choose anything: "It is with deep grief that I watch the clattering down of the British Empire, with all its glories, and all the services it has rendered to mankind . . . Many have defended Britain against her foes. None can defend her against herself."

'Jawaharlal Nehru was the undisputed leader of the Indian National Congress and the great battle for India's freedom was surely accomplished and India firmly decided upon a democratic constitution; but that terrible religious, political spectre, which Winston Churchill was ever prophesying, began to grow and threaten. Mohammed Ali Jinnah, at the head of his Muslim League, was not to be denied: "By all the canons of international law we Muslims are a nation."

'And a leader of the extreme Hindu Mahasabha movement didn't help when he shot back: "India is the abode of the Hindu nation!"

'And Jawaharlal kept repeating: "As long as I am at the helm of affairs, India will not become a Hindu state!"

'Jinnah was relentless: "Never have we in the Muslim League done anything except by constitutional methods. But this day we bid goodbye to constitutional methods. I will give the British and the Indian Congress a demonstration of bloodshed and civil war!" And in Calcutta alone, over five thousand people were promptly murdered. Hindus and Muslims.

'Jawaharlal Nehru hastened to the Punjab, one of the sensitive provinces where over two thousand lay dead: "I have seen ghastly sights and I have heard of behaviour by human beings which would degrade brutes. If there is a grain of intelligence in any person he must realise that whatever political objective he may aim at, this is not the way to attain it."

'As the Indian nightmare grew, the British Government took drastic action and despatched a new Viceroy eastward: Lord Louis Mountbatten. It was a poetic appointment; he was a great-grandson of the first British Imperial ruler of India: Queen Victoria.

'The charming Lord met Jawaharlal and Mountbatten said: "Mr Nehru, I want you to regard me not as the last Viceroy winding up the British Raj, but as the first Viceroy to lead the way to the new India."

'Nehru: "Now I know what they mean when they speak of your charm being dangerous."'

Now, before I go in front of the camera to communicate each piece, I detach myself from everyone else and I ponder the incipient sequence as finely as I possibly can. Yes, I have researched it and thoughtfully written it, but now I must *become* it, and whatever I experience, inside my head and choreographically, that experience will be finally engraved on film, which probably millions of people will look at. And during this last spasm of pondering, new truths can occur to me. On this occasion, I suddenly realised that the above dialogue between Mountbatten and Nehru was, significantly, that between two sophisticated British public schoolboys. The exchange contains the humour, the sensitivity and the audacious honesty that is the best of that old educational arrangement, which I had observed at Harrow School.

'And then Mountbatten met Jinnah and after the lethal chat was over, the Viceroy remarked: "My God! He was cold. It took most of the interview to unfreeze him . . . I had not thought it possible that a man with such a complete lack of a sense of responsibility could hold the power which he has."

'Nehru, Mountbatten and Gandhi fought to retain the blessed union of the Indian sub-continent; but Jinnah, at the helm of the Muslim League, was glacially adamant: "India stands on the brink of a ruinous civil war. Pakistan is the only solution."

'The sailor in the Viceroy expressed the situation graphically: "India is a ship on fire in mid-ocean with ammunition in the hold."

'Horrified, the Viceroy addressed the British Secretary of State for India: "I realise that all this partition business is madness. No one would ever induce me to agree to it were it not for this fantastic religious madness that has seized everybody."

'Jawaharlal simply said: "My country has gone mad."

'And so Nehru addressed Mountbatten: "As you know, we are passionately attached to the idea of a united India, but we now accept the partition of India in order to avoid conflict and compulsion."

'At midnight, on the 14th August, 1947, British rule over the sub-continent of India came to an end and here in this Constituent Assembly Chamber in Delhi, Jawaharlal Nehru began to speak: "Long years ago we made a tryst with destiny and now the time comes when we shall redeem our pledge . . . At the stroke of the midnight hour, when the world sleeps, India will awake to life and freedom."'

And at this point of our film-making the troublesome Government officials of India dealt us an almost lethal blow. I have learnt over the past two years or so that these people are a far greater danger to the survival of India than, say, Pakistan. And whenever they came near our film on the life of Jawaharlal Nehru they injured the project mercilessly.

At this juncture of our film – being made for the Government of India, remember – the story was face to face, as it were, with Nehru's great positive achievements. No longer was it the passive battle for the right to steer India's own course; now it was the monumental course itself. And by the very fact that Nehru was now the leader of India, most of those momentous acts were carried out in the Constituent Assembly and in the Parliament Chamber, which is called the Lok Sabha.

For a year, Doordarshan had had the time to make their arrangements for our filming. The key members of our film crew, Alan Birkinshaw, Venu Gopal and I, had been escorted by Indian officials through the great chambers and we had discussed our various camera positions very fully. The place was ideal and we knew that the great climax of Nehru's life was safe and sound in our film arrangements.

Of course, we were to film during a period when the politicians were absent. The vast, empty edifice was ours to do final justice to Nehru's major policies. The dates for filming were fixed and agreed and then – as it seems to invariably happen in official India – something went wrong.

Gradually, it emerged that vague officials with power, bureaucrats, were stating that we could take our cameras into the Constituent Assembly and the Lok Sabha generally, but that I, the storyteller, must be neither seen nor heard.

We learnt the judgement on the very morning that we were due to start work. Inefficient, vague Indian mumblings were all that reached my ears. I begged to see these priggish obstructionists. Had they viewed one of 'my' films? Would they quickly view, a year after they should have, one of the films now? Nothing except that mulligatawny fog that is bureaucratic India.

I informed the Prime Minister's office. Serious attention was given to the emergency and I understand that appeals were made to the thick-headed officials at the highest level. But they were adamant: no one is to be recorded within the precincts. I desperately pointed out that I had been made welcome inside the National Assembly of France (for films about Napoleon and Thomas Paine); that I had been courteously invited into the Israeli Parliament, the Knesset, in Jerusalem (for the film on the life of David Ben Gurion); and that I had been kindly received into the parliament and apartments of the Prime Minister of South Africa, in Cape Town (a film about the Second Anglo-Boer War). And that I was given invaluable access to the White House in Washington (the Thomas Paine film). And that in this Nehru saga, the great Imperial doors of Britain had been thrown open and that we, Indian and British film-makers, were affectionately made to feel at home. I reminded them that, from an interior scenic point of view, Winston Churchill's speeches in the film would come out far more effectively than Jawaharlal Nehru's, simply because Britain was anxious to help the project while India continuously hindered it. But those Indian officials wouldn't budge. They were too important in their own small minds to even see me. I appealed enough. I pointed out that if I had been informed a year earlier that I was to be barred from the Lok Sabha I would have cancelled the film.

And so we were compelled to fake large and important parts of the film. Never before have I faked one of these films. And what is even more tragic for Nehru's memorial, as far as our film epic is concerned, is that we had to remove some of his most significant and moving statements because those calcified officials would not allow me to record them where they were spoken.

'And immediately the massive obscenity of religious slaughter began. As Hindus and Sikhs made their escape from Pakistan southward and Muslims hurried northward to the safety of Pakistan, perhaps half a million people were butchered. No one knows the correct number of casualties or ever will.

'Jawaharlal Nehru walked among raging Sikhs and Hindus begging them to find peace: "During these last few days in the Punjab and in Delhi, I have supped my fill of horrors. People with destructive weapons shouted Long live Mahatma Gandhi!; long live Jawaharlal! I feel ashamed to hear these cries from people who might have just committed murder . . . I never knew that my admirers were beasts. My heart is soaked with sorrow and the monstrous riots have degraded my country. I went to meet Bapu [Gandhi], but I could not look him in the face. I was full of shame."

'Here in Delhi, Muslim refugees took what shelter they could in the ancient ruins of Purana Qila and here at the Mogul Emperor Humayun's tomb. Jawaharlal and Gandhi walked among them, giving what comfort they could. An old Muslim and his wife, in ragged clothes and both suffering from knife wounds, stood to greet the good Hindu. The Mahatma said: "I hang my head in shame!"

'Nehru towered above religious bias and, enraged, he said: "I will not tolerate this! I want Hindus, Sikhs and Muslims to live like brothers!" The Mahatma immediately commenced to starve himself and Jawaharlal joined him and the mass murders began to cease.

'In Karachi, in the new State of Pakistan, Mohammed Ali Jinnah, the first Governor-General, was about to enter his official residence when he suddenly turned to an officer: "Do you know, I never expected to see Pakistan in my lifetime. We have to be very grateful to God for what we have achieved."'

We had planned to travel to Pakistan to film the above sequence but the relationship between that country and India was in too parlous a condition; so our Delhi authorities edged away from even a formal request. And so we also faked this Pakistan piece, in India.

I should mention that my adviser, Doctor B. R. Nanda, a highly responsible Hindu, kindly murmured to me that he felt that my presentation of Jinnah was more unsympathetic than it might have been. I say this because it is a fact that the Government of India's representative with me, Doctor Nanda, did not want a hint of injustice in my script towards Pakistan. I think that this is worth mentioning. *I* am responsible, Pakistan!

'And Prime Minister Nehru announced: "We join the Commonwealth because we think it is beneficial to us and to certain causes in the world that we wish to advance.

'"I think that it is a good augury for the future that the old conflict between India and England should be resolved in this friendly way."

'The Russians, through their newspaper, *Pravda*, came out with the predictable cliché: "Nehru is the running dog of Imperialism."

'But Jawaharlal was nobody's running dog. He had certainly said, "Life under Communism would be a joyless and soulless thing, regulated to the minutest detail by rules and orders, framed by the all-powerful official."

'However, on the other hand, while being entertained by some American businessmen in New York City, he was shocked when the host said: "Mr Prime Minister, do you realise that you are eating dinner with at least twenty billion dollars?"

'And Jawaharlal was to say: "I have no respect for property at all; except for some personal belongings. I cannot appreciate America's tremendous attachment to property."'

At this juncture of Nehru's life I wore a Jaipur suit exactly as Nehru did during his premiership. And also I wore a red rose through one of the button holes as he did.

Though my change of dress in our film is a dramatic image, I hope that it eases properly on to the screen.

'Everything may have appeared to be on course for a peaceful future, but Gandhi had a premonition: "If I am to die by the bullet of a madman, I must do so smiling, There must be no anger in me. God must be in my heart and on my lips."

'The madman's name was Nathuram Godse and as the Mahatma walked through this garden on the 30th January, 1948, Godse made an obeisance and then fired three bullets into the old man's chest. As he fell, and momentarily before death, the Mahatma was able to say: "Hey Ram", which means, "Oh God". The murderer was a Hindu Brahmin, closely associated with an extreme Hindu organisation. Godse felt that Gandhi had demonstrated too much sympathy for the Muslims. After a painstaking trial, Godse was hanged; a retribution which the Mahatma would not have approved of.

'Nehru, Patel and Mountbatten hastened to the body of the Mahatma. Jawaharlal held the dead hand and wept uncontrollably. The Englishman, Mountbatten, addressed the two Indian patriots, who had recently experienced disagreements: "At my last interview with Gandhiji, he told me that his dearest wish was to bring about a full reconciliation between the two of you." And the two sometime adversaries quietly embraced and vowed to remain united.'

The death of Gandhi was filmed at Birla House in New Delhi, both in the garden, on the exact place where he was shot, and then in Gandhi's room where the body had lain.

Alan Birkinshaw wanted to film me walking along the pathway that the Mahatma took and to re-enact the terrible moment when he was shot. I am always extremely wary of such reconstructions. The art is to avoid the viewer becoming conscious of 'acting'. I protested mildly and urged Alan and Venu Gopal to film it, if they must, in slow motion. In this way we would stylise the moment and thereby avoid a naked piece of conventional film drama. Slow motion would have been a poetic impression; but because of some technical mix-up, it was not done. I believe that it will prove to be a critical moment in our film, when we may lose the support of many viewers. I know that our form of film argument rests on a very sharp knife's edge. How do we win belief? That is the fine, ultimate battle. We will see; I may be wrong. I hope so.

'Shortly afterwards Jawaharlal broadcast to the Indian nation: "Friends and comrades, the light has gone out of our lives and there is darkness everywhere . . . The light has gone out, I said, and yet I was wrong. For the light that shone in the country was no ordinary light . . . it represented the living, the eternal truths, reminding us of the right path."

'And then, virtually alone, Jawaharlal Nehru took the helm of the biggest democracy in the wide world and he began to work towards enlightenment: "If we look back at India's long history we find that our forefathers made wonderful progress whenever they looked out on the world. And, in later periods, when they grew narrow and shrank from outside influences, India suffered politically and culturally."

'The new Prime Minister immediately looked toward the potential future of India: "When I look at the Himalayan range of mountains, I think of the vast power concentrated there . . . But before we release power, we have to know how to control it and then use it in the proper way."

'Nehru was an idealist: "I am influenced by the idea that if a person does the right thing, the right results will flow from it." And apparently he believed that a nation – India – could also operate along such ethical, moral lines. But that disturbing, ever-pervasive political *reality* now began to confront him. On the sub-continent there were 562 so-called princely states, most of them run by Rajahs and Nawabs, often along disconcertingly feudal patterns. And at the transference of power from Britain to India, certain promises were made by the British to the respective princely rulers about their guaranteed future status. But now that British-promised status was anathema to the new Indian Government. Nehru said: "The Indian Princes represent, probably, the extremest type of autocracy existing in the world." In short, there was an uncomfortable compulsion by the Indian

Government to absorb even ruthlessly the princely states into the new nation of India. The enormous and sometimes cruel task was given to Sardar Patel, the unshiftable realist, who suffered no twinges of discomfort; and his job was softened up by Lord Louis Mountbatten. British royalty has always had its uses.

'The acquisition of the princely states was pushed through with remarkable success – though it did involve the new Indian Army here and there. The big exception to ease of acquisition was here, in beautiful Kashmir, where Nehru's ancestors had hailed from. The debate was whether Kashmir would accede to India or Pakistan. The majority of the population was Muslim. There was a shady and murderous invasion of Kashmir by Muslim Pathan tribesmen from Pakistan and Nehru painfully ordered the Indian Army to counter it. On the 2nd October, 1947, he spoke on India's radio: "I can assure the people of Pakistan that India has no aggressive designs against any country, least of all against Pakistan. But there has been aggression of a brutal kind; aggression against the people of Kashmir and against the Indian Union. We met that aggression as any self-respecting country was bound to meet it."

'Nehru had said, many years before: "As I gazed at Kashmir, it seemed to me like the hopes and desires that fill us and yet so seldom find fulfilment."

'Now, in the middle of a threatening conflict, Jawaharlal said: "I am called a Kashmiri – in the sense that ten generations ago my people came down from Kashmir to India. That is not the bond I have in mind when I think of Kashmir . . . Kashmir, because of her geographical position, with her frontiers adjacent to three countries, the Soviet Union, China and Afghanistan, is intimately connected with the history and the international contacts of India . . . We have only two objectives in the Kashmir State. To ensure the freedom and progress of the people here and to prevent anything happening that might endanger the security of India."

'Here, in his official residence in Delhi, the good man,

Jawaharlal Nehru, was now battling with the rough and ready of bitter political truth. He struggled with his conscience: "So unfortunately, but inevitably, compromises have to take place."

'And then Jawaharlal sent a message to his beloved sister, Mrs Pandit, who was India's outstanding ambassador to the United States of America: "Don't talk too much about our high ideals; for our immediate past and present are not in consonance with these high ideals and we may lay ourselves open to a courteous retort."

'During 1948, Lord and Lady Mountbatten left India and in particular they left their friend, Prime Minister Jawaharlal Nehru. A vast concourse of Indians expressed their affection and respect for the British royal couple who had tried so hard to ease the transition of India to independence. At the great farewell function Jawaharlal said: "I have wondered how it was possible that an Englishman and an Englishwoman could become so popular in India during this brief period of time. You may have many gifts and presents, but there is nothing more precious than the love and affection of the people." Certainly, all three of these outstanding people loved each other.

'But the pressure of the world outside India continued to harass Nehru and he proceeded to confront the hard facts: "There are the problems of what are called foreign possessions in India: French Pondicherry and Portuguese Goa and the rest. We want a peaceful solution. But it is quite clear that there is only one future for these possessions and that is complete integration with India."

'Well, the French left quietly, but the Portuguese, under their dictator, Salazar, did not wish to move. They had made Goa part of Portugal some four hundred years before and a very large proportion of the population were Roman Catholics. Nehru reiterated his pacifist nature: "We do not want to use force and we shall follow that principle in Goa." He waited for fifteen years and then influences in his Indian Government pushed him, and into Goa went the Indian Army and the Navy and the Air Force. There was little resistance from the Portuguese. But world opinion was surprised. And Jawaharlal was not happy; not happy at all. He said: "The fact that a war is a little war does not make it less of a war."

'President Kennedy of the United States of America is reputed to have said of Prime Minister Nehru: "It is like finding a priest in a brothel!" It was not even a courteous retort.'

I was asked to remove the last paragraph from the film. I begged that it should remain. I pointed out that such international tensions and conflicts are the stuff of drama. That without the shocks of life a film can become innocuous and boring. I happily conceded that President Kennedy's humorous stricture was unfair and that the viewer cannot fail to recognise this fact, having seen and heard Nehru's feelings and words in context around Kennedy's Irish-American joke. But Doctor Nanda was adamant. Latterly I have pleaded that the piece should remain in the international version of the film, but not in the longer Indian one. But 'No!' and so it is out of both films. A pity, I suspect.

'But how high Jawaharlal Nehru soared above the usual details of petty national disagreement! And he brought a new concept to contemporary international thinking. Why commit India to the democratic capitalist powers *or* to the Communist totalitarian régimes? Would the interests of humanity be served by the world being divided into two power-blocks? What about love? he seemed to ask. The shade of Gandhi must have been very pleased. Jawaharlal travelled to the United States and said: "I have repeatedly been impressed during my visits to the Soviet Union and to the United States, by the many things the two peoples – the Russians and the Americans – have in common. They are both frank and hospitable and are exceedingly friendly. I think that once they get over the present day political difficulties the peoples of the Soviet Union and the United States are likely to come nearer to each other than possibly other countries might."'

This prophetic and warming statement by Nehru, in view

of the advent of Mikhail Gorbachev and his apparent vision of a freer Soviet Union, is one of the pieces that we have lost from our film, because of the pin-headed intransigence of the little people who lord over India's parliament. We film-makers did our utmost to counter their pompous destructiveness; we filmed it effectively elsewhere, but during the editing period (sticking the story pieces together) we found that prolonged faking was not acceptable. And so Nehru's Indian vision of invaluable optimism for our world is lost to the film.

'Nehru explained the difficult international road that he was constructing: "We have sought to avoid foreign entanglements by not joining one ideological bloc or the other. The natural result has been that neither the Russians nor the Americans look on us with favour. Nevertheless, we intend co-operating with the United States of America and we intend co-operating, fully, with the Soviet Union."

'However, for most of his life, Jawaharlal did favour one country above all others – China. Way back, during 1939, when the Indian National Congress was struggling desperately for India's independence, the Congress managed to send medical aid to the fighting Chinese Communists and Jawaharlal received a letter in reply: "China takes this opportunity to thank your great Indian people. Heartiest greetings, Mao Tse-tung."

'And during the dark days of 1942, Nehru said: "I see the future filled with hope because China and India are friends and comrades in the great adventure of man."

'And then, in 1950, the first shock was experienced: China brutally invaded Tibet. The truth is, Nehru was hurt and ominously puzzled. His decency couldn't quite comprehend how his beloved China could have perpetrated such an act. Jawaharlal's words were mild: "The Chinese have acted rather foolishly. It is natural that our enthusiasm for supporting China wanes somewhat; but our general policy towards China remains the same."

'In 1954, Chou En-lai, reconfirmed the ancient respect of the two vast nations for each other: "The friendship of

960 million Chinese and Indian people constitutes a mighty force for peace in Asia and the world."

'But now Jawaharlal was faltering. He wanted to believe such words but his faith in humankind had been disturbed. He had always, since a child, suffered a degree of loneliness. But now he could not turn to his father, Motilal; nor to his devout mother; nor to his loving wife, Kamala; nor, above all, to Mahatma Gandhi. His devoted daughter, Indira Gandhi, was ever at his side; but he was inclined to spare her from his self-doubts. Nehru made an agonising effort to resign from the premiership of India: "I feel now that I must have a period when I can free myself from this daily burden." India had long ago raised the frightening question: "After Nehru, who?" And so Jawaharlal was persuaded to stay on.

'But events were moving from bad to worse. Inside Tibet the Chinese were waving Mao Tse-tung's "little red book" and they were systematically destroying Tibet's ancient, invaluable culture. And then, unexpectedly and quietly, over India's northern border came the smiling, dignified Dalai Lama, with a great trail of suffering, patient Tibetans. Nehru stood up in the Lok Sabha: "We have every desire to maintain the friendship between India and China; but, at the same time, we have every sympathy for the people of Tibet, and we are greatly distressed at their hapless plight." It was a compassionate and courageous statement; Jawaharlal had begun to digest the bitter fact that his beloved China was now unpredictable. He was right; sometime later the Chinese Army began to pour over India's border, high up in these Himalayan Mountains and eventually in massive array.

'The disciple of Gandhi was put to a stark test: "There is no alternative for us Indians but to defend our borders. What is happening in China today is the arrogance of power . . . India can never concede to making a gift of the Himalayas to the Chinese . . . But I hope that our Indian nation will never be brutalised. I hope that India, which is essentially a gentle and peace-loving country, will be able to retain that state of mind."

'The truth is that Jawaharlal Nehru was still clinging to

his high ethical, indeed spiritual, idealism. His words, in the blast of arrogant Chinese aggression, were again gentle, even as the Chinese legions – completely prepared for high altitude warfare – drove the ill-prepared Indians back towards their vast but vulnerable plains: "Perhaps there are not many instances in history where one country, that is India, has gone out of her way to be friendly with the Chinese Government and to plead their cause in the councils of the world, and then for the Chinese to return evil for good and even go to the extent of invading our sacred land."

'But he was never without humour: "However, I may sometimes lose my temper, but I never lose my nerve."

'Sinister mystery piled upon sinister mystery. Suddenly the Chinese military avalanche halted, and then, without explanation, withdrew in good military order. No one, to this day, is quite certain why they did what they did, or understands the psychology of why they did it. But the harm was done.

'Nehru tended to work for about sixteen hours per day. One of his secretaries said: "I am unable to find a purely physiological explanation for the amount of work that Nehru is able to achieve day after day. It is really a case of the utter triumph of the spirit over the body; of a consuming passion to work for India."

'Nehru's target was: "To convert India's economy into that of a modern state and to fit my country into the Nuclear Age" – but no nuclear bombs! After seventeen years in control of India's destiny, food production had risen from 55 million tonnes to nearly 90 million tonnes; industrial output had risen ninety-four per cent; and life expectancy had increased from thirty-two to fifty years. Yes, the sixteen hours each day had been worthwhile.

'Jawaharlal Nehru pushed and pushed India into the world of science and technology, but not without reservation. In 1959 he spoke to the Indian Science Congress: "May I offer my respectful congratulations to the great scientists of the Soviet Union, of the United States of America and of the United Kingdom of Great Britain, for the magnificent advances that they have brought about recently. And yet an odd thought comes to mind. We are stretching our hands to the moon and some day we shall go to Mars or Venus, and yet, perhaps, we forget what is happening to this earth."

'During 1960, Prime Minister Nehru visited Britain to attend the Commonwealth Prime Ministers' Conference. He visited his widower friend, Lord Louis Mountbatten, and he revisited Harrow School, where he resang the old school songs, in the vicinity of that other old boy, Winston Churchill. Churchill remarked, with tears of astonishment in his eyes: "Nehru demonstrates no resentment towards me."'

This piece we filmed in the Assembly Hall of Harrow School. Around the curved wall at the back of the auditorium are – six? – oil paintings of old boys who became Prime Ministers of Great Britain. And then there is one other portrait – of Prime Minister Nehru, of India. We were allowed to reshuffle the great portraits so that Nehru was next to Churchill. And so our film shot began on Nehru as I started to speak and then down on to me and then back up on to Churchill as I said: "In the vicinity of that other old boy." We were tying history to the film moment, which is part of our style.

'During this traumatic period, Jawaharlal spoke to a Marxist journalist: "We must find ethical and spiritual solutions."

'Journalist: "What you say raises visions of Mr Nehru in search of God in the evening of his life."

'Nehru: "Yes, I have changed. The human mind is hungry for something deeper in terms of moral and spiritual development, without which all the material advances may not be worthwhile. The old Hindu idea that there is a divine essence in the world and that every individual possesses something of it and can develop it, appeals to me. And there is the message of the Buddha; a message of peace that is particularly necessary for the world today."

'Jawaharlal would not, could not, relinquish the values of the Buddha or of Mahatma Gandhi – or, for that matter, of himself. He continued to urge India forward, though the Chinese invasion had broken him physically: "Old as we are, with our Indian memory stretching back to the early dawn of human history, we have to grow young again, with the irrepressible spirit and joy of youth and its faith in the future. And we Indians should not become self-righteous. We Indians think that every evil is being done by Pakistan and China and that we are completely free from wrong-doing."

'And he declared his final life's creed in very simple language: "I am not wedded to any dogma or religion; but I do believe in the innate spirituality of human beings. I do believe that every individual should be given equal opportunity . . . I dislike the vulgarity of the rich as much as I dislike the poverty of the poor."

'Suddenly it was the end. His daughter, Indira, was at his side. Her blood was transfused into his stricken body, but to no avail.

'Jawaharlal Nehru died in this room on the 27th May, 1964. He was seventy-four years old. By the side of this bed, on this table, was a verse of poetry written by the American, Robert Frost :

> The woods are lovely, dark and deep,
> But I have promises to keep,
> And miles to go before I sleep,
> And miles to go before I sleep.

'Jawaharlal had been carrying this poem, in his pocket, for some days.

'He had addressed the students of Allahabad University: "I may have only a short while to live and the only ambition I have is that to the end of my days, I shall work my hardest for India and humankind, and then, when I have done my job, there is no need to bother about me further."

'About noon on the day of the traditional cremation, an earthquake shuddered through Delhi. And Hindu priests chanted mantras and Buddhist priests muttered their prayer and the Jat Regiment played Mahatma Gandhi's favourite Christian hymn: "Abide With Me" and Muslims spoke the Prayer for the Dead. There were muffled drums and gun salutes were fired, and the military played "The Last Post".

'Jawaharlal Nehru's will and testament was published. "I wish to declare that I do not want any religious ceremonies performed for me after my death. I do not believe in any such ceremonies." And then he had inscribed a list of instructions which no reasonable Hindu could disagree with: "I am conscious that I too, like all of us, am a link in the unbroken chain which goes back to the dawn of history in the immemorial past of India . . . I am making this request: that a handful of my ashes be thrown into the Ganges River at Allahabad to be carried to the great ocean that washes India's shores.

'"The major portion of my ashes should, however, be carried high up into the air and scattered from that height over the fields, where the peasants of India toil, and so become an indistinguishable part of India."

'Jawaharlal had kept some of the ashes of his beloved wife, Kamala, for twenty-eight years, and now these, too, entered the ancient ritual.'

And so the above, as it were, ends my discovery of Nehru as far as my commission to make a film about his life was concerned. Those words that I wrote and spoke and their implications sum up everything that I carried in me about Jawaharlal Nehru to the day we completed filming. Of course, there are many other vital contributions: where Alan Birkinshaw chose to place the camera; how Venu Gopal chose to photograph the film; the work of Shri Das, our sound man; and Chiara Peretti's watchful eyes to make sure that we made no continuity blunders and to help guide our editress Reena Mohan through her perceptive work in the cutting room. (Incidentally, I have never observed a better-run editing operation.) And then Surendra Dhir nursing us all along under unhelpful circumstances. Finally, of the thirty men from the Indian

Film Division in Bombay, I choose to single out Shri Chiplunkar, who helped me wherever and whenever he could with dedicated sensitivity. This dependable young friend is described in the film credits as 'light boy'; he was a damned sight more than that!

But, as long as I am on this earth, I will go on discovering more about Nehru. With every subject that I tackle, as a film, I never cease to enquire about and think about and assess the various subjects – long after the final print is accepted and transmitted. Today I know more about Nehru than I did when the last word was recorded for our film.

CHAPTER FOUR

An Unexpected Happiness

Everything connected with the Nehru film, every single event, was different from my experiences on every other film that I have ever worked on. That is India. Normally I remain with the various projects – usually in Britain – while they go through their irrevocable final processings. But we discovered that India hasn't got the sophisticated technical arrangements that we require for sixteen millimetre film, which is what we were using. And so this work had to be done in Britain. Alan Birkinshaw returned to Britain with the film and with him went Reena Mohan and Surendra Dhir; all of them to supervise this work. Finally Venu Gopal went, to help grade the film (balance the colour) as he had wished it to be. I usually keep a watching brief on this period of the film operation, though as unobtrusively as possible. Under these unexpected circumstances I decided to remain in India until the two films were delivered by our contracted delivery date.

Of course, the films were edited in India at Delhi and the music was composed and recorded in India, at Bombay. And before the work could be taken to Britain it had to be viewed and passed by the Indians in authority. This was a trauma for us all; particularly me! I had come to India to make a film which I calculated would take me seven months to complete. Now, two years later, it was to be judged by Shri Sharada Prasad, on behalf of the Prime Minister; by two distinguished Indian historians: Doctor Bal Ram Nanda, the first Director of the Nehru Memorial Museum and Library, and Professor Ravinder Kumar, the present Director; by the then Director-General of India's television service, Shri Baskar Ghose; and finally by Jawaharlal Nehru's personal secretary – the one I had quoted in the film about Nehru working sixteen hours per day. And none of these gentlemen was familiar with the complicated business of film-making.

We assembled in Reena Mohan's makeshift cutting-room and these distinguished gentlemen faced the paraphernalia of a film-cutting table. As far as I remember there were six reels of film, which meant that they saw the film in six separate parts and after each one Reena removed the section of the film and replaced it with the next and, of course, painstakingly synchronised the sound with my lip movements. Later, in London, the sound and the picture would be married on one single strip. Our Indian adjudicators then watched these broken sequences on a small screen attached to the cutting table.

No lay person should ever see a film in this unfinished state. I myself, the producer, am reluctant to watch and judge a film at this rough juncture. But the representatives of the Indian Government had to look at it. Alan Birkinshaw sat to the left of the worktable and fed in the recorded music by hand-control at the approximate places in the film where he thought that it might be used in the dubbing theatre (where the use of sound is finally 'engraved') in London. Wow!

At half-time we were all served coffee and cream cakes. I rather naughtily remarked that this was the first time that the Government of India had directly supplied me with such titbits. The learned men made no comment to me, except Nehru's old secretary, who smilingly took my arm and said: 'You've got the man's spirit right.'

And a load melted away from my mind. I told Nehru's old secretary that for me his remark was all-important. It was devoid of political considerations; it was an assurance to me that I had been faithful to a man he obviously loved. I tried to explain this to him: 'If Jawaharlal walked through this door now and having looked round at all of us, I suspect that he would embrace you first.'

Before this strange film-show commenced I said a few

words. I explained the awkward technical process that we would all have to suffer over the next four hours or so. (With the change-overs it would take this length of time.) That the film was a delicate and hard-considered structure. That the removal of one 'brick' now would be far more serious for the overall value of the film than any non film-maker could imagine. I reminded everyone, ever so gently, that I would soon have been in India for two years and that there was other work that I must do in other parts of the world. Yes, it was a nervous time.

At the end of the whole film-show, there was a silence and once again I leapt to the front. I briefly spoke about the dangers of platitudes in a film. That provocation or conflict was as much an ingredient of a film as it was of life itself. Then I remembered to be a wee bit inspired: 'And, of course, it is a *foreigner's* point of view. I am aware that eight hundred million Indians will have eight hundred million different opinions. And that in the Lok Sabha if all I had said in the film was 'Yes', there would have been massive rage from some quarter of the House and exactly the same rage from another quarter if all I had said was 'No'. And at this point Doctor Nanda intervened and said he had always understood this fact about my subjective role and that while bearing this in mind, he had personally passed every word I had spoken in the film. I really like my friend, Doctor Nanda.

Professor Kumar took me to task about my interpretation of the explosive subject of the massacre at Jallianwala Bagh, which he had made a particular study of. But I stood my ground, pointing out that I had personally collected evidence from Indian survivors and that my version of the subject had been passed. Shri Prasad quietly said: 'I would like the words used in the Chinese-Tibetan sequence changed from "China brutally invaded Tibet" to "China brutally overran Tibet." ' That change made little difference to me and since it was voice over archive film of the tragic event, there was no serious technical problem.

Professor Kumar, who has been a good friend to me, said

as everyone was dispersing: 'Now you didn't want us to simply tell you how good the film is, did you?' It was all a happy resolution of a prolonged trial. Shri Ghose seemed to be trying to persuade Shri Prasad, as he got into his car to depart, to ask the Prime Minister to make some television appearance. I, who had just appeared in front of them all as some twenty-five different historical characters, rather sportingly offered to impersonate the Prime Minister for Shri Ghose. Shri Ghose – like so many other people – doesn't seem to love me too much; all I hope is that he simply hasn't got the time.

Well, it was goodbye film; goodbye Alan – with that last forlorn message at Indira Gandhi Airport, Delhi: 'Go easy on the music!' I've become something of a fatalist; I now think that it's the Hindu in me.

The problem for me was what precisely to do with my time and where was I to do my work most effectively until my contract with the Indian Government expired. The first of those questions pointed clearly towards a greater understanding of what was going on in India and thereby an even more rounded understanding of Nehru.

I had gathered together a vast amount of research material that was beyond the direct perimeter of our film and this I turned to. And where to work on it? The only place of peace I had found in Delhi to work in was the Nehru Library. But really I could do it anywhere. I thought about moving back up to the houseboat on the lake at Srinagar and then I mused I would move to Dona Paula in Goa, where I had written my Thomas Paine script long ago and where I had met Chiara Peretti for the first time. I considered moving south-west when the ice appeared on the Kashmir lake, but the disruption! So I went straight to my little cottage at Dona Paula, where the monsoon was doing its worst. But the bending palm trees and the torrential rain beating into the Arabian Sea was a beautiful event. I did my hours of work towards deeper appreciation of India and Nehru every single day.

I am drawn to Goa for an interesting historical, sociological reason. I am not Portuguese, I am not a Roman Catholic; indeed now I please to call myself an agnostic. But I am happily pulled towards Goa because I feel at home there. The Portuguese have left an indelible mark on Goa. During the four hundred odd years of their presence they created a hybrid European culture which is full of fish and delight. And what an understanding of Greater India can one get if the myriad evolvements are understood. Again it is an example of the old European cultural link.

Goa was invaded by India, though it is safer these days to say 'liberated', at the end of 1961; but the real invasion is taking place now. The Portuguese arrived in Goa under the astounding leadership of Alfonso de Albuquerque and St Francis Xavier. Portugal perpetrated the unspeakable 'Holy' Inquisition of Goa against their own Christians, but more cruelly against the indigenous Hindus. But once that obscene aberration had ended, the Portuguese and the native inhabitants of Goa and the mixed blood that ensued became a remarkably attractive amalgam. Somehow the mixture was an easy-going innocence. But now, a massive invasion has broken across Goa's frontiers: the foreign tourists from Europe and America and, most dangerously, the beady-eyed Indian money-makers from all over the great sub-continent.

Each morning at Dona Paula I read a local newspaper called the *Herald*. Quickly I realised that I was reading the best newspaper that I had seen in India. It was everything that the big Indian newspapers were not. It was fighting for the poor bloody people; what the Soviet Union calls the 'exploited'. The editorials went straight at the throats of the police, the business boys and, above all, the local politicians and what they have most at heart which, incidentally, is not the welfare of Goa. 'Who runs this six sides of print?' I demanded. 'Rajan Narayan,' I was told. And soon, while sitting in a small restaurant and entirely alone, with the monsoon thrashing the palm trees, a man came and went like a whisper. The manager of the rain-beleaguered place said: 'That's Rajan Narayan, whom you admire so much.' Today he is a Best Friend.

The political and business assault on Goa – particularly from the Hindu Maharashtra state – seemed, so I am told, overwhelming, till Rajan Narayan, at the helm of the *Herald*, began to attack their lusts. From the north to the south of Goa I have been told by ordinary Goans that Rajan Narayan did more to secure statehood for Goa and to make the local language, Konkani, the first language of the new state than anyone else. Strangely, Rajan Narayan is not a Goan by birth; he is one of those Bombay energetics; but *his* beady eyes are not focused on money or on the material benefits of political power; they are gimleting for the welfare of the Goan underdog.

One day I heard a middle-aged American say to Rajan Narayan: 'Are you the editor of this paper?' He was flourishing the slim *Herald*. 'This is the best newspaper that I have read in India!'

Yes, Goa very recently got its statehood and by another of those endless incalculable coincidences that pepper my life I arrived at the Governor of Goa's residence, where I had been invited for supper, as His Excellency, Gopal Singh, listened to the momentous news of statehood on a portable radio. Is all of this relevant to a deeper understanding of Jawaharlal Nehru? I think so. Whither goest thou? And a young waiter slapped some fried mackerel in front of me. 'Ah! Indian mackerels!' I exclaimed.

'*Goan* mackerels!' he shouted; but pleasantly enough.

One of the many subjects relevant to Nehru's battles for Indian independence which did not touch our film was the mutiny of some sections of the Indian armed forces after the Second World War, particularly of the Indian Navy. My interest in this event brought me into the company of a number of distinguished servicemen and ex-servicemen; this was easy for me to achieve through the good offices of my two old friends: Admirals Singh and Ghandhi (the latter being personally involved in the naval threat to the extent –

so rumour has it – that he contemplated shelling the Bombay Yacht Club). Among the bevy of senior men that I had the privilege of meeting was Vice-Admiral J. P. Govil and his wife, Jyotsna, and they happened to mention to me that the Admiral had recently been appointed the Fortress Commander of the Andaman Islands and wouldn't Chiara and I visit the Andamans? The Andaman Islands, and to their south, the Nicobar Islands, lie along the eastern side of the Bay of Bengal; they begin, at their northern extremity, not too far from Burma and stretch southward to within forty-four miles of Sumatra, Indonesia. I knew just enough about these mysterious places to clinch the visit speedily.

Across India we flew, with Indian Home Office blessing, and at Port Blair's simple airport we were received by Admiral Govil's handsome and smiling Flag Lieutenant. We stayed, initially, at a Government Rest House, quaintly called the Megapode Nest; the megapode being an eccentric bird.

Everything about these exotic islands is redolent of ancient times and more recent vivid history. Of course, the British acquired the islands on behalf of the English East India Company and it was a Lieutenant Archibald Blair of the British Indian Navy who ran up the Union Jack on the 25th October, 1789. Many years ago I asked a distinguished British Foreign Office official, Ewart Biggs, what he had been doing in Dubai in the Persian Gulf. 'Discouraging slave-runners,' came the reply, without a flicker. My very civilised and kindly friend was later assassinated by the Provisional Irish Republican Army. Anyway, 'to discourage slave-runners' and so on was why the Brits went there; and no doubt for Imperial profit.

The British began to build a penal settlement at Port Blair in 1858, a significant date, bearing in mind that the Indian Mutiny broke out in 1857. Sadly, Port Blair is most famous for its prison, which culminated in an ingenious structure, completed in 1910, called the Cellular Jail; so called because there were 698 separate cells.

I visited this place several times and I tried to contemplate its significance, particularly as far as our British responsibility was concerned. Today it has been largely converted into an Indian national shrine, though prisoners are still held in portions of it – such as foreign Asian fishing trespassers, to whom I gave the wink and a thumbs up, which was received with a very Oriental smile. Again, why are they 'inside' and me outside?

I believe that every political prisoner from the time of Nehru's freedom struggle has now got his photograph hanging on the walls. I spent several hours gazing at these images of people who had once been incarcerated within the walls where I stood. I remarked to Chiara: 'What fine characters they look generally.'

On one occasion two Indians were close to me and were emotionally peering at these photographs of their martyrs when they came to a long batch of men who had been executed. 'Shot, shot, hanged, shot,' they repeated, with an odd accusatory glance at my British face.

I could not resist the temptation: '1943, 1943, 1943, 1943, while your fellow Asians, the Japanese, were occupying these islands.' Yes, all things are relative.

Another Indian I met told me that he had planned for most of his life to visit the Cellular Jail, only to pray in remembrance of the freedom-fighters. Well, I am no defender of the concept of Imperialism, so I kept quiet.

On the 23rd March, 1942, the Japanese took over Port Blair and a sub-human regime began. I do not want to repeat in this book details of Japanese depravity on the Andaman and Nicobar Islands; suffice it to report that their minds often focused on brutal obscenity and females were popular with them. The four remaining Britishers were broken first and then the Japanese began to turn their attention to the Indians.

One of the leaders of the Indian community was a Sikh medical doctor, Diwan Singh. He was an exemplary man and the chairman of a well-meaning local organisation called the Citizens' Peace Council. While the Japanese were torturing Doctor Singh to death their honoured ally, Subhas Chandra Bose, as head of the Indian National Army, was a guest of Admiral Ishikawa, the Japanese Commander of the Andamans, at Port Blair and there was a ceremonial reception for Bose. Doctor Singh was guilty of nothing, except human goodwill. It is clear that Subhas Chandra Bose did not even bother or perhaps dare to ask after the welfare of Doctor Singh. Recently, an Indian lady and a friend of mine wrote a historical piece about the Japanese atrocities on the islands and she recorded her revulsion against Subhas Chandra Bose. Privately, she was asked to remove that Bose portion from her work. I appeal to Greater India to win back their self-respect by removing this wretched man, Subhas Chandra Bose, from their pantheon of heroes. Start with the ridiculous memorial to him that faces the Red Fort in Delhi; it brings India into disrepute.

A few years ago I was working in West Berlin and on many evenings Chiara and I saw television programmes in which the Germans criticised their sometime Nazi role, particularly their policy of genocide towards the Jews. Chiara asked: 'Why do the Germans have to go on flagellating themselves?' I thought that it was a good thing and I admired the Germans' hard road to absolution. But never had I heard of one squeak of remorse out of the Japanese for their setting of new standards of human degradation. And then in Port Blair I did. The manager of a hotel told me that he has one Japanese guest, of the war generation, who visits Port Blair each year; he does nothing on the Andamans except visit the Cellular Jail each morning, stays there all day, and returns to the hotel in the evening. My informant said: 'I understand he prays each day.' Someone else at Port Blair told me that many Japanese now visited the islands and, in one case he knew of, the visitor was a young man who had been sent by an old Japanese soldier who had served at Port Blair. The ex-soldier was now too ill to travel himself and the young emissary had been provided with a list of names and addresses, which he had been instructed to trace, and if successful, he was to ask for forgiveness and also to ask the long-ago victims if they would accept presents which the old man had sent for them. I was told that when Japanese first visited the islands after the war, the local people would not serve them in the shops or speak to them; now they will. This was an important piece of news for me that I heard at Port Blair.

Just off Port Blair is a small island called Ross. The British set up their headquarters there in 1858. It is perfectly placed for the administration of a penal settlement; from Ross Island you can view the Cellular Jail across the water – there was once, I believe, a signalling arrangement between them – and the prison personnel could also see their headquarters. It was Alcatraz in reverse. Today Ross is an astounding sight; it is a small British colonial town with secretariat, Governor's mansion, Anglican Church of Gothic persuasion, military barracks, graveyard, social club for officers and wives or other, ballroom, and commissariat; you name it, Ross has it. And the jungle is devouring the town. It is an image of British Imperialism being eaten piecemeal by an Asian jungle. It is hazardous to enter the church – not because of snakes but because the spire and all are being held upright only by the lianas and what have you. What a staggering image of lost empire it is. I gazed and gazed. Wild deer wandered amid the fantastic ruins. Chiara and I did something rather charming. At considerable risk to our lives we entered the root-shattered ballroom and, while I hummed a gentle waltz, we did a few turns. The last dancers. As a friend, who is a resident of Port Blair, said: 'Remove the trees and the town will collapse; remove the town and the trees will collapse.' Perhaps it is not – first and foremost – the last Asian assault on the old British Empire; but the final consummating embrace of an often passionate love affair.

The Andaman and Nicobar Islands are mainly a 'prohibited area'. There are several obvious reasons for this.

They are of strategic significance, they have extraordinary flora and fauna, particularly the former, and their human tribal life is precious.

Not far from Port Blair is an island named Sentinel (must have been a British man-o'-war) where, if you attempt to land, dark-skinned, naked islanders will possibly dance a threat and if you persist they will probably fire a shower of lethal arrows. They seem vehemently to say: 'Keep your bloody televisions off our patch.' The Indian Government is handling the situation with great care.

Chiara and I were presented with a rare and indeed wonderful opportunity. We were given special dispensation to travel south on a Government ship to the very tip of Great Nicobar Island, calling at Hut Bay on Little Andaman, Car Nicobar Island, Camorta, Trinkat and Katchall Islands and finally to Campbell Bay on Great Nicobar. I could not help feeling that the moment I was free of Doordarshan and the Ministry, India became my helpful and affectionate friend.

This ship also was called *Sentinel* and that six days aboard, in itself, was a tremendous experience. It seemed that the entire ship's company was personally concerned about our happiness. Very few Europeans had travelled that way since 1947 (and not many before that!). The ship was in no way prepared for European tastes, and they hovered over us and performed their memorable best. It might be true to say that we were as happy on that ship with that Indian crew as we have ever been. There are at least two, very contrasting, Indias.

On Little Andaman Island I had the precious experience of kneeling down in a darkened hut beside a small glowing fire and looking closely at a member of the Onge tribe, who was as near to the Stone Age as any human could be in 1987. We held hands and when I smiled the person smiled back at me. I had the opportunity of being with one of our universally common ancestors who had barely been touched by what we have chosen to call civilisation. It was a profound experience. I am grateful to those who got me there.

At Car Nicobar Island we visited the Church and grave of Bishop John Richardson, who worked so successfully to spread the Christian message over the island. Again, as in Goa, the social result is reminiscent of Polynesia and those such as I, feel strangely at home.

Chaura Island created an atmosphere that made it difficult for me to believe that it was quite real. Through the heaving sea sped magnificent war canoes, or so they seemed, with a long, regular row of white stars painted on the sides of the black boats. There is no landing stage attached to the island. The men, women, babies, chickens, and large, live pigs tied to stout poles and carried by two men, were transferred from ship to narrow canoe as the sea lifted and sank alarmingly. As we peered down at the hazardous transfer I thought that 1987 could not have been expected to produce such a dangerous spectacle outside of a war or some great physical disaster. The islanders handling the canoes were consummate seamen; whenever necessary they slipped from the canoes into the surging sea, sometimes holding valuables with one hand high over their heads as they still managed to swim, and swiftly. Some of them had exceptionally large feet, which aided their versatility in the water.

Marco Polo wrote: 'You may take it for a fact that all the men of this island have heads like dogs and teeth and eyes like dogs; for I assure you that the whole aspect of their faces is that of big mastiffs. They are a very cruel race: whenever they get hold of a man who is not one of their kind, they devour him.' I don't know about the latter, but as Chiara and I looked at some of these extraordinary people we could not avoid noting the thought of mastiffs. Large, flat faces but with pronounced and formidable jaws. They believe in a legend that they are descended from a Burmese princess and a dog. We also noted that they chose to wear sarongs with tails hanging from behind and bandanas round their heads with two pieces of cloth pricked up to represent ears. We were told that they wanted to emphasise this idea.

And are the big feet of the swimmers part of a land-sea evolutionary process?

As the ship and the canoes rose high and fell, I witnessed babies being held out by one hand and grasped by another before the point of contact disappeared. Great courage was shown by men and women, young and old. The ship's siren blared its anxiety to depart. As the slender canoes departed for the distant shoreline crammed with humanity and pigs, I was aware that I had witnessed an heroic, breathtaking act and so I cheered with all of my sometime Old Vic Shakesperian experience. The surprised canoe-men turned, smiled and waved. Oh! And Chaura Island is the centre of unadulterated witchcraft.

On the Island of Katchall it was arranged that we should be looked after by Chief Abu Soul who was, so a government official told me, immensely rich, mainly through owning thousands of coconut trees. Chief Abu Soul was a very big man and he didn't speak much English. He kindly drove us about his island, very fast, in some four-wheel-drive vehicle. I sat by his side and sang to him, as far as I could remember the words: 'I've got a lovely bunch of coconuts, See them standing in a row, Big ones, small ones, some as big as your head, Tiddly dum, tiddly dum, That's what the showman said!' I felt the song was very apt and I sang it loudly several times. Chief Abu Soul looked straight ahead with his foot firmly on the accelerator. Later, at his coconut headquarters in a clearing close to the sea, I enjoyed a swing, which was attached to a high tree, and Chiara felt that the Chief might have thought me eccentric.

Before leaving this island we were invited to join a Christian ceremony held for the purpose of 'welcoming' a dead man's spirit. It was a happy occasion, the singing was beautiful and we foreigners were treated with fine graciousness.

As our ship approached Nancowry Island our good captain invited Chiara and me up on to the bridge to view the spectacular passage through the 'West Gate'. This is the narrow entrance between two jungle-laden headlands into a vast, natural harbour. The captain must judge the cross current and the wind of an open sea in order to 'sail' through the centre into sheltered spaciousness. The truth is that for some minutes an essential risk has to be taken; should there be any engine trouble or other unforeseen incident during that brief interval there is really no time even to get the anchor down. Incidentally, the rain forests are the most magnificent that I have ever seen.

On Nancowry I saw a simple memorial commemorating the place where the Japanese were 'forced to surrender'. And here we had the good fortune to be invited to visit the Rani (Queen). We were taken across the black choppy water and walked to her residence. She is a very pretty old lady who received us, with members of her family, in her sitting room. This matriarchal arrangement is a bit of a mystery. As far as I can gather the Rani's grandmother (who was the British 'agent' on the island and was not of island stock; so how did she get there and hold this important position?) observed the arrival of the German warship *Emden* during the First World War. No thought of retreating into the jungle entered her head; instead she raised the Union Jack and the Germans, presuming that this signal presaged the firing of a salvo from a hidden British artillery battery (there were, in fact, no guns whatever) beat a hasty retreat through the West or the East Gate, I know not. Naturally, the British authorities, when they eventually digested these facts, were delighted and the Rani was again honoured for service to the British Crown.

After coffee and cake and a kindly chat, one of the Rani's very pretty daughters or grand-daughters presented us with a present of large local cowrie and other exotic shells. I was unprepared for this visit so, as I was leaving, I gave the Rani my Rajasthan shoulder bag. Whether it is true or not I have not been able to verify, but I was told, as we walked back to the jetty through the tropical night, that the Rani had 'had several husbands'.

Finally, the ship sailed into Campbell Bay on Great Nicobar Island. Arrangements were speedily put into operation to transport us on quite a lengthy journey along a newly-constructed road to the most southern tip of the island, which the British called Pygmalion Point, but which has recently been renamed Indira Point. It is the most southern tip of all Indian territory. We stared southward over the hot sea towards Sumatra, not so very distant.

Chiara, who is extremely brave in most respects, plunged into the tropical ocean and swam through its muscular waves. A lone fisherman gesticulated and I learnt from our government escort that he was saying Chiara must be care-full to avoid – predictably – the sharks, but more especially the great crocodiles that patrolled the southern coastline. Oh yes, it was nature all right.

We picked papayas out of the jungle. And we were very fortunate again to meet members of the Aboriginal tribe, the Shompens. They looked a handsome people to me. Some anthropologists believe that they have Dravidian blood; but no one really knows. We bought some honey that they had collected from the jungle.

I took work with me to the Andaman and Nicobar Islands, but apart from an odd chat with naval friends about the old mutiny, I did nothing except ardently appreciate the experience which I have just given you a résumé of.

India's bureaucracy, which unhappily extends to the Andamans and Nicobars, did briefly stroke me, however. I went to buy a 'tender' coconut from a Government-owned plantation. 'How much?' I asked.

'Two rupees,' said the jungle official, 'but first sign this form.'

I silently and carefully wrote Kenneth Griffith. And then this lone representative of Delhi took my signed form and immediately, in front of my disbelieving eyes, destroyed it! I have written a letter to the *Herald* of Goa, relating this pioneering breakthrough by this unknown, unsung iconoclast in his jungle hut. 'Cannot we get the news of this Andaman system through to Delhi? Immediately destroy the endless millions of heart-breaking forms! And perhaps the rupee might drop: there are warehouses full of forms that might never have to be signed in the first place!' My message to the *Herald* was answered in the letter columns from as far afield as Bombay! For thirty-six hours I was deliriously hopeful that I had set India alight. I saw myself as the saviour of the sub-continent. Brit that I am, perhaps my statue pointing at that coconut hut could replace all of the empty pedestals that had once held up a jack-booted Subhas Chandra Bhose. But no, the fire died out in Bombay and that coconut man must wait for an alternative John the Baptist.

And so Chiara and I returned to our cottage at Dona Paula in Goa to await any orders that Doordarshan and the ministry might issue to us from Delhi. Or, for that matter, from the Prime Minister himself. When might the Prime Minister deem it fit to comment on the film? Well, he hadn't seen an inch of it yet. Shri Prasad, who had already seen the film assembled in an unfinished state on the cutting room table in Delhi, had informed me that he had reported his impressions to the Prime Minister. And very soon the final polished version would arrive from Alan Birkinshaw and my other colleagues in London. My contract with the Indian Government expired on the last day of February 1988. I would simply wait in beautiful Goa, surrounded by compatible Goan friends (Roman Catholic priests predominated; the majority of them being Jesuits) for orders from Delhi or the expiry of that contract.

I gave my time to thinking about the preceding, often bitter time, of working for the Indian Government and the endless struggle against that Indian system while trying to tell the filmed story of Jawaharlal Nehru's life. I pondered the unavoidable irony that our biggest enemy in achieving a just story of Nehru's life was the independent country of India that he had won. I pondered this book. As the weeks and months went by, I lightly wondered what my exit from India would be: a red carpet or a discreet smuggle. Well, little is predictable in India.

My life in Goa was extraordinarily full. A large part of the reason for this happy fact was my close friendship with Rajan Narayan, the editor of the *Herald*. With him I visited the Konkani (native Goan) Theatre. I visited a Soviet Union pop entertainment in the capital city of Panjim, various Goan social occasions, I was ushered into the mysterious presence of a powerful Indian political figure (very like being in the heated presence of a Mogul prince), and Rajan took me to a Goan bullfight.

The Konkani Theatre is unique in my experience. A domestic drama is played out which conveys a popular contemporary morality. Since Gulf Oil has come to the fore in this world, thousands of adventurous Goans have worked in the Middle East. They have long been travellers; the first Goans I ever met was thirty odd years ago on passenger ships plying the big oceans. They were often excellent crew members. The last Konkani play I saw was about a simple (but not stupid) Goan fisherman's family whose children and in-laws had become infected with high material expectancy from that Persian Gulf source. The play was about culture shocks. It was very funny; I believe that Konkani plays are almost invariably funny. Of course, the ambitious lost sheep of the drama all came a cropper and finally crept home to Mum and Dad. I could easily follow the universal human plot of the play, though I speak no Konkani. And always there was a kind friend at either my right ear (Rajan) or at my left ear (Father Antonio Pereira, SJ) to interpret the nuances.

But that was certainly not all! After each of many, many scenes, there would be a music-hall entertainment of song and dance. Sometimes the 'turn' would be relevant to the drama of the evening, sometimes it would not. The backdrop to these song and dance entertainments was always – in my experience – the Portuguese balustraded promenade of the Mandavi River, which runs through Panjim. The songs and dances were an unbroken link with Portugal. The idea that lay behind these musical intermissions was that the audience needed a regular rest from the intellectual argument of the drama. I loved the Konkani plays. When I return to Goa (please God) I shall hasten to watch another one.

Goan bullfights are very Goan. Men in Goa are not called upon to fight bulls; bulls are encouraged to fight bulls. And more often than not, a Goan bull does not relish fighting another bull. A suitable field is canvassed off and into the makeshift arena come the two beasts. Each of the bulls is accompanied by at least one human handler. Frequently, when one bull sees the other he unashamedly bolts for an exit and sometimes they both flee. However, every so often the bulls are persuaded to lock horns and the tussle is not unlike human wrestling: they push and grunt it out. Some blood may be raised around their respective necks because they are being prodded by the adversary's horns. An umpire decides when and which bull is clearly dominant and he announces his judgement. There is no dark red death in the bull arenas of Goa. Quite incidentally, the bull's human accomplice not only pushes his gladiator into a direct head-on confrontation (I have presumed he does this to avoid any dangerous injury to the animal's vulnerable flanks) but he also regularly sticks a finger into the bull's arse, which apparently encourages the bull to push even harder. Watching this combat I dwelt on the fantasy that matadors in Spain might have an assistant with them in the bull ring, his finger placed in a similar manner in order to provoke the bull-fighter to greater flashes of daring bravado.

I spent more time with Roman Catholic priests in Goa than I have with any clerics in the preceding part of my entire life; and of course more time in Roman Catholic churches than ever before. The Roman Church is everywhere and seems to be an essential, hard-working and friendly keystone which holds the Goan culture upright. Generally, these priests proved to be invaluable company for me because of their perceptive concern and intelligence. I call myself, these days, an agnostic. While discussing my wanderings through and around this astounding human experience a Jesuit priest said to me: 'Do you know, Kenneth, what St Augustine said about you?' 'What did St Augustine say about me?' 'He said, "Any person who is searching for God has already found God." ' I find that statement by St Augustine a show-stopper.

As I left Goa on my journey back to Britain, I carried with me a handful of Rajan's editorials; I did this simply because they are clearly full of wonder. Rajan Narayan is a candidate for being the best newspaper man that I have ever met. And I have known a few of the best: James Cameron, Hugh Cudlipp, Harold Evans and Anthony Holden among others. Here is one of the editorials, for the 9th February, 1988. I have selected this one because it is aimed at the Indian government system that I endured for more than two years, and it is just as well to read the thoughts of an *Indian* sufferer in this book, which is primarily about the tribulations of a European. When I have expressed my outrage against India's official ill-treatment of me and my working colleagues I have usually received one of two customary replies: 'You British taught us our system of bureaucracy.'

To which I reply: 'If we inflicted this system of behaviour on India, we certainly didn't inflict it on ourselves!'

Or an Indian will often reply: 'You have had to suffer these bureaucratic outrages for only a year or so; how would you like to suffer them for your entire life, as we have to do?'

Here is an extract from the thinking of Rajan Narayan on behalf of the masses of India. The editorial is headed: 'Masters and Knaves'.

> And sometimes I wonder whether all the efforts and all the time and all the energy spent in investigating the sins of omission and commission by the government and the political establishment is worth our while. And sometimes I despair that nothing that we do and nothing that we say can push back the floodtide of corruption and venality and political immorality. And sometimes I feel that bureaucrats and politicians are so thick-skinned that nothing affects them. That they are so shameless that you cannot humiliate them. That they have become so habituated to stealing from the

> public that nothing can reform them. Indeed, every time a politician or a bureaucrat is caught with his hand in the till, he will sound very penitent and very apologetic and promise never to do it again. Until the next time. And all the honest and conscientious and good bureaucrats inevitably find themselves total misfits in a system which unabashedly glorifies and celebrates corruption. Indeed, it has become easier for a camel to pass through the eye of a needle than to find an honest politician or an honest bureaucrat.
>
> Corruption in the country has become institutionalised. Corruption starts from the top and goes through to the bottommost rungs. Corruption perpetuates itself because the watch-dogs are themselves inevitably even more corrupt than those whom they are supposed to watch. The politician who is at the top of the pyramid believes that he has a congenital right to loot and plunder. The people's representatives believe that they have an obligation to loot and plunder the people who bestowed them with power.
>
> But, fortunately, there is a small, tiny, little flame still glimmering at the end of the tunnel. Fortunately, within every system there are a few conscientious objectors. Within every system there are a few people who still have a conscience. Fortunately, there are a few individuals who care. Individuals who refuse to be intimidated. Individuals who, at very grave risk to themselves, are willing to unmask corruption. And it is these honourable gentlemen and women who sustain our faith. Who keep us going. Who renew our faith in our battle against corruption. Who much to the despair of corrupt bureaucrats and representatives of the people refuse to be cowed. I understand, for instance, that at every meeting the Inspector-General of Police cajoles and threatens his officers not to inform the *Herald* of the corruption in the department. Indeed, I understand that the honourable Inspector-General has even started an investigation into how the *Herald* gets the news. To all those who have been helping *Herald* in its fight against corruption, a very big Dev Borem Korum.

I believe that the fundamental cause of this ghastly predicament is that the laws and rules of Official India today are fundamentally the ones inflicted upon subject India long ago by, principally, the Master Moguls and the Master British, during their tenures of paramountcy. And, understandably, because the Moguls and British were in India by force of conquest, these laws and rules, formulated by them, were devised in a spirit of distrust of the conquered

Indian people. And these laws and rules – when 'independence' and 'freedom' came – were not promptly destroyed and new laws and rules, implying that the new free Indians were innocent until proved guilty, were not put in their place. The suspicious attitude of the Moguls and British towards the Indians still pertains. Every Indian official attitude is framed in a spirit of total distrust. The Indian people suffer it twenty-four hours per day for the rest of their lives and we guests and visitors have to suffer it while we are there. Come the revolution against the system.

Also, at 'independence', India failed to carry out Lord Louis Mountbatten's pleading to 'Pay your Government servants properly or you will be asking for corruption.' And, of course, this, together with the innumerable religious, ethnic and political variations on the sub-continent, held together by a democratic structure trying hard not to use dictatorial force, are the basic sum of reasons why the Indian system is in an ugly shambles, which has recently aged me – as it is daily ageing almost every poor bloody human being who comes near it.

Poor Rajiv Gandhi. He has the hardest job on the face of this planet. Harder than Mr Bush's job, harder than Mr Gorbachev's job and, in fact, harder than Mr Botha's or Mr Shamir's.

Of course, each day that I quietly worked and delightfully lived in Dona Paula, I was basically standing by for any instructions that might come from my employers in Delhi. Hardly anything happened from that direction, for which I was profoundly grateful. The film had been accepted by the powers-that-had-been-appointed and was now at the laboratories in London, receiving its final polish. But an intermediary stage of this technical process had arrived in Delhi and I was handed a telegram from the Director-General of Doordarshan, Bhaskar Ghose, which informed me that the film had been 'viewed by the highest authority' (which I erroneously took as a vague euphemism for the Prime Minister) and that a sequence had to be changed in the film. I hurried back to my city of dreadful night, New Delhi, fearing the worst, which was what always seemed to happen with my associates there.

'The highest authority' turned out to be a few of the senior men at Doordarshan for whom my respect had long evaporated. Apparently, a number of questions about the film had been raised by these gentlemen now very late in the day; indeed I had feared that it was too late to change anything even if the argument for a change was ethically valid. But it turned out that technically it was not too late, which was the first relief for me. The passage that worried Shri Shiv Sharma (or so I was told that it was he) was about India's war with Pakistan over which of the newly-born countries should own Kashmir. The relevant passage in the film stated: 'There was a shady and murderous invasion of Kashmir by Muslim Pathan tribesmen from Pakistan and Nehru painfully ordered the Indian Army to counter it. . . .'

Of course, the historical facts of this critical event for both India and Pakistan are highly complicated and, if anything, my necessary film shorthand was more merciful to India than it was to Pakistan. But there was now a request-cum-order to make it clear in the film that Nehru gave orders for the Indian Army to invade Kashmir at the specific request of the Maharajah of Kashmir, who was the Hindu ruler of a population that was overwhelmingly Muslim and which population might understandably lean towards Muslim Pakistan if it came to a democratic vote. Now I didn't get into all of that in the film because I knew that once the details were started they would have to be followed through. These details and the basic facts are still lethal questions on the sub-continent to this day; they are, at this moment, the most dangerous stimulus for armed conflict between the two countries.

What Shri Shiv Sharma and company at Doordarshan wanted was the Hindu Maharajah's request to Nehru for Indian Army help and nothing more. Now by this time I had, perhaps, already gone beyond the end of my tether. I was beginning to capitulate; I was beginning to join the hundreds of millions of Indians who had given up hope and the will to oppose the System. It is a step on the hopeless and disgraceful road to total apathy. Eighteen months earlier I might have uncompromisingly opposed this Doordarshan request. Now I compromised and inserted the information about the Hindu Maharajah's request for Indian Army help and I got this insertion passed by Doctor Bal Ram Nanda. But, though I was crumbling fast and waiting as quietly as possible to leave India, I am glad to state that I had not become totally abject. In presenting the insert to Doordarshan I wrote a warning letter to Shri Ghose (of course, you get very few replies in India) and I verbally addressed, eyeball to eyeball, Shri Lele (the Deputy Director-General) and company: 'Now we all know, Shri Lele, that the Maharajah of Kashmir didn't want India to take over his country.' I made it seem as if this was the end of my statement; I created a long, long pause and I did not speak again until I sensed the shock of such a statement had penetrated to an uncomfortable degree and then I added, as if it were an unnecessary oversight: 'Nor, of course, did His Highness wish to join Pakistan! As we *all* know, he dreamt of remaining independent of both countries. A plague on both your houses, as it were. Now if I simply add that the Maharajah asked India to come into his country, Kashmir, without any further explanation, I submit that millions of Muslims are going to want to ask me why I kept silent and misled people. And I will only be able to reply that "I confess my guilt" and that "I never wanted to mislead television viewers so dangerously". And that I did it against my original judgement because you [Doordarshan] asked me to do it and that some of my principles have evaporated since I came to India!' After forty-eight hours or so Shri Lele informed me that the film's text should remain as it was. Again I was greatly relieved and I fled back to the trustworthy peace of affectionate Goa.

My contract ended on the last day of February, 1988. Our

living expenses were due on the 1st February and didn't arrive. I had learnt always to expect the very worst from Doordarshan and the Ministry, so I became neurotically worried – I had hotel bills to pay. I telephoned, I telegraphed, I wrote letters and in the middle of February one quarter of what was due on the 1st February arrived. Chiara Peretti and I were in a desperate position. I reluctantly telephoned Shri Sharada Prasad at the Prime Minister's South Block. Shri Prasad said that he would enquire into what was going on; but no further funds arrived. And we had no access to our money in Europe.

Fortunately, two Goans learnt of our predicament and smilingly offered to lend us any money that we required. That was my cue to inform my friend Rajan Narayan to send one of his journalists to see me because I wished to give his newspaper an exclusive interview about how I had been mistreated over the preceding two years while struggling to produce for the Government of India two films on the life of Jawaharlal Nehru. I told the story as I remembered it; no holds barred. I said: 'And you have exclusive rights on this; you can syndicate it; do what you please with it.'

Of course, there were some Indians who were very kind and helpful as families and individuals; notably Admiral and Shrimati Satyindra Singh, the Gopal Sharmans and others whom I have mentioned in the text. One of my problems now, when thinking of India, is that I daily suffered at the hands of people who worked for the State and it is very difficult for me to see the general Indian character unaffected by the soulless behaviour of the Government people who dealt with me. Mine is a very jaundiced view; circumstances condemned me to this.

The last parting insult to me as I left India was that Shri Lele and company refused to make themselves responsible for the return of my wardrobe worn in the film, my research library and other personal effects; which wardrobe and books they had anxiously transported into India a long while before. I addressed some of these Indian colleagues: 'I have often wondered whether I would leave India on a red carpet or whether I would be quietly smuggled out. I never calculated that you would commit highway robbery on me en route to Indira Gandhi Airport.'

Alan Birkinshaw and I had often said to each other: 'If we complete these films and are proud of them and if we are paid for our work, it will be a miracle.' The miracle has been achieved.

I hope that this story and the two films do something to help the seven hundred and ninety nine million Indians who are probably smilingly and patiently suffering the creatures of the Indian Government at this very moment.

EPILOGUE

On my first return to Britain to film the English sequences of Nehru's life (at Harrow, Cambridge and the Inns of Court), Mr David Elstein, the Director of Programmes for Thames Television, had asked me if I would return to India, when I was free, to make a film for Thames about the 'Untouchables' of India. I replied that this would be impossible even if I were given twelve hours' screen time (I would be lucky to get a full hour). I reasoned that Untouchability was such an ancient religious-social structure that no one could be certain of even its origins. There were many theories, as one will always find in the East, but most of them flickered in the depths of legend. I also explained that the organisation of Hindu caste and outcaste was so woven into the breathing existence of Hindu people that no one, leave alone me, was competent to unravel firmly or to explain it.

But Thames persisted with the hope and I returned to them stating that what I was qualified to do – and would like to do – was a life of Doctor Ambedkar. 'Who is Doctor Ambedkar?' David, not surprisingly, asked. I explained that he had been born an Untouchable and incredibly had fought his way to becoming, possibly, the best educated man on the sub-continent of India and who had then spent the rest of his life fighting for the full emancipation of his Untouchable brothers and sisters. It is an extraordinary and noble saga. And so I was taken on by Thames Television to do it.

I researched the subject and wrote the script. I was offered assistance from good Indian Jesuits, from Buddhists and from Indian sociologists; three groups that are still labouring in this difficult and often cruel field.

However, when we came to apply for entry into India to begin our filming, we came slap into conflict with that old obstructionist attitude that I had only recently escaped from. First the Indian Government demanded nine copies of the script to peruse back in Delhi. India is the only so-called democracy I know of that would make such demands. 'Everything will be all right, Mr Griffith. It is a normal procedure. Just a few weeks.' And the months rolled by and we agreed to postpone our departure to film in India until January, 1989. It was then September, 1988 and I decided to slope off quickly to South Africa and make a simple film about the apparent cruelties that the African National Congress and the Anti-Apartheid Movement have inflicted on Miss Zola Budd, the distinguished Afrikaner athlete. I saw this project as advocating the point of view of a South African 'Untouchable' (i.e. Miss Zola Budd) as much as my other wish to be the spokesman for Indian Untouchables. I suppose I could be defined as a very simple humanist who has no allegiance to anything except what my head, heart and soul tell me. Certainly, I am out of step with all conformists.

Just before I left India, having seen the completion of the Nehru film, I visited Doctor and Shrimarti Nanda to say goodbye. The good doctor said he hoped that we would all meet again soon. I replied: 'I expect to be back within the year.'

'I am very pleased. Are you coming on holiday?'

'I hope to make a film on the life of Doctor Ambedkar for British television.' The atmosphere that then filled their usually friendly room astonished me.

Finally, Doctor Nanda spoke in a most ominous tone: 'Be very careful, Kenneth; you could easily make Ambedkar look like a hero.'

I stood among that cultured company momentarily transfixed. All that hurried through my mind was that it would be impossible to make Ambedkar anything less than a hero. And that mentality was the main hidden reason for the delaying tactics of the Hindu Establishment. Recently I was with another Brahmin Hindu, again a man of great intelligence and sensitivity, and he was being pressed by an 'ex-Untouchable' activist friend of mine, who was good-humouredly trying to pin him down about the morals and ethics of the caste system. My Brahmin friend weaved, ducked and counter-punched with brilliant dexterity. A British woman later asked me: 'Why doesn't that man, who is so decent and intelligent, admit that the caste system is wrong?'

I replied, like the over-seasoned Western observer that I am: 'It is as if you were demanding that a solid Roman Catholic should categorically deny the Immaculate Conception. You are striking deeply and lethally at Faith.'

I am surrounded, like Douglas Fairbanks Senior, by widely differing ironies. For several months British Television have refused to transmit my film about Zola Budd because I am supporting her innocent case and she is a white Afrikaner woman. The truth is, even today, that it would be easier to show a sympathetic film about Mrs Winnie Mandela. Fair play all round has long gone out of the window. Of course, there are also some personal animosities against me and I understand that.

At this same time I am being prohibited from entering India by the Indian Government, to speak up for the Pariahs, the Untouchables, the Harijans, the Scheduled Castes – call them what you will. Should we not put our double standards and hypocrisy very firmly aside and look at the *whole* truth? India is so busy viciously criticising the South African cultural predicament that they barely have time to confront their own. Well, they haven't the *will* to do it.

Many Indians visit me these days to ask me if they can see the Nehru film – say six per week, the Tagore Society, the Jawaharlal Centenary Committee and so on. I show them the film willingly but warn them that its availability is in the hands of India's impossible Government. A few weeks ago two of these Indians arrived by appointment and I settled them comfortably in front of a television monitor. 'It is a long film,' I warned them.

They stared at me in surprise: 'No, no, we have not come to see your Nehru film, we are Untouchables – or ex-Untouchables. We have read that the Indian Government won't allow you into India to make a film about Baba Sahib [Ambedkar]. Is that true?'

'Yes.'

'Have you got a script, Mr Griffith? May we borrow it and return it in two days' time?'

They returned two days later with the script, assuring me that while it was not being read it had been kept in a safe. 'Mr Griffith, several of us who have now read it have wept. Everything that should be in it is there. Now, Mr Griffith, you *are* going to India to make this film. There are over one hundred thousand of us ex-Untouchables in Britain, a quarter of a million of us in America and sixty million in India – and this is election year.'

And one of my friends shyly added: 'And quite a few of us are millionaires.'

I quickly informed Thames of this new Indian intervention. I have attended a number of Indian luncheons and formal meetings with these loyal, humorous ex-Untouchables. At one of them I gave the usual Ambedkar salutation: 'Jai Bhim!'

'Oh no!' hastened my host 'Mr . . . is a Brahmin and Mr . . . is a Muslim.'

And so I added '*Namaskar*' and '*Salaam*'. It was a moving, ecumenical gathering in the name of fair play.

These people have now informed me that they are about to meet the Indian High Commissioner in Britain and that they are going to insist I am allowed to relate the true facts about Doctor Ambedkar's life, on the historical locations in India, otherwise they will publicly burn a copy of the Indian Constitution in front of the Indian High Commission at the Aldwych, London. I have muttered that I will be present.

INDEX

Index compiled by Peva Keane